Inside

Their

Hearts

By

Elizabeth Baillie

Copyright© 2016 Elizabeth Baillie

VJKBooks

First Edition

Cover by Vera Soroka

Photos by Kimberly Palmer and Wtamas

ISBN 978-0-9948218-3-6

Chapter One

I've seen souls lined up in jars and promises of true love stuffed into used pill bottles. Both for sale to the desperate and lonely. There are those who desire eternity, and they are easily led down a garden path lined with dead black roses that they are too blind to see.

When they are trapped or too far gone, blood lust fills their empty souls or Hades keeps them as a part of his Hunt.

My choice was made for me. I was given the gift of blood lust and it was my true love that gave this gift or curse to me. However you look at it, I don't remember him so the hate and pain that I carry is a dull ache.

Even who I was I have no idea. My memories are like staring at old faded black and white photos-unrecognizable and forgotten. I am forever frozen in this body of a young man of nineteen with dark brown hair and green-blue eyes.

I keep to myself for the most part and feed on the desolate and outcast humans to kill the blood lust. I've looked at other men and want to be with them but when I get near the blood that flows through their veins wakes the monster that lives inside me.

Solitude keeps the beast quiet and arouses nothing.

Keeping to myself also keeps me out of reach of Hade's Hunt. They're always wild and thirsty for terror. Although humans are the ones they lure and entice for their play, they will sometimes hunt one of my kind for pure sport. I have no desire to end up as a plaything for one of them to drain me of my blood and leave me a desiccated corpse to rip to pieces and wear my bones around their necks.

Even though I keep to myself I am forced to be in the same circle as the demons. It's a gift of fate given to us monsters living with monsters. And when I am near I can't help but stare at one in particular. My attraction to him is dangerous.

He's charismatic and portrays leadership that others dare not challenge. His sexuality is seductive and yet poisonous. I even fantasize what it would be like to be held in his arms or to lay naked in bed with him. Would his touch feel like pure fire to my cold skin? He always makes me shiver.

I stay in the safety at the edge of town near a forest. Abandoned farms and an old cemetery in particular are my hang outs. Tonight, I sense others out there.

A scream rings out in the black moonless night. Someone was being killed. I circled around the Hunt masquerading as black mist in the cold darkness. I followed a creek that went into the dense forest. I would be safe there.

In the distance I could hear wolf like howls. I sat crouched down close to the ground. A strong scent came my way sending a burning sensation down my throat. That all too familiar smell of copper pennies filled me-blood. The need to feed was getting stronger.

Getting away from here to make my way to the old abandoned bridge had to happen soon. It was a popular place for vagrants and drunks-easy prey.

My senses were focused on the Hunt, and just as my legs were about to lift me, the faint sound of crunching leaves and breaking twigs brought me to a halt. My body held still like a frightened deer.

A tall dark figure appeared in the clearing. Despite the blackness he seemed to shine like the moon's reflection on still water. From the look of his hair that was thick and wild–it was him and he smelled of what I craved, blood.

My legs instantly went back down to make me become a part of the darkness. My senses told me that he had picked something up. *Could he feel my presence?*

I had to get out of here and running was pointless. I would have to play with illusions and trickery to make my escape. In my mind I threw out an owl sound. He jerked his head in the sounds direction. He started away. I made the sound again and this time added flapping wings. He walked faster but I was instantly stopped.

My eyes were held by silky black eyes with red pupils that flickered like the flame of a candle. His smile sent a shiver through my cold body.

He tilted his head slightly at me never losing that smile. His voice was low but soft. "Hello, are you hunting alone?"

Silence wafted between us like tendrils of smoke. I looked straight into his handsome face. His high cheek bones offset those black red eyes. The fire in his pupils burned with seduction.

I was pulled back into the fantasies that I had of him. His lips made me think about what it would be like…no! I turned to leave him. In a split second he was right in front of me breathing warmth down on my face.

"Are you always this quiet?" he whispered in my ear. Our cheeks almost touched. I could feel the heat from his face. I closed my eyes and almost leaned into him but I stopped myself.

Not meaning to sound nervous as I know I did I said, "I should go." Shifting away from him there was once again a space between us. It was uncomfortable and I wanted nothing more than to close it. *What was wrong with me?*

"You do talk" he said. He closed the gap between us and I held my breath. "Are you afraid of me?"

"What do you want?" I tried to make my voice sharp as a knife.

"I like the sound of your voice, keep talking to me."

He practically sang the words out. Christ, he's found a new toy. What do you do with a demon who wants to play with you?

He stepped back and gave me some space and just to spice things up he held out his hand. "My name is Elijah."

I looked down at his hand. The ends of his fingers were red talons. Very slowly and cautiously I set my hand in his. His hand felt heavy and those talons gave me the impression they served him well as a deadly weapon.

"And what do they call you love?" My head jerked up to his eyes when he said the word '*love*'. He was waiting. "Avian."

"Well it's a pleasure to meet you Avian." Now that we played the introduction game, what was next? I backed a few steps away from him but it seemed my departure was not yet to happen.

"I should be on my way."

"What's the hurry," he spoke out into the black night.

I decided to take a chance and keep walking and for a brief moment I thought he had let me go. The smell of blood enveloped me making me dizzy. A low growl escaped from my throat.

"Hungry, are we?" He sighed like he was yawning. "Let's get you fed then."

I kept walking. I wasn't sure where my feet were going but we started to go towards where I first heard the cry. I didn't want left overs.

I wasn't a dog to be handed scraps. I started to feel an anger build inside me. But instead he passed the remains of the kill and started down a path to town. I didn't want to go there either so I asked, "Where are we going?"

"My special spot." *Could he feel my apprehension?* "You'll like it, trust me."

I think *'trust'* was a delicate word to be used around Elijah. At the end of a cobblestone street was a small pub.

The old door looked like it had been opened and closed many times, clearly a few kicks thrown in. The light was dim and a grey smoke hovered in the air burning my eyes.

He sauntered over to a table, looked back at me and gestured for me to sit down. A dusty wine bottle sat in the middle holding a burning dripping candle. Pooled wax sealed to the base of the wine bottle sticking it to the table. The rest of the table was scratched and dirty. The smell of blood was as also hidden in the table. I guess from too many disagreements.

Elijah beckoned over to a gaunt looking girl behind the bar. Her eyes looked like two empty sockets. She poured some red thick liquid into two large crystal goblets. When she came from behind the bar it was like a walking skeleton coming towards us.

Her boney little fingers placed one glass in front of each of us. Elijah placed some coins in her boney little hand which clamped with a clicking noise.

Elijah lifted his glass up. "Let's drink to new adventures, love."

He said the word *'love'* again. I lifted my glass up to my lips. The liquid inside was warm. My throat caught fire. I threw back the warm liquid. Elijah's red and black eyes were watching me.

The boney little skeletal girl placed another pitcher in front of us. Elijah poured me another. I drank until the pitcher was empty. Elijah sipped at his like he was savoring it, or savoring me. He smiled at me, pleased with me and him.

"That's better isn't it?" He let a low laugh that seemed hollow and empty. I nodded and in a low murmur thanked him.

"You're quite welcome." I started to shift away. I didn't look at him. "I should go now."

"We just got here Avian. Our night has just begun. Relax and enjoy it." His gaze settled on me making me uncomfortable.

"Come Avian, I promised you a night of fun." The door opened with a loud bang. Their black scent washed over my cold skin. I didn't have to look to know that the Hunt was here. Elijah smiled at me. "Now the fun begins Avian." I just wanted out of this place. They never came over and joined us which relieved me. Elijah did get up. "Wait here."

This was my chance to get away. There was another door in the back. In a blink I was in front of it. It was old and rusted shut but I didn't care. I placed my hand on the latch. With the strength I possessed I opened the door making a scraping metal sound and then it popped open. I flew into the night and sought the darkness of the woods.

I was at the edge of the forest. As I looked back I could see the dim lights of the small town. I wouldn't be going back. I walked into the forest on my way to the old bridge. It was on route to the old cemetery. It was a quiet place. I shook off those feelings that Elijah stirred in me. I wouldn't be seeing him again.

Chapter Two

THE WROUGHT IRON GATES of the old cemetery towered over me. The metal grew like a vine up into the air and around rooting itself to the crumbling stone wall. The rusted once black metal wrapped around the small cemetery imprisoning it's dead with its cold grip. I was just about to unlatch the gate when I was stopped by a voice.

"I thought this would be a favorite place of yours."

Out the corner of my eye I could see his black and red eyes with a flicker of fire in them.

He sauntered up to me and I thought he was going to reach out to my hand that was on the latch. I held my breath but instead he let his red talon fingers rest on one of the metal scrolls right next to my hand.

"You didn't think I would forget you?"

By the look on his face he seemed amused but there was an underlying danger to his tone. He came very close to me. His warm breath felt light as a feather and brushed against my cheek. "Shall we go in?"

I let the weight of my hand fall against the latch releasing the gate. It opened with an eerie groan. He followed me in.

Tall grass in the cemetery blew in the cold fall wind. A crumbling stone angel stood tall in the middle-one of her wings was missing. She looked down upon her dead with blank eyes. Wild vines wrapped around her feet rooting her fate here. A small chapel was in the back of the cemetery. Its crumbling stone façade was partly caved in and now served as a refuge to foxes.

I walked down a well-used worn path that was used by foxes, coyotes and other creatures. Near the old chapel there was a row of above ground tombstones. My favorite was nearest the chapel. I hopped up and sat down. The large faded chipped tombstone served as a nice back rest.

Elijah observed my fancy couch.

"You are such a creature of comfort, aren't you?"

I ignored the sarcasm and leaned back breathing in the crisp air. The dampness from the night air settled into my bones. Soon the mist would climb through the grass and join me. At times I would imagine the ghosts of this cemetery are the mist, rising to keep me company. Elijah scraped the top of the tomb with one of his red talons as if he was checking for dust. Then light as a cat, he jumped up. He sat cross legged facing me.

"So, this is what you do?"

I shrugged.

"Okay, Avian, you need some spice in your life."

I half opened my eyes hoping that maybe the mist had absorbed him but that was wishful thinking. *How was I going to shake off his fascination of me?*

"Do you like games Avian?"

His facial expression was soft and I found myself transfixed by him. If I had a beating heart it would be racing now.

"I like you Avian and I want you and me to be...," he paused for a moment like he was thinking what word he would like to use. At last he said '*intimate*'. He smiled like he was happy with his choice and was looking straight into my eyes. He grinned mischievously. "When you hear me say it out loud, you like it don't you?"

Swallowing hard I averted my eyes away from him. Elijah let out a soft gentle laugh.

"Have you ever played cards, Avian?"

I nodded.

He reached into his pocket and pulled out and old deck of cards and set them down in front of me. They looked tattered and used. Elijah no doubt cheated and won a few souls with those cards. The symbols on top of the cards represented black magic that demons favored.

Whenever I saw cards of this nature, visions of games being played for souls played out in my mind. The other player always went in with the attitude that they would beat them.

They would soon learn otherwise. The Hunt would always gather around the intended victim and watch with delight while they were allowed to win and then at the last minute have it all swept from under them. I always walked away when the first initial scream started followed by the howls of the Hunt.

He glanced up at me. His black and red eyes danced.

"Ever play poker?"

"Yeah, I've played but why do you want to play with me? I have no soul for you to take."

Elijah leaned in toward me. "Who said anything about playing for souls love?"

I shifted away from him. I kept my tone even and calm. "What do you want from me?"

Elijah grinned, "Let's make this more interesting, shall we?"

I tilted my head up listening.

"Let's play for," He paused and leaned in close, touching my arm, "a night of passion—then freedom. That's if you win." He smiled. The fire in his eyes burned right through me. "If you lose, you spend eternity by my side and become a part of my Hunt."

"You're playing with me," I growled. "You don't have vampires in your Hunt."

He grinned to himself at my accusation as if we were having some kind of lovers spat. At this moment I was ready for anything, but mostly I wanted him gone.

The mist now had risen and shrouded the angel. He looked down and in that moment it was as if the darkness had consumed him but I knew he was right in front of me. I flew off the tomb and disappeared into the old chapel.

I sat on a rotting pew. The mist had settled in the old chapel with me. I didn't think a demon like him would venture into a sacred place despite it being in ruins.

I heard my name. Elijah's voice seemed to seep through the walls. When I heard his voice again it was much louder. The third time his voice sent a tremor through the chapel sending some loose plaster to the ground. He wanted me.

I met him at the entrance way staying just inside.

His face was still. His thick black hair had settled around his face in disarray and those black and red eyes were wild. "I'm sorry," he said. "I don't want you to leave. Let's go back and just talk. I promise no more games."

The desperation in his voice danced on my skin. I nodded and he waited for me to come beside him. Then we walked back. His hand brushed against mine. Neither one of us took our hand away for that brief second.

Once again Elijah and I were sitting on the stone slab. It was barely visible now with the mist. He looked at the name on the stone.

"James McKinnon," he said.

I chuckled. "Did you know him?"

He shrugged. "I knew lots like him."

"What do you mean *like him?*"

Elijah grinned and moved over next to me resting himself against James McKinnon's head stone.

"Let's just say that your dead companion here would be a favorite of my fathers."

From the corner of my eye I looked at him, "Your father" I asked.

He nodded. "Yeah, my father always knew what rich men did in their spare time and it usually was some kind of trouble."

The bones that lay under me never got me wondering to what kind of man he was. He simply provided a resting place and a contemplative spot.

"Are you close to your father?"

He grabbed my hand. "My father is everything that made me, love."

I didn't flinch when he said '*love*' this time. I turned my head to face him. Our noses were almost touching. His face was alive and fire flickered in his pupils. "When you're one of Hade's boy's, you're special."

Chapter Three

ELIJAH GRIPPED MY HAND tighter digging his talons into my palm. I gritted my teeth. Black droplets fell on top of the tomb. He brought my hand up to his mouth. His tongue traced over the wound. I quivered slightly despite my fear.

"Become a part of the Hunt with me," he whispered in my mind.

"We can be lovers…I know it's what you want. Father won't mind that you're a vampire. If it makes me happy to have you by my side Father will allow it." His eyes were dangerous. His tongue continued to move along my wound. I wasn't saying anything and his tongue felt rough, like a cat's tongue.

"Yes," I breathed out.

His rough tongue was replaced by the softness of his lips. My wound healed. Elijah placed my hand back on my lap.

He shifted very close to me. I looked down at his lips. I could almost feel and taste them. I waited. Abruptly he pulled back. A playful smile lit up his face. "Anticipation tastes the best."

"No," I gasped. Elijah was in my face again.

"No," he asked playfully. "You want to be kissed don't you? I knew you were full of fire, love." In a blink he cupped my face with his red talon hands and looked me straight in the eyes. Blood black eyes looked deep into me. "I promise you that when you've become a part of my Hunt, you will share my bed for all eternity."

Elijah's nose was touching mine. His lips felt like they were giving off the heat of a fire. His tongue swept across the bottom of my lip making my sharp teeth sink into the corner of my mouth. A drop of blood slid down my chin like a tear drop.

Elijah licked it off and sucked ever so gently on my mouth. I groaned and his lips of fire smothered mine. A growl erupted from my core. I fell into his arms as we were starting to get lost.

Then a sudden chill drenched both of us. Elijah gasped like he was trying to find his breath. I pulled away and looked around. A soft voice spoke through the chill.

"You two look like you need to cool off." A tall young man was coming towards us. His black coat dragged on the grass. The dampness from the mist clung to his straight dirty blond hair that framed a face with sharp features. When he got close to us I could see his eyes were black and empty.

He grinned at both of us and then he tilted his head at Elijah. "So, since when are you into *dead things*?"

His empty black eyes casually fell on me. He said light heartily, "no offense."

I backed off. Elijah sighed. "Go away, Zak."

Zak gave an exaggerated frown and shook his head. "Not in this life time." Then he laughed at his own joke. "Does *Daddy* know about him?"

Elijah's eyes glowed.

Zak smiled. "I didn't think so." He threaded his fingers together. His nails were perfectly manicured and coated in the blackest lacquer that I've ever seen.

Elijah's cards were still on the tomb. Zak narrowed in on them. "You two playing a friendly game?"

"We were going to but changed our minds," mumbled Elijah. Zak gathered them up and placed them neatly in a pile and gave them a gentle pat. "Why don't we all play?"

"Play what?" Elijah perked up and suddenly seemed interested in this little card game.

"Hmm, let's play poker, Elijah." I could feel the thrum of dark magic roll off him.

"Let's put your *love* here up for stakes."

Elijah was expressionless. I was waiting for him to say something. Instead he said, "What do you have in mind?"

"If you win, I'll keep your little secret about your *love* here and if I win, he becomes the hunt."

Elijah and I locked eyes. He shook his head but only slightly. "Okay… I'll play you a game but let's up the stakes even more."

Zak gave him a wicked grin. "Sure, why not. What have you got in mind?"

Elijah traced with his red talons a pattern on the top of the tomb. It was a symbol of sorts like a ruin for summoning. As Zak watched Elijah his empty black eyes widened. I thought for a moment that it scared him and he would back off, but he smiled.

"You're on," he said.

Elijah didn't give any indication of ending this deadly game he was about to play.

I leaped down and left them. I didn't get to the gate when Elijah and Zak were behind me.

"Where are you going," Elijah asked.

"I've had enough of your games and company. Good night gentlemen."

Suddenly, they stood, one on each side of me. Zak's playful manner was replaced by an animal that was ready to pounce. I turned my back on him and faced Elijah. A slight wind had picked up, no doubt by Elijah, blowing his thick unruly hair around his face concealing those black red eyes. I wanted to very gently slip my fingers through his hair so I could see his eyes. He came very close and I caught a glimpse of them.

"It's not what you think," he whispered under his breath.

"Then what is it?" I kept my tone dead.

"I want to protect you," he replied.

I glanced over at Zak. "What about him?"

Chapter Four

ZAK'S MISCHIEVIOUS GRIN was back and he winked at me.

"Zak will keep our little secret, Avian."

I wondered what had transcribed after I left.

My eyes locked in with Elijah. "What happened to your little bet?"

Zak's breath was hot on my neck. "We decided that wasn't much fun after all."

I stepped over beside Elijah and faced Zak. "So, now what?" I looked for clues as to what new games they conjured up that involved me or not. Zak raised his hands in the air like a surrender.

"Nothing," Zak said.

I shifted my gaze back to Elijah. He just smiled at me and took my hand.

"That's right, love, nothing. But I want you to stay with me for the rest of the night." He paused a moment. "I want to show you my place. Zak stays there too."

They both read my hesitancy.

Zak smirked, "Oh come on, Avian. You'll get to do more of what I caught you two doing." He chuckled.

Elijah squeezed my hand. Energy vibrated inside me and I wanted more. I nodded numbly.

All three of us walked silently into the black night. Elijah kept my hand in his. His warmth went through my coldness. The more we walked, the more I could feel and sense my surroundings. The darkness was thick like smoke and the air was acidic. I swallowed hard choking down what tasted like bitter wine. I coughed once. They both looked at me and then each other.

All I could think was that I should not be here.

We stopped at the end of a deserted road. There was nothing but bush and tall leafless dead trees. Elijah waved his hand in the air. The dead leafless tree branches that hung down above us like knotted skeleton claws transformed into tall black metal gates. It towered over us like a black monster.

Grey smoky mist swirled around and through the gate. I half expected metal fingers to come out from the mist and grab us.

The gate split open. Elijah and Zak escorted me in. It shut behind us with a heavy metal clank. I was locked in. We walked along the gravel lane. The gravel crunched under our feet echoing into the dark. An eerie glow rose out of the blackness. An old Victorian house came into view. As ghostly and forbidden as it looked I'm sure it was a fine estate in its day. It resonated with me for some reason.

Zak dashed ahead of us leaving the two of us alone.

Elijah slipped his arm around my waist and pulled me near him. A spicy scent wafted from him. Our bodies fell against each other. We shared a moment of looking into each other's eyes.

"Hey!" Zak shouted. "You two can make out when we get inside." Whatever spell that Elijah just used fell away. I pulled away but only slightly. There was something happening to me. How was I going to get out of this?

Zak jumped up onto the landing and opened the door for us. Elijah went in behind him. I stood at the doorway looking in. A burgundy and gold rug filled the foyer, covering the dark wood floors underneath. A massive staircase with a thick oak banister appeared, vanishing into the darkness of the interior. The smell of mold and dust wafted past me.

Zak nudged Elijah and instantly he flew to the door. "Come in Avian, I am sorry I didn't invite you in right away."

He reached his hand out to me and I took it. I took the first step into the house. A waft of memory flew through me. It quickly disappeared when the floor creaked under my weight. Ornate but worn furniture adorned the large foyer. A heavy layer of dust covered everything. To my right there was a large formal dining room. The room was in darkness but I could see a large dining room table sitting in the middle of the room. Behind the table against the wall was a large china cabinet. The glass doors of the cabinet were open. Some of the panes of glass were broken and the china inside was in the same shape. The velvet curtains hung heavy with dust. They looked like played out ballroom dancers.

Elijah gripped my hand tighter before my other foot touched the floor. He led me up the large stairs. Double doors stood at the end of the hall way. They opened without him touching them. He kept hold of my hand. When we were in the room, the double doors shut.

I jerked, swinging my head towards the doors. Before I could say anything Elijah pulled me towards him, kissing me. We melted into each other's arms. His kisses sent a fire down my throat. While he still held me he pulled me towards the bed. He pushed me down and I felt the weight of his body on top of me. I moaned and he kissed me harder almost bruising my lips. His hand traveled down my side and I felt my shirt being pulled up. He was touching my bare skin. The tips of his red talons along my skin ignited a backdraft that only he could put out. I felt my body wanting to push into his. The smell of his skin reminded me of a hot summer night— sultry and spicy.

Elijah slid off me to the side. His hand slid to my pants and when he started to undo the zipper my eyes flew open. I jumped up into a sitting position. I was catching my breath like I just broke water.

"What is it my love," he whispered into my ear. His breath was fire. I was actually shaking. What was I doing? I shouldn't be here!

Very tenderly, he placed a trail of kisses down from my temple to my cheek over to the corner of my lips. I leaned into him drunk with passion and desire. He pulled me back down and continued his act of seduction.

I didn't stop him this time. The sound of my zipper seemed loud in the room. He pulled my jeans apart revealing my aching bulge. I held my breath when his talon fingers pulled the band of my underwear down releasing my hard cock. Elijah stroked my hard swollen member and every once in while one of his talons would glide down my shaft sending a pain through me that left me desperately wanting more.

I sucked in air when I felt his hot wet mouth slide down my shaft. I heard myself let out a whimper. I was losing control. I had fantasized about Elijah and now it was actually happening. I closed my eyes and tried to breathe while my mind raced. My mind was enclosed in his touch. My skin felt like a pane of glass, his touch was the rain beating against it. He gently kissed my bare skin. We were fire and ice hitting each other sending up a cloud of steam.

Elijah slid his hot wet mouth over my heard cock, sucking hard. He made me raise my hips as I thrust myself into the back of his mouth.

Elijah worked his magic with his tongue. I felt like I was on the edge of a cliff ready to fall. The sound of his wet mouth moving hard up and down on me sent me over the edge. The rush to the bottom of the cliff blew me apart as the world exploded into tiny pieces of ecstasy.

I laid there in a state of exhaustion. I never felt so spent. Elijah held me for a while as shared gentle kisses. Soon sleep took me to another world.

There was music and laughter. The room looked younger and newer than it did now. The house was alive and bright. Smiling faces were everywhere. It was like time traveling back into a Victorian period. The ladies wore ball gowns and men in suits. It filtered through my mind that I had worn one of those suits. The room smelled like champagne and strawberries with a hint of spice that came from the bouquets of roses.

My eyes blinked and that's when I spied Elijah. He didn't look the same but I knew it was him. He smiled at me and started to walk towards me. The anticipation grew inside me waiting for him. My chest inside thumped quite lively. It was my heart-a sound that I had almost forgotten.

Now he was in front of me. He looked down at me with eyes that were a brilliant chestnut brown. They were beautiful. My breath held still for a brief second as I took him all in. His wild unruly waves were tied neatly into a pony tail. He smelled of sandalwood and jasmine. "Let's dance."

My heart took another jump. Elijah led me proudly into the dance floor and we waltzed. The last sound I heard was the violin.

When the violin music faded I opened my eyes and looked into black red eyes.

"Sleep well love?"

He kissed me pushing his tongue deep into my mouth.

I moaned as he tasted me and I him. He reached down and rubbed his cock up against mine bringing wetness to the surface.

He had stripped of my clothes last night after I blanked out from the orgasm he gave me. I was now under the covers with him and were both naked. Our bodies were touching. It was going to happen all over again. I wanted him and he knew it.

He continued to rub out cocks together and smearing his wetness with mine. His touch was sending live currents through my body.

Elijah moved in closer to me sliding his hand across to my lower back and down to my buttocks. He squeezed me and one of his fingers slipped in and started to spread me apart. I squirmed. "Are you a virgin," he whispered in my ear.

I didn't answer.

"Well, then you are in for an erotic ride then love. You will enjoy it I promise."

I pushed my hand against his chest. "I don't think I'm ready yet."

His breath was warm against my cheek. "I want you Avian. I want to claim every part of you and that includes your sexy ass."

He rolled me onto my stomach. I shifted but he grabbed my hips and held me. He spread my legs apart and started to massage my sac. Despite the pleasure he was giving me, every nerve in my body was tense.

"Relax Avian, I'm going to pour a little of this almond oil over you and massage you with it."

The smell of sweet almonds filled my senses. The warm oil almost made me feel like my cold skin would steam. His red talons dug into my lower back making me wince and groan at the same time.

He spread my buttocks apart and I found myself raising myself up to him. Now I wanted his fingers to explore me at least.

One finger slipped in part way pulling me and stretching me. Another moan escaped from me as he went as far as he could with his finger and then two fingers were deep inside me moving and twisting all the while stretching.

He hit an erotic spot that made me scream out.

"We found your sweet spot, that's good. I can make you spill your seed right now Avian with just massaging that sweet spot of yours. But I won't." His fingers slipped out. I lifted my hips even higher as if I was protesting.

Then I felt the tip of his hard cock slide in part way burying his tip inside me. I gasped at the feeling.

"Relax love and let me go farther." He massaged my lower back and every time he moved a little forward he entered farther into me.

I wanted him to reach that sweet spot again, with his cock this time. I pushed myself up against him.

He chuckled softly. "You want my cock don't you?"

"Yes, I do, please take me."

He mercifully thrust himself deep inside me making me cry out in pain. I couldn't believe that the pain and sensuous feeling I was feeling could be combined.

He moved in and out of slowly so I could feel every inch of him. He moaned as his thrusts got hungrier and faster.

"Oh Avian, I'm going to fill you soon. You ready for some hot seed inside you?"

"Yes," I breathed out. "Fill me Elijah."

Now he was thrusting hard and hitting that special spot that drove the pain and ecstasy into another dimension. He let up for a moment and leaned over me grabbing my cock. "You have to come first."

He started to rub me as he was deeply inside me rubbing against my erotic spot. I wasn't long spilling out over his hand and over the bed one stream after another.

He rubbed my spilled seed from his hand onto my sac. Then he picked up his thrusts again. He was pounding me and hitting me with his sac.

In one howl he filled me and I never expected the heat that was released in me would be so hot and intense. I collapsed under his weight.

He stayed deep inside me.

"I want you to remember. I have now claimed you. My scent is on you now and every demon and vampire will know who you belong to. So Avian, tell *daddy* who you belong to?"

In a very weak voice I replied, "I belong to you, Elijah and only you."

He nuzzled his head against my neck kissing me. "That's what I want to hear love. Never forget it."

I fell into darkness and once again I was transported into another world where it seemed both of us lived another life.
The living room was alive with activity. The crystal on the table glittered in the sunlight that shone through the large window. Elijah was overseeing everything. I was at awe at it all. Our eyes spotted each other and he came over to me and we kissed. What is all this I asked him? He smiled but then everything went blurry and I fell into darkness.

I woke up in a bleary haze like I had been on a drunk all night. Elijah had left me all alone in the room. Where was he? My clothes were folded neatly on a chair. In one swift movement I was sitting on the chair pulling on my underwear and pants. My head was swimming, *what did I just do? I gave myself to Elijah last night. He fucked me and claimed my ass for god's sake! I have to get a grip here. You can't allow yourself to love him. He will own you forever. Do you want that?* I pulled my shirt on and headed for the door thinking the answer to my own question.

Yes.

I practically ran down the stairs keeping my sights on the front door. My hands were trembling as I reached for the knob.

Suddenly a voice stopped me.

"You're in a hurry?"

I spun around. Zak was leaning casually against the doorway to the kitchen.

"I have to go," I blurted out.

In a low voice Zak said, "Elijah will miss you. You two had quite the night."

I looked away and looked at the door almost willing it to open. Zak sauntered up to me and opened the door. Bright light blinded me throwing me back. I didn't burn but I found it intolerable. He shut the door, like he knew. He sighed.

"Come into the kitchen, I will give you something to eat. Elijah said that you would need feeding."

I had to admit that my insides ached. He sat me down at the table and brought out a crystal pitcher with thick red liquid. He poured some into a tall crystal glass. He shoved the glass towards me.

"Drink Avian."

I took the glass and gulped it down. The liquid inside was warm and my body wanted more. He poured me another. I kept drinking until I was completely full. The pitcher was empty. Zak grinned.

"I guess Elijah should have fed you earlier," he said.

"Where is he?" I looked around almost expecting Elijah to come through the doors.

"He's out taking care of some business-that's all." Zak's voice was casual like Elijah had just stepped out for the paper. I got up and walked over to the window. The day now had cast over. It was better than sun. I thought I could tolerate it though.

Black lacquered nails came into view and shut the curtain dimming the room of its light. He came close to my ear. "You're not going anywhere."

"I'll see Elijah later." I went in the direction that would take me to the front door. Suddenly Zak was blocking the way. His grin was full of mischief. He shook his finger at me. "No, no, you don't. Turn around and I'll find a way to entertain you till Elijah gets back." Zak reached out and turned me around by the shoulders and marched me into the study.

Zak led me over to what looked like a gaming table. Brief images of a couple of guy's playing cards flew into my mind. My head jerked and the images vanished. In front of me all I saw was the old table with chipped ends and peeling stain. I cupped my hand over the chair back to pull it out. It was smooth under my fingers like it had been grasped by many hands and again brief images sprung to life in front of my eyes. I saw an older man but I didn't get a good look at his face.

I slowly sat down in the chair looking around the room. Dark dust covered the curtains weighing them down. A large desk sat in front of the curtains.

One leg was cracked making it lean to the side. Books appeared cemented into the bookshelves, their names obscured with a thick coat of dust. Everything seemed entombed.

I watched Zak go to another little table and he unlocked the drawer with an old skeleton key. The drawer was stiff and when he pulled it out with some force a cloud of dust hung in the air. He took out a black velvet box and brought it over to me. His black eyes watched me to see what reaction I would have upon seeing it. I showed none as I had never seen the box before. He proceeded to open it and take out some metal trinkets. One was a rocking horse, another was a dragon fly and the third was a tiny dagger.

"What is this," I asked.

Zak neatly arranged the ornaments in a row and placed the card in front me keeping silent. I stared down at the tarnished silver pieces like I was trying to remember them. I looked over at Zak whose eyes were endless black pools of black water. I broke away.

"This is a game of chance," he explained.

I could feel the energy rising in Zak. He liked nothing better than to play for stakes but that wasn't me. I was about to open my mouth when the door burst open and Elijah came marching into the room. His eyes were a dark storm.

"What are you doing?" He roared at Zak.

I flinched back but Zak didn't bat an eye. "We're just about to play an interesting game, Elijah." His voice was smooth but there was an underlying challenge. "Why don't you join us?"

In one fast furious motion Elijah scooped up the tarnished trinkets and cards and threw them into the box. He slammed the top down shaking the table and rattling the trinkets inside. He held out his hand to Zak. Elijah's long talons meant business. Zak sighed like a yawn and dropped the key into Elijah's hand, whose talon fingers wrapped around it. Elijah walked over to the little table where Zak had got the game. He locked the drawer and placed the key in his pocket.

"I trusted you to look after him." His gaze towards Zak was poisonous.

Zak rolled his eyes.

"You are so possessive of him. He's okay."

The tension in Elijah's shoulders softened and he bent down and kissed me. "I'm sorry I had to leave you this morning. It wasn't my choice. I'll make it up to you tonight."

Zak snickered.

My eyes widened slightly but I didn't say anything. Zak kept quiet as I'm sure it was more fun to watch the shiny new toy squirm. His black eyes casually glanced up at Elijah and then back to me. I stared back. *What does he expect, that I throw myself at Elijah's feet?*

I was trapped. The way I felt about him was getting to me. Sitting back in my chair I chilled for a second.

"It's starting to get twilight out now, let's go for a walk, my love." Elijah then turned to go. Zak leaned over and in a low voice and whispered, "So much for leaving, huh?" He chuckled to himself. I got up abruptly and went to the door where Elijah was waiting for me to join him.

Chapter Five

THE AIR WAS COOLING off outside creating moisture that clung to our skins.

Elijah took my hand in his sending a shiver through me. We meandered through garden beds that towered over with grasses, weeds and perennials that had seeded themselves with abandon. The long grass in the old lawn laid over on its side. Patches here and there were stunted. We kept walking and came across a path. Elijah led me down a pebbled weed invested path. It led to an old gazebo.

I froze. Suddenly images flashed in front of my eyes. I could barely see what they were but the gazebo was definitely the focus.

Old rose vines and ivy clamored over one side of the old white gazebo. A faint smell of spice from the old roses filled the air. The stairs where still there although one was broken. He led me up onto the decaying structure. You could look all around the yard and back to the house from where we stood. I placed my hand on the ledge and felt the crumbling wood underneath my fingers. I could smell the damp rot of the wood.

Elijah pulled me close to him. His warm breath fell on my face. I leaned in to him. His voice was low but his words made it to my ears.

"I'm so glad I found you."

I pulled back slightly. "What?"

Before I could ask what he meant, his lips were over mine. I was caught up in the passion of the embrace when memories lightly touched my mind. Standing here in Elijah's arms in this gazebo gave me the feeling I had been here before with Elijah. I just couldn't put it all into focus.

We went back to the house just before dark. He showed me a bit more of this place of theirs. As we walked and my eyes scanned the old paintings on the wall something inside me started to think. *I've been here before and I've seen these painting before—many times. How did I know that?* My hand brushed against the walls trying to touch memories and bring them to life but I couldn't draw them out. The secrets were buried too deep inside these walls.

The feeling of familiarity wouldn't leave me and I didn't know why. Old paintings on the walls reminded me of things I had seen in my dreams of Elijah and me. I ran my fingers along the edge of the paintings feeling the dust and rough cracked oil paint. I was hoping something would touch me back. Yet nothing would come out and tell me anything.

At the end of one hall hung a large painting of a woman. She was beautiful. Thick dark hair framed a fragile face. Bright blue eyes that almost looked frightened stared back at me. I wondered who she was.

The hallway rugs were burnt reds and gold. Down the middle was thread bare and in some places so worn you could see the wood floors beneath.

I wanted to ask Elijah about the state of the house. I didn't know how to ask or how he would react. I would have to wait till Elijah was in a vulnerable state to ask these delicate questions.

There was another study on the second floor. It was open to the main floor. It was tucked in between two rooms so it just consisted of three walls with a place to sit and look out the window that faced the garden. The other walls were book shelves from floor to ceiling. I think at one time it was a crisp white but now what showed was a tea stained wall with peeling paint.

The draped hung sadly over the window. Even the window panes were covered in a dusty haze. The smell of old dust filled this little space. Despite that I could still see to the garden below. The moon's bright light cast shadows over the entire expanse of the garden.

I could see the gazebo where we had kissed and the path that we took to get there. I could see a hoe, a square shovel and pruners on the old flagstone path. A pot lay on its side. *Did this place die suddenly?*

Elijah came and sat next to me. He pulled me away from the window and towards him. He kissed the top of my head and mumbled something that I couldn't make out. There was a quiet stillness between us.

Later back in the bedroom I stared from the window out at the garden. Silvery moonlight bathed the plants and gave the blackness an iridescent glow. White flowers bloomed sporadically in the garden glowing in the darkness like tiny white lights.

Elijah came up behind me and slid his arms around my waist. I leaned my head back and rested against him. The scent of sandalwood drifted from him filling me with thoughts of him. His lips grazed my neck and then his tongue did the same. His tongue got a little rougher with each movement making me protest. He kissed my neck to make things better. I just started to relax again in his arms and closed my eyes when I felt his sharp teeth sink into my neck. He bit me!

My eyes flew open. He had a firm hold of my neck in his mouth. I could feel the flow of my blood being sucked out of me. I held still as it became more intimate between us.

He turned me. His lips fell on mine. I moaned and as he pulled away from me and whispered. "Feed on me."

Elijah offered me his wrist. I sunk my teeth in and instantly the flow of his demon blood burned my mouth. He held his wrist at my mouth firmly. I gasped for air when he took his wrist way. I turned to him in anger.

"What the hell was that about?"

"We're part blood bound now," he said. There was blood running down the corner of his mouth. I reached up and rubbed the blood away with my finger which he grabbed and placed my finger in his mouth sucking the blood off. His eyes were pure acid red. The warmth of his skin felt like fire. He pulled me towards the bed. "I want you naked and underneath me. I want our bare skins to touch."

He started pulling at my t- shirt. With his talon finger he traced around my right nipple. I laid back on the bed and he smiled looking very pleased.

Within minutes I was naked in bed with him. His touches were needy and hungry. He fed one more time on me and I fed from him. His blood didn't burn me this time-just left me with a slight high.

Elijah aggressively pushed my legs apart with his knee. I braced myself for his harness to drive his way inside me again but he held back. Instead he went down and with his tongue probed me and with his fingers spread and stretched apart preparing me for his lustful take.

He looked down at me for a moment. "Are you ready love? I want to fill you so bad." He eased himself inside and I caught my breath as the pain and sexual sensation combined as he hit my erotic spot. His eyes closed as he took in the moment and then he bared his sharp teeth at me and started his thrusting. I screamed with the crash of his body against me. His body pushed into mine crushing me as he filled me with his roaring heat and pulling out just in time to smother me with his hot cream. Elijah grinned down at me. "Now you get to take me. Make it good."

Elijah positioned himself on all fours on the bed. I came up behind him and spread his buttocks apart and slid deep inside him. He hissed as I went as deep as I could. I couldn't believe how he good he felt. My own lust took hold and my thrusting picked up a hungry speed.

I screamed his name as I filled him and covered his lower back. I collapsed on the bed and him beside me. Elijah pulled me close to him, wrapping me protectively in his arms.

Elijah was calm now, his energy spent. His eyes were back to their black red and where half closed as he lazily looked at me. His smile was one of contentment. "I love you so much, love. You have no idea." His lips softly brushed my forehead. His unruly thick hair fell in his eyes. I reached up and brushed his hair aside.

Elijah had bold cheekbone structure that defined his stature. He was taller than me by a good half foot. I loved nothing more than to rest my head against his broad chest and feel every ripple of his muscles under my cheek. I let my fingers trace down the side of his jaw all the way down his shoulder to his talon fingers. He slightly closed his eyes enjoying my gentle touch.

"I love you too," I whispered softly. He swallowed hard and pulled me close. "I will never let you go". There was fierceness in his voice that made me think that Zak was right-he was very possessive.

Chapter Six

THE HUNGER THAT WAS OUR lovemaking earlier was replaced with a much gentler love. This time was spent taking our time to explore each other and no blood feeding. We both fell into a sleep wrapped in each other's arms. No dreams this time.

Something woke me up in the night. Elijah was resting peacefully next to me. I could feel his warm breath. The moon's light shone brightly almost lighting up the room. Quietly, I slid out of bed making sure I didn't disturb Elijah and went to peer out the window. The whole garden was bathed in white light making the garden even more ghostly. The white blooms now seemed like they were hovering like spirits. An old oak tree that was nearest the house stretched out its gnarled fingers in the air ready to snatch what flew in the air. An owl came and perched on one of its limbs. It was eyeing something moving in the flowerbed. Before long, the owl dropped and flew off with its prey.

Elijah stirred behind me drawing my attention to him. His half opened black red eyes shimmered in the moon's light. He groaned as he beckoned me to come back. I slid in beside him.

"Can't sleep?"

"No, the moonlight drew me to the window. I couldn't resist," I said.

Elijah's hand slid down my hip and across my abdomen, getting lower and lower.

"I know something that is better than the moon. Something you definitely won't be able to resist." Elijah's voice was velvet smooth inside my head and I let out a small moan as he cupped my sac and gently squeezed and massaged me. I grew hard in his hand. He was right, I couldn't resist.

My breath hitched when Elijah's red talon ran down the length of my shaft. He rubbed me and played with my throbbing head. Pushing myself against him gave him the message of what I wanted from him.

Elijah pushed me onto my stomach and started massaging my buttocks. He did get some oil and as I felt the oil fall over my skin as I lifted myself to him.

"Anxious are we? Well, I won't keep my love waiting." He entered me and drove himself deep. I grabbed onto the bed sheets as now the pain I felt before was all gone. It was all pleasure now and I wanted more.

The two of us moved together bringing us both to an incredible climax. He was amazing. I collapsed in his arms and this time Elijah made sure sleep took me.

I was back in that dream world with Elijah in the garden. This garden was definitely not dead. The roses were in full bloom and their perfume filled the air. Elijah looked at me with those chestnut eyes and smiled. He had told me he had a surprise for me and I was excited.

He led me over to the rose laden gazebo. A table and two chairs were waiting for us. Beside the table was a bucket of ice with a bottle of champagne chilling in it.

"Are we celebrating something," I asked.

Elijah turned around. "I certainly hope so."

There was an air of mischief to him. *What was he up to?*

"Come sit over here beside me." He patted the seat next to him. My heart was pounding and I could feel the palms in my hand ringing with sweat. I quickly wiped my hands on my pants.

Elijah took my left hand and kissed my fingers sending a quiver through me. He reached into his pocket and took out a dark navy velvet box. He held it front of me watching my eyes go wide. He opened it and took out a thick band ring with a sapphire mounted on top of a cluster of small diamonds. "I would be honored if you accepted this and became my…"

My eyes flew open and bolted up into a sitting position. I looked around at my surroundings and then down at Elijah who was a sleep. I laid back down trying to calm my breathing down. My mind was racing with images-the garden, the gazebo, the ring and those chestnut eyes. *Why did these dreams come to me?*

I turned over on my side to face Elijah who stirred and rolled over to come face to face with me. His sleepy eyes opened and a lazy smile formed on his lips.

"Good morning love."

He kissed me and those images dissolved away leaving me in his arms to sleep again.

The next time I awoke, I was looking into red black eyes. We kissed leaving a burning sensation down my throat. I made an uncomfortable noise and rubbed my throat.

"You're hungry." He rolled off the bed and brought over a carafe. He poured some thick red liquid out into a glass and handed it to me. I didn't hesitate to down it and held out my glass for a refill. He poured me another. I still wanted more. I looked into his black red eyes and could see that he was thinking about something.

When I held out the glass once more he set the carafe down. He took the glass out of my hand. "I'll give you what's left if you do something for me."

I felt a chill and shifted under the covers. "What do you want me to do?" I could feel an uneasy prickle go through me.

"I want us to feed off each other again and blood bond us more." His voice was seductive with lustful undertones. His tongue traced along his bottom lip like I was the hunt. I held still but ready to move. He swallowed and quietly came back under the covers next to me.

As quick as hunting his prey he pinned me down and bit into my neck. His fingers laced through mine holding my hands above my head on the bed. I could feel my blood flowing into his mouth. I could feel him grow hard against me. When he pulled away blood dripped from his chin and his black red eyes burned with fire. The fresh blood from my neck made him moan.

He rolled me over and after rubbing my buttocks with warm oil he entered me from behind. I held still as his lust grew into a hungry beast. His red talons dug into my hips as his thrusting became an uncontrollable need. A growl erupted from him when he finally released.

He laid on top of me breathing hard. He closed his mouth over my neck and very gently fed again.

Elijah, still behind me, pulled me onto my side. He poured some of that warm oil on my hard cock and started rubbing me up and down my shaft. He entered me again and together we created a rhythm that brought us to a climax.

We weren't done yet. "Feed off of me and I'll give you the rest of the blood and I'll suck that cock of yours till you fill my mouth with your sweet cream." He offered his neck to me. I bent down and fed on him. His warm blood filled me with a darkness that like the drugs that sold on the street. Most of them killed you.

When I was satisfied and had drunk the rest of the blood in the carafe, Elijah kept his promise. He pleasured me and sucked me till I let off a load in his mouth that made me scream.

Elijah rested beside me with his eyes closed. I looked up at the ceiling with his it's chipped paint. I felt more alive than I had for a very long time.

Avian, you have allowed yourself to be blood bound to Elijah, a demon. Why? What is it about him that draws you to him, like a moth to light? I know he is someone from my past. I must have loved him from before. I have to find out more about him and us or what we used to be.

I rolled over and kissed his cheek and told him, "I love you just as much now as I know I ever did before."

He didn't look over at me, he just smiled.

Chapter Seven

WHEN I WOKE I HEARD VOICES. I lifted myself up and rested on my elbows. Zak was in the room. He and Elijah were having a quiet conversation. Zak glanced casually over at me. "You're mate has finally wakened." Elijah turned and smiled. "Yes, my mate has."

I think *mate* had a nice ring to it for Elijah. I flopped on my back forgetting that I was fully exposed. I notice Zak was eyeing me up. I pulled the sheet over. He grinned.

"Don't worry love, I got a good look at you before," Zak said.

Zak Leaned slightly over to Elijah. "Anytime you want a threesome."

Elijah grinned. "Let's give our boy some time, okay?"

Zak chuckled softly but gave me a playful glance before he left.

When the door shut softly, Elijah silently joined me on the bed. "How are you feeling, love?" "I'm fine." I'm not sure what he wanted to know but I just kept my answer simple.

He leaned over and kissed me and we just sat there and kissed for a while. Elijah slipped his hand under the sheet and held me. I started to grow hard. Elijah's lips formed a smile as he pulled away the sheet and my hardness was there for him to see. His breath hitched. I could see desire in his eyes. He bent down and slipped his mouth over my shaft. His sucking was strong and soon I gave him what he desired. He swallowed what he called was my sweet cream.

It was like candy to him.

After we both sat up, we let our foreheads touch. I could feel a connection to Elijah that was stronger now. It was probably the blood feeding. I looked deep into Elijah's eyes. In my mind it was like opening a door into Elijah's life. I entered into his past. That's when it happened, it was very brief but it was a very clear image. I saw a different time. He looked at me-with chestnut brown eyes. When he pulled his forehead away the image vanished. I didn't say anything, and neither did he. I wondered if he saw the same thing. I kept the image to myself.

When he looked at me with those beautiful red black eyes, I smiled. A softening in his face seemed to almost warm the room. The moment was disturbed by a quiet knock at the door. Zak didn't wait for an invitation, he walked in carrying a tray that held glasses and a full decanter. I smelled the blood right away. Zak grinned at me.

"I thought you would be hungry." He poured a glass and handed it to me. He also poured Elijah one. For the first time Elijah drank quite thirstily. The blood seemed to give Elijah a renewed energy. He gestured for Zak to come join us. My chest jerked. Elijah noticed and took my hand and whispered in my head. "When you're ready, love."

I relaxed a bit. Elijah bent over and kissed Zak. He moaned like he was starving. When Elijah pulled away, I could tell Zak wanted more by the look in his eyes.

I could feel Zak's desires in my head. I shut him out but he was strong.

"Take it easy on him Zak. I know you're hungry. Give him time and we'll all be together soon." Zak's black eyes gazed over me with seductive lure to join them. I quivered and looked away. He rested his head on Elijah's shoulder. I could feel the disappointment in my head. His gaze made me uncomfortable. Elijah then pulled him down. I knew Elijah was going to make love to him. I could feel their thoughts coming through me. They hungered for me to join them.

I shut their yearning out. It was a relief that I could do that. I slipped out of bed quietly. Before getting to the door Zak's soft voice wafted over to me.

"Please come back to bed. Lay between us."

My eyes settled on them for a moment. The need for fresh air and some time alone was stronger. I would seek the garden out and find some solitude there.

I walked out.

It was early morning by the feel of the air. I walked out and took one of the old paths. I stood there and looked over the over grown expanse.

The garden had a grey look to it like there was a spider's web draped over with a heavy blanket of dew weighing it down. Tiny dew drops hung like pearls adding to the ghostly garden.

I took one of the old paths that had pea gravel on it. It actually held up not too bad. There were only a few weeds. It crunched loudly under my feet. The pompous grass towered up into the sky and dew dripped like rain droplets onto the pea gravel making its own song.

Dampness stuck to my hair and skin as I explored this strangely familiar place.

The image that I had seen in Elijah's head only confirmed that we had lived another life together before this one. This garden wasn't going to tell its secrets, I had to find them myself.

Behind a flower bed I spied what looked like the top of a giant head stone. I walked over but the path was blocked by brambles. Looking over and through the over grown plants I could see it was a family plot.

If I could get inside, maybe this would provide some answers. The damn brambles were acting like a fence to keep out intruders. I walked around and there was a small chapel at one end. Next to the outside wall was a metal gate that was leaned up against the old stone wall. It must have been the entrance to this little cemetery.

I decided to use it as a ladder to get over those brambles. The grass had grown through the gate tying it down. It was hard pulling it free, but I did it. I carefully leaned it against the still existing fence, climbed it and then effortlessly leapt, landing on the other side.

Tombstones peaked up through the grass. Most of them were broken and leaning over. In some cases the lettering was gone like the stone had been chipped away. There was an eerie feeling of death here. My mind picked up images of other people as I touched the tombstones. *Did I know these people?* I continued to walk around the broken stones. The chapel seemed to have eyes that was watching me. I felt like I had come back to something. My eyes looked up at the trees that towered over. Even the dead leaves that still hung on the trees held memories of this place that had died. *How did this all happen?*

I could feel something else. I wasn't alone. It wasn't Elijah or Zak but something…someone else and whatever or whoever it was, it wasn't happy.

I jerked around at a noise. Something was in the grass. It was coming straight for me. I leaped up into the tree. I surveyed the area. Whatever was hiding in the grass, I could hear grunts and growl. I edged over the tree's largest limb. It reached out over the brambles onto the other side. All of a sudden I heard shouting in my head. "Jump!"

Silently I landed on the other side. I could hear panting in my head. They were coming towards me and as I turned I saw Elijah and Zak running. Both of them looked at me with wild eyes.

"What were you doing?" Elijah held me at arm's length making sure I was alright. Zak walked around in front of me and looked me in the eyes. His endless black pools sent a shiver through me. I backed up slightly.

"Don't ever go there love," he said.

That was the first time Zak called me love. I looked at them both. "Why?"

They exchanged glances then Elijah spoke. "You don't want to tick off the gatekeeper."

"Gatekeeper? Who or what is that?"

They both stood in front of me. Elijah rested his hand on my arm. "Behind those brambles lives the Death Witch. She's father's plaything and the gatekeeper is her pet. That is her domain and we stay away from there. That's how it is." His voice grew softer. "Love, you have to be careful where you walk here. Please don't go for *walks* without one of us with you. This is no ordinary garden." There was a certain amount of eeriness in his tone. His face was slightly pale and his skin was even a bit clammy. Zak shared a look with Elijah that I interpreted as a fear that they didn't want to face.

One came on each side of me and slid their arms around my waist. Together they pulled me away from the little cemetery. We walked back towards the house. Zak's hand was rubbing me softly on my lower back. When we got to the entrance way of the house, Elijah stopped.

"I'm going to go check on something. I'll join you two in a bit." Before I could ask him where he was going he was gone. Zak faced me and leaned in without hesitation. His lips brushed against my cheek. The softness of his cheek hovered against mine for just a mere moment. He smelled like morning dew. I think I could feel a flush in my cheeks. He pulled away taking my hand and led me through the door. We stood in the foyer and my body went stiff. In a blur he came up behind me and slid his arms around my waist burying his face in my neck. I could hear a moan escape him followed by a whisper of suggestion that we go upstairs. Without thinking I leaned into him enjoying the kisses. It was like I wasn't in my own mind or body. His hand slid down to my jeans where he undid the top button. I tensed.

"Let me," he whispered. His hand slid effortless down inside my jeans.

"Zak, I don't know." Even though my breath was getting faster I still needed to put up some protest. He pushed me towards the stairs and I numbly went up them.

We went inside the bedroom and he took my hand and led me to the bed. I backed up slightly knowing what was going to take place but he didn't take my resistance as a no. He pushed my shoulders down making me sit on the edge of the bed. Without effort he pushed me onto my back. I could hear my zipper unzip. My hard cock bulged through. Zak wasn't long finding me with his hot wet mouth. I grabbed hold of the sheets as I sucked in air. I could smell the scent of lavender and old rose. It reminded me of a Summer June afternoon. *How did he do that?* It was a tidal wave of emotion as I felt his suck getting stronger and *his* emotions were swimming in my head. An image of him and I holding hands fluttered in front of my eyes. *Yes, Zak, I will hold hands with you and more...* He dug his nails into my thigh as his suck got faster. It wasn't long before I arched in ecstasy. I couldn't believe that I did this with Zak but I did and I returned the pleasure to him, tasting him.

Elijah came back and slipped into bed with us. Zak was half asleep so Elijah nudged him. He moaned and rolled over. Elijah kissed him and then me. I was in the middle as they both let their hands glided over my naked body exploring me and each other. The three of us experienced a connection that made us as one now, in an odd erotic way. The love making was pure to us, thus connecting us with the tiniest thread.

I laid in between them feeling the warmth of their bodies seep into me. Zak was fast asleep. His breathing was an even rhythm. Elijah watched him then turned to me. We gazed into each other's eyes.

"Tell me about this place, Elijah. Why is everything here in a state of death?"

His black red eyes blinked in surprise searching for words to tell me. Finally he sighed. "In time Avian I will tell you more but right now let's just enjoy what we have."

He said it like we wouldn't have it for long. Zak stirred and he rolled over and looked at us with sleepy black eyes. He grinned. "This is more like it." He kissed my cheek and Elijah kissed the other side of my cheek.

I was firmly wedged between them-just where they wanted me. Their gentle touches sent traces of fire running through me. I felt nervous but both of them whispered in my head calming me into a relaxed state. They both sent kisses down one each side of my neck. Zak's hand slid down my stomach all the way between my legs. He squeezed my inner thigh while Elijah cupped my sac and massaged me until I was hard. Then he stroked me till his fingertips were wet from my cream. Zak slid down and sucked me for a bit while Elijah held me firmly in Zak's mouth.

"Give us a taste," Elijah whispered.

I shuddered as both their hot mouths took turns sucking me and sucking on my sac making me crazy. I fell asleep in their arms.

I knew when I woke up it was the middle of the night. I was still in-between them. I moved and Zak shifted but his arm tightened around me. When he relaxed I gently put his arm over to his side. He protested a bit but soon fell back into his slumber. I went to slide out but I was quickly grabbed. Elijah was alert.

"Where do you think you're going?" He pulled me back and looked down at me. His black red eyes glowed in the dark.

"Nowhere," I replied.

He grinned. "I don't believe you." He kissed me and when he did I felt my mind being flooded by him. It was like he was exploring every corner of my being. I tried to pull away but he wouldn't let go.

When he did I gasped. "You're too curious. We have to fix that." There was an underlying darkness to his tone.

"What do you mean?" I was getting nervous.

"You have to learn that now that we are bonded that you can't go off to where ever you want and that includes exploring that creepy little cemetery. You're my mate and I want to know where you are at all times. You understand love?"

Zak's off comment about Elijah being very possessive echoed through my head, again.

I didn't go anywhere that night even though every fiber of my being wanted to be out there a part of the black night's solitude. I fell asleep finally in Elijah's restrictive arms. Zak rolled over and threw his arm around me securing me where they wanted me.

Filtered sunlight made my eyes flutter. I half opened them, pulling away from the light, not that it was burning but the room was a blur. Dust hung in the filtered sunlight casting a room that looked abandoned. The chair by the desk adorned a spider web in the crook of its leg. The sunlight highlighted the tiny black spot in the corner. I guess she was sleeping. The table cloth that draped over the small table beside the chair was probably white at one time but now looked tea stained and frayed. My eyes traveled over to behind the chair and table to a tall book shelf that was built into the wall. It stood floor to ceiling tall. The books were squeezed tightly together. I tried to read the spines but the dust clung to them hiding the titles except for one. It was like it repelled the dust and I could tell it was a black velvet cover. How could that be? I felt compelled to go to it. Elijah and Zak were sleeping so I carefully slid out through the bottom of the bed as silently as I could. Neither one of them shifted. I walked over to the bookshelf and reached up for the book. I almost was touching it.

"Are you going to start to read now, love?"

The sleepy voice from behind me made me pull my hand back. I looked over at Elijah who was sitting up on one arm. His unruly dark hair was even more unruly and was partly obscuring those black red eyes of his. He tilted his head slightly at me. "Although, I don't mind watching you read there like that." I remembered I was naked. "You look beautiful in the sunlight, Avian."
His voice was caressing my mind and I reacted without realizing.
"Come over here and stand by me, love."

I walked over and when I looked down at myself I realized why he wanted me over. He reached over and wrapped his talon hand around my hard cock and guided it around his tongue. With his tongue he flicked and licked my head making me groan. Then his entire mouth slid over my shaft making me suck in air. By this time Zak had stirred and saw what was going on. He got up out of bed and came up behind me. He cupped my sac massaging me and sending kisses down my neck. I could feel Zak's hard cock rubbing up against me leaving wetness on my lower back. His cock was so wet he slid in between my buttocks. The guys had a rhythm going. Zak would give my sac a squeeze every now and then until I was ready. Just before I came Zak pulled out and bent down on his knees and Elijah let Zak put his mouth over my head and sucked for a minute. When I came they both enjoyed taking turns devouring me.

I flopped on the bed face down. Zak kissed a trail up my spine. Elijah came and laid beside me. "That's what you get for crawling out of bed like that." He kissed my temple and with that brief touch I saw an image of Elijah, he was looking at me smiling with love in his chestnut brown eyes. I blinked and the image was gone.

Zak rolled off the bed. "I'll meet you guys down in the kitchen?"

Elijah nodded.

"Let's get dressed and get you fed, you must be starving." I watched him dress as I lay there. He glanced over at me. "I'm not leaving without you, you know." He grinned but I knew he meant it. I pushed myself off the bed and went to reach for my clothes when Elijah grabbed them first. I was standing in front of him naked. His eyes took all of me in.

"You're so beautiful, Avian." He sighed and came close to me. He gently held my sac which was a bit tender and he knew it. He gently massaged me.

"Is that better?"

I nodded. I felt very breakable in his hands.

Elijah and I went down stairs to the kitchen. Zak, of course was not there like he said he would. Elijah brought out a pitcher of the thickest black red liquid. My throat burned. He poured me a mug and I couldn't wait. He handed it to me and in one gulp I had it down.

"Take it easy love." He refilled my mug. I slowed down this time thinking he might again use my blood lust as leverage for one of his desires. He poured one for himself and leisurely sipped. I could tell by the vibe that thrummed through me that he was thinking about something. Elijah silently walked over to the kitchen widow and took a couple of sips. He gently set his mug on the counter wrapping his red talon hands around it as if keeping the contents warm.

In a blur he was in front of me. I startled. Elijah looked down at me with a predatory hunger in his black red eyes. He cupped my face with those red talon hands and I felt this energy go through me. It didn't hurt but it made me suck in air. The tip of his nose was now touching mine and all I could see was black red. "I want to take you hunting." Then he kissed me and calmness settled into me.

The front door rattled and banged announcing Zak's arrival. He bounded in full of hellish spirit wearing an evil smile fit for a demon. He asked Elijah, "Are we all going?"

Elijah looked down at me and grinned. "I believe so."

Chapter Eight

I COULD INSTANTLY SMELL that familiar smell-the night air with its sharp edge of fresh coldness that could cling to skin. The airs cold touch flowed through me down to my toes. Purely exhilarating. Twilight was here now and soon we would be in darkness.

Zak walked beside us with a lively step. He was up for the hunt. Elijah laced his fingers through mine and gently squeezed. Looking up at him I could see black red eyes that shone back at me. They were dangerous and evil. We looked straight ahead. Elijah leaned in and whispered, "You're not afraid are you?"

I just grinned at him.

"Didn't think so." He laughed.

Just as the sun went down a scream filled the air. Zak leaped ahead of us. We stopped to listen. Another shrill cry filled the night. A wicked smile danced across Zak's face. "The boys have found the hunt."

Elijah squeezed my hand. "There is a surprise waiting for you."

Apart of me already knew what it was. As we got closer the sound of someone being dragged got louder. Then we came to a clearing where there were five others. The acidity in the air burnt my eyes. These were demons. My body instantly pushed close to Elijah. A body lay on the ground at their feet and it was still alive. It was a female, no doubt seduced by one of them.

They looked at us when we came into view. They all smiled and greeted Elijah and Zak.

Then all eyes were on me.

Elijah pulled me close. "This is my mate Avian." A few muffled murmurs came from the group. One stepped ahead and I held my breath.

"Your *mate* is a vampire."

The demon's black eyes settled on me. After a pause he smiled revealing sharp teeth. "Welcome" he said. He stepped back with the others.

Elijah laughed, "I brought my love here to celebrate and give my new love a gift." He walked over to the girl who was still lying on the ground. He roughly grabbed her by the arm and dragged her over to my feet.

"This is for you love, feed well." Elijah kneeled down to her and propped her up sweeping her hair back from her neck exposing her main vein. "Come love, for you."

My insides froze as I stared at the girl who shook with fear. *Why was Elijah doing this? I don't feed on the innocent, only the drug users and drunks that* die *anyway.*

"Is something wrong love?"

My body shook itself out of its daze and I kneeled down. She jerked back when she saw me but Elijah violently grabbed her by the hair holding her still. His black red eyes were alive and evil. There was no choice for me. Her bare neck was exposed and so without thinking anymore I leaned over and sunk my teeth into her neck. Elijah covered her mouth to muffle her scream. Warm blood flew into my mouth and down my throat. There was one last shudder from her body before she went limp. She was dead. As I fell back, Zak pulled me up and now was standing beside me. Elijah was standing in front of me. This time Zak offered me his wrist. My eyes flew to Elijah shaking my head no. Suddenly Elijah leaned in close letting his cheek rest on mine. He whispered in my ear, "Feed from him love." His voice was cold and dangerous.

Zak wanted me to feed from him and Elijah wasn't letting me go anywhere till I did what I was told. Zak held his wrist up to me, pushing against my lips. His black eyes made my skin even colder.

"Enjoy me," he whispered. The rest of them were snickering and whispering things that sounded like metal being clawed in my ears. I sunk my teeth into Zak's wrist. A burning sensation erupted inside me. I almost spit it out but between Zak and Elijah, Zak's wrist was held firmly in place making me swallow. Zak hissed in my face, "That's it love, take more."

I didn't think it was ever going to end. Finally Zak and Elijah let go and I gasped. My mouth felt like it was burnt away. My shaking hand went to my lips half thinking I wouldn't find anything but I did. Elijah was inches from my face now. He kissed and licked the blood around my mouth. His tongue felt rough. I could see a flicker of fire in his black red eyes.

"Why did his blood burn me?"

"Zak's blood is full of underworld drugs. That's what burned you but don't worry, unless you have taste for his addictions, you only have to feed off me."

I must have had some look of horror on my face. His black red eyes narrowed slightly at me. "Are you scared of me now?"

Before I could say anything Zak came up behind me slapping my shoulder. "He's got you running through his veins, he's numb to fear, right love?"

The rest of them howled like barbaric wolves. One of the members of the Hunt grabbed Zak by the arm and took him off to join them. Two of them dragged the body away, vanishing into the darkness. There would be no evidence when they were through with it.

Elijah and I were alone standing in front of each other. The cold air embraced us as he ran his red talon fingers through my hair. I shivered. A low growl escaped him as he kissed me hard.

"Come and let's celebrate love." This time he tenderly kissed me. I believe this was his way of shoving aside any notions of trying to leave.

When we met up with the others they were waiting for us at the edge of town. Elijah had his arm around my waist keeping me close to him. His presence was in my head and he wanted me to know it. I kept my thoughts quiet and desires hidden.

We ended up back at the drinking hole. Tonight was alive with members of gangs, more demons and some dangerous looking vampires.

There was entertainment in the form of fights and a few explicit sex forays played out to the delight of the audience members. I stayed back in the dark corner where nobody would bother me. Everyone in the room knew now that I belonged to Elijah. They would never risk getting on his bad side by tormenting his mate. That would be suicide.

Elijah mingled with the others but every once in a while he threw me a glance. He talked to me in my mind telling me how special I was and the things he wanted to do to me tonight. He was explicit. He sent me images of his hard cock that begged to be sucked. His voice filled my head.

I want to bend you over and fuck you on all fours like you're my bitch.

I took a gulp of the cold drink in my hands trying to douse his erotic thoughts.

Let me claim your ass again and again and fill you with my heat.

My eyes stared at him trying to tell him to stop but he was only getting started.

Silently I absorbed his desires much to his pleasure. Within a split second he was beside me filling my mind with even more explicit play. My hands tightened around the glass and my hand started to shake. The glass shattered and fell to the floor. There was a small cut on my hand. My eyes flew up to Elijah who looked at my blood with hunger.

Being careful I placed my hand up to his mouth. It was making him fevered. His mouth covered my cut and he sucked the blood making him moan. When he let my hand go my cut was healed.

Elijah took my other hand and placed it down on his hardness that was pushing through his pants. He made it clear he wanted me now. Images of us naked in front of everybody made me shake my head no. Still he made it very clear if we didn't head back to the house he would take me here in front of everyone. That was a promise I knew he would keep.

Waiting for us outside was a black sports car-ready to pick us up. The back door opened and Elijah gently pushed me in.

I couldn't see the driver. The driver was either very short or the car was possessed. The gates were open like they were waiting for us. The car never made a noise on the gravel driveway and stopped at the entrance. The door opened and Elijah was there of course to take my hand and escort me out of the car and into the house where deadly passion awaited.

Instead of going upstairs he led me to a room on the main floor. I believe it was the remains of a study. There were candles lit everywhere giving the room a soft glow. A table was set up with two wine glasses and a bottle that was already opened. What took my breath away was this massive four poster bed that sat in the middle of the room. My chest slightly tightened as Elijah came up behind me. His breath was on fire. "I want you so bad. I'm going to show you just how much I want you."

He walked to around to the front of me. With one of his red talons he slid into the top openings of my white shirt and pulled it open revealing my bare chest. He cut into my flesh a fine line across my breast bone. A trickle of blood went down to my abdomen. His tongue followed the blood up to the cut where he healed it. He was drunk with passion and I could go nowhere.

He pushed me towards the bed. "Take off your clothes and lay on the bed. I want to admire what is mine."

Slowly, I took off my clothes and lay on the bed. I could tell by Elijah's eyes that he liked what he saw. He sat at the edge of the bed and just stared. Then he came a little closer. His eyes felt like the tips of his talons. In my mind I could feel the sharp edge of his talon against my skin. I almost flinched.

"Get hard for me," he whispered. I did. To add to his lust I placed images of me with my legs spread apart and his breathing got faster.

Finally, he had to have me.

Elijah's hand slid up from my ankle stopping under the curve of my knee. His red talons dug into the soft flesh. I flinched and he instantly let go and continued up my leg. This time he stopped at my thigh. He gently squeezed gliding his hand to the inside of my thigh. His hand rested there, felling the beat of my blood. He closed his eyes as the vibration of my blood softly thrummed into his fingers sending little electrical shocks up his arm.

Elijah's talons dug in but not to the point of breaking skin. His half opened eyes peered at my swollen member. He bent down and flicked his tongue at my throbbing head. With his tongue he pulled me into his mouth and sucked concentrating on the tip.

I threaded my fingers through his hair gently pushing him down making him take more of me into his mouth. He obliged taking all of me. I cried out.

He stopped to spread my legs apart. Taking one side of my sac at a time he sucked and teased. The sheets underneath my hands were bunched up in a tight ball. "Take me Elijah, please."

He came up and towered over me. "Don't worry love, I will take you over and over until you collapse in my arms."

He took out his favorite oil and massaged me from the tips of my toes to my face. I pulled my legs up and reached for his cock but he moved out of my reach. He was driving me crazy. His fingers slid inside me easily. A moan escaped from both of us. "Avian, I need to fill you love."

Elijah's pants were undone but not pulled down. I sat up and pulled them down and he eased out of them. I grabbed his shirt and undone it letting the back of my fingers brush against his skin as I worked my way down to the last button.

Grabbing his swollen member I rubbed his tip with my thumb where already he was leaking his wetness. "Come inside me, now," I breathed in his face.

Rocking back I took him with me and he thrust himself inside me as I wrapped my legs around him holding him there. I moved my hips and he moved his creating an erotic sensation for both of us.

I eased my hold and his hungry thrusts drove into me filling me with his heat that only he could give me.

Elijah was trying to catch his breath but I didn't let him. I made him go on all fours where I oiled him and myself. He hung onto the bed railing while I fucked him. I cursed out his name when I was finally rewarded with my release. When I pulled out I spanked him.

Now we were both on the bed lying side by side trying to catch our breaths. I turned my head to him, "So, how many more times are you going to take me?"

He laughed. His black red eyes flickered with mischief. "We've only just begun love. I haven't bought out the sex toys yet."

I was exhausted and he was pleased. Elijah was content holding me in his arms. The room glowed in the candle light. "My precious love, you're mine forever." He whispered to me over and over. He was obsessed, I could feel it. I kissed him gently and he moaned with pleasure at what I did.

I whispered softly into his ear, "Do you love me?"

"I have always loved you."

I don't know if he realized it or not but that was a hidden past memory surfacing. I laid my head on his chest and slipped into a dream.

It was a sunny bright afternoon and it was one of those windy days. I was in the garden with Elijah. He looked so handsome and happy. He had asked me to the party his family was having the next night. He was excited about it because he was hoping to make an announcement. I wanted to know what it was but he wouldn't tell me. He led me to the gazebo where a tray of sweets and wine waited for us. He was up to something.

I asked but he still wouldn't say. I had one raspberry tart and some wine. Then I could hear my voice say it. I had asked one more time what he was up to. I looked into his chestnut brown eyes for a fleeting moment and that's when the wind picked up. Our nice sunny day was gone and it seemed a storm was coming up fast. Elijah's hair was blowing all around his face. The smile he had on his face was gone. I asked him what was wrong and all he said was "evil."

My eyes opened and looking down at me was Elijah. His black red eyes bored into me. I wondered if he knew what I dreamed. He didn't say anything but maybe he put the dream there?

I pulled him down for a kiss and I felt this warmth flood over me. It was coming from him. It was like he was letting his guard down. *Is this a glimpse of who he used to be?*

"Hey, wake up love birds." Zak came crashing through the doors. He grabbed a hold of the beds posts, one in each hand and swung himself forward like a drunk man. His white shirt was half open and stained red. His hair was a mess with a bit of blood caked into it. He had "partied" all night.

"Elijah, have you had your fill yet? You were positively salivating over him last night." He swung himself around one of the bed posts. I thought he was going to land on the bed but he managed to stand. Zak's black eyes looked down over Elijah's naked body. He ran his tongue along his bottom lip. Elijah didn't move or say anything. Zak came around to Elijah's side and leaned down and wrapped his hand around Elijah's shaft and devoured him in his mouth. He sucked hard. Elijah grabbed hold of the bed sheet. Zak was being forceful. Why didn't Elijah stop him?

Finally they both relaxed and Zak brought Elijah into orgasm filling him with what he wanted. He looked over at me and winked. "I got a little taste of you there too."

Elijah waved him out of the room. Zak blew us both a kiss before he left. Elijah stared up at the ceiling trying to catch breath. "Zak can be an ass at times but he is loyal."

He ran his hand though my hair and firmly held my cheek in the palm of his hand.

"I hope you can be just as loyal because there is nothing worse than betrayal. I don't handle it well love. It would a nasty little thing if you get my drift." His words were ice.

"I would never…" I began when he finished for me with a smile on his face. "I know you would never do anything love. You love me and only me." I nodded and he smiled again. I could feel how happy he was. He pushed me back on the bed and made love to me sending me the message that I was his and only his.

As I picked up his vibe I knew where I stood. *I am yours Elijah forever and a day. Blood bound to you is my fate. The day you decide that I am not yours is the day that my life as it has existed will end. Without you there is no existence for me.*

Chapter Nine

THE DAY AND NIGHT MELDED into one with Elijah. He pretty much kept me close by and of course he was in my mind-always. He did let me wander around the house a little more.

It was getting dark out now but I didn't want to for a walk in the garden. I remembered the bookshelf in the bedroom. When I walked into the room it was like no one had ever been here. We had been sleeping in the other bed for a while. Dust lay thick on the table by the bookshelf. The bedding looked decayed and torn, not like it was when Elijah and I were here. Even the floor had a layer of dust on it. I walked over to the bookcase and that's when I saw it, the black velvet book.

I remembered it now. It had no layer of dust anywhere near it. I pulled the book down. It was a thick book with not a speck of dust stuck to it. It seemed to repel it or something. It weighed heavy in my hand. I put it on the table and opened it. The language in the front page was foreign. The paper of the book was thick and I could feel something on my fingers like grit but I couldn't see anything on the paper. I turned some more pages and these had no print on them at all. I couldn't figure out this book but then it was like the book told me. It was a book of black magic. A chill went through me. I wondered if it belonged to Elijah. When my hands touched the paper the book felt alive. The velvet jacket felt warm like clothing against a person's skin. My hand jumped off the pages when they started to turn themselves and then stopped. The pages were blank. I stared at the book waiting to see what the book would show me.

In the middle of the two pages ink started to crawl out like a spider crawling out of the spine as if hiding in there somewhere. The ink slithered across the two pages forming words.

On the page read, "HOW TO LIFT CURSES".

I started to read it and it told me I had to collect items that belonged to the ones affected and place these items in a jar along with certain herbs. Then with a chant to a spell, drop a match in the jar. How would that lift a curse? Then I read the ingredients, the herbs, wolfs bane being one was poison to demons and if put with an item that meant something to them, it was very effective in removing the curse that they put on you but also could kill them.

This was not Elijah's book.

I backed up as if the book might attack. Then I noticed something slithered across the bottom. It read "You're not one of them."

The door opened and I quickly snapped the book shut. I held the book behind my back.

"You like to read do you?"

He smiled softly. "I'm sorry love I didn't mean to startle you," he chuckled.

Elijah looked over the books himself and reached up and pulled down a book. "Do you like Shakespeare?" I looked at what he had pulled down-Romeo & Juliet. I grinned at him. "You know they both die at the end?"

He just shrugged his shoulders. "I like to think that they lived on forever in another world-after their death." I think he was making a reference to us-maybe. I still clung to the black velvet book behind my back. This book felt like it had a life form as it got warm against my back.

Elijah put the book back and continued his search for me. That's when I noticed the bed.

It was like everything was replaced. The bedding was fresh, I couldn't help but stare. Elijah came close to me. "Oh my love, I love it when you have thoughts of us in that bed together. That makes me happy."

I just smiled and nodded in agreement. Elijah tilted his head at me. "What's behind your back love?"

"Nothing," I replied.

He chuckled and reached behind me. The velvet book snatched itself out of my hands and landed on the floor. Elijah bent down and picked it up. I watched him look at the book. He thumbed through it but of course all he saw was blank pages. Then he smiled at me. "This is a journal. Where you going to write about us, love?" His voice was smooth and soft. He leaned over and kissed me. "You can write whatever you want love about us. Don't leave out any details."

His grin was wicked. He pulled me into his arms and kissed me deeply which led to the bed and him saying, "Let me help you with the first journal entry."

My love showered me kisses and his hand slid between my legs squeezing me and made me very hard. I moaned as he continued on. After begging many times to take off his clothes, my love finally did giving way for our skin to touch sending us both into a raging passion.

"How's that for a first entry love?"

I smiled at him. "I like it but I want to be underneath you, lying on my back while you fuck me. Make me scream and I'll put that in as well with lots of explanation points."

Elijah laughed and proceeded to carry out the deed. I did indeed scream when he finally granted me my release. Elijah gathered me in his arms and kissed the top of my head. My eyes closed to darkness.

I was in a dream and this time I was not alone. Elijah was with me. It was summer as always and the garden was beautiful. The smell of the old roses filled the breeze that blew against my face. Elijah and I were holding hands. My hand felt light and small in his. We walked for a while. I'm taking in the view and wondering and I thought out loud. "Why doesn't the garden look like this anymore?"

Elijah sighed in a melancholy way like he was thinking back, "Things happen love but don't worry about the garden, and we have each other forever, love."

"We'll be together forever?" My voice sounded far away but I did feel Elijah squeeze my hand.

"Yes love, we will always have each other. You're mine. You were his gift to me."

A slight chill ran down my spine like something about that wasn't right.

I woke up with the smell of rose and my nose twitched. I sat up and there were literally vases full of old fashioned roses everywhere. Their scent was heavy with spice. Silky petals of cream, pale pink and crimson filled the room with color and somehow brought the room back from the dead.

The door opened and Elijah came in with a tray. A crystal pitcher filled with red liquid caught my eyes. The scent of blood stirred the blood beast within me and my throat started to burn. Elijah laid the tray on the nightstand and silently poured a glass for me. I took it and let the warm liquid flow down my throat feeding me. He leaned over and kissed me. I noticed that his cheeks were flushed. I touched them and they were very warm.

"That's the glow that you give me. You fill me with such love." I smiled and kissed him. Our kiss lasted a little while. I slid my arms around his neck and held him. My eyes roamed the room while I held on to him. "Thanks for the roses love."

He smiled down at me. "You're welcome. I wanted to bring some of the dream back to you."

"Dream? You saw the dream I had?"

"Just a glimpse, not sure what it was about but I smelled the roses." He smiled.

I laid back on the bed and Elijah watched me. I don't know why but my eyes drifted over to the bookshelf. The black velvet book stood out and I could feel a pull to it. Elijah's eyes followed to where I was looking.

"You want to write something in the journal? Let me help inspire you." He reached under the covers and took hold of my cock. "Get hard in my hands love." He bent over and starting sucking and that did it. "I think you need a good massage love."

He grinned at me with a look that told me I was in for a ride. Elijah went and got some of that almond oil he liked and started to rub it all over me. He was talented with his hands. I closed my eyes enjoying his touch and exploration of my body. I think he was enjoying it as well. He licked my nipples and teased them making me groan. Down on the inside of my thigh, I had a tender spot that made me shiver.

He was now naked and had me in a position to have anal sex with me. He slowly massaged my buttocks working his fingers to the inside trying to relax me and is finger found that special spot inside that made me want more. He entered slowly but I was relaxed enough that I accepted all of him. He moaned with pleasure. He had applied plenty of oil to himself and me. He moved in a rhythm that brought us both pleasure. Elijah's breath got faster as he took hold of my hips and went faster and faster until he came with an explosion. He pulled out and came all over my lower back. With his fingers he massaged his warm cream all over and down to my hard cock where he rubbed me till I spilled my load.

We both laid in each other's arms trying to catch our breath. "Now you have something to write in that journal," he whispered in my ear.

"You can also write down that we're getting married."

"What?" I choked.

"You heard me love, we're getting married. I can't wait for you to be my husband." He kissed my temple and wrapped his arm and leg around me securely leaving me with thoughts of becoming a husband to Elijah.

Chapter Ten

I WOKE TO THE MOON'S LIGHT. It bathed the whole room in a
blue white ghostly light. I looked over at Elijah who was sleeping
peacefully. The moons light blanketed him with a soft glow. Then
my eyes wondered over to the bookshelf and instantly the black
velvet book looked at me like it had eyes.

Quietly, I got out of bed and went to the bookshelf and touched
the book's velvet spine. With my fore finger I pulled it out and it felt
heavy in my hands. I went over to the table and set it down carefully
to not wake Elijah. Carefully I opened the book in no particular
place as I thought it would go to where it wanted anyway. My eyes
stayed focused on it. Then it was like it yawned and woke up. The
ink seeped up through the binding and stretched out across the pages.
At first it was blurry but soon became readable.

"Can't sleep darling?" I could almost hear a soft laugh like a
woman. More words formed.

"How about a bedtime story?" There was another soft chuckle
and I swear it was a woman who made the noise. Like rain falling

against a window pane the words formed on the pages of the book. The story was titled-*A Lover's Night.*

My gaze shifted over to Elijah and his statement of getting married.

They met under the red moon with the woman that would grant them their eternity. The two lovers stood before the woman. She was ominous with blood red eyes that peered down at them. They clung to one another with fear shaking in their chests. The woman let their fear seep and crawl under her skin with much delight. Fear of the unknown was the most delicious to her. She instructed them to hold out their hands palms facing up. She laid a glass dagger across their palms.

The woman started to chant, waking up the dead silent night that only existed after midnight. Out of the shadows crept a pair of large wolf like dogs with red eyes. They laid at the woman's feet with sharp teeth showing with grey saliva dripping from their mouths. The two lovers shivered. From behind the woman stepped out of the forest what looked like tall spindly bodies with twisted limbs and knotted up fingers. Where the eyes should be where hollow black holes. Spider like creatures with many eyes came out of the grass and clung to the woman's skirt. Flits of light darted around her head. The lovers almost dropped the dagger. Her red eyes narrowed and her pointed ears bent back slightly. The two lovers froze.

She quickly softened and almost smiled at them. Then she closed her eyes and started to chant. The creatures around her did the same and without warning she took the glass dagger from their hands and slashed across their palms. Blood flowed and the wolf like creatures howled at the sight of the blood. The two lovers cried out but it was too late. Everything around them grew darker and darker. The two lovers dropped to the ground. They died at her feet in a pool of their own blood. The woman walked away leaving the night creatures to their treat.

I could hear a sigh. The story disappeared leaving a little note. "Wasn't that a lovely tale?" I could hear a wicked laugh. I slammed the book shut. Damn her.

I walked back to the bed and laid beside Elijah. His arm slid over me and this wave of calmness settled over me. I fell asleep with my eyes on the book.

A crack of thunder startled me. Elijah and I were wrapped up in each other's arms and tangled in the blanket. There was an eerie silence that hung in the room.

When the lightning struck the room followed by the crack of thunder, the room shook. Elijah lay still. What the hell?

I had never heard a storm here and soon the lightening gave light to the rain that started to pound against the window followed with ping noises against the glass. It was hale. Why couldn't Elijah hear it? I picked up a strange vibe from him. It was like he had gone to another world. My eyes frantically went to the book. It was open now. I knew I had slammed it shut but now it was like it wanted me to go over to it. I pulled myself away from Elijah without as much as a whimper. I untangled myself from the sheets and walked over to the book. The words were waiting for me.

Don't let Hades rule. The words never moved they just stayed. A muffled moan jerked my attention over to Elijah. He was now stirring and his black red eyes settled on me. The book shut itself, startling me.

"Come over here, love," said Elijah in a groggy voice. I crawled into bed and into his warm arms. Elijah glanced over at the window noticing what was going on outside. He snapped his fingers and the old heavy velvet curtains closed shutting out the storm making the room black. "That's better," he said.

He pulled me close so that our bare skin was touching. "Was it the storm that woke you?" I nodded. "I never heard a storm here before."

"Hmm, yeah, well every once in a while it happens." I could tell Elijah didn't want to elaborate on the subject so I didn't push it. I softly kissed him making him groan.

I wrapped myself around him before he could take it as anything more. He accepted that and kissed the top of my head taking in a deep breath. "In the morning love, I will have you."

Being in his arms eased the uneasiness of the book. I knew it was a woman who wrote that and she knew Hades. Who was she and how was I going to find out?

My head rested on Elijah's chest and the black room soon swallowed me.

When I woke the next morning, light shone through the sheet I was under. I pulled the sheet away from my face to see Elijah standing naked looking over the garden. His face was solemn. He looked over my way and smiled when he heard me shift in the bed. His grave look had disappeared. I wondered what he was thinking about. He looked beautiful standing there. He had strong lean muscles and chest hair that travelled down his abdomen to his most sensual part that aroused me most. He was getting hard in front of me. He knew I was watching him.

He strode over to the bed and stood there wanting me to touch. I reached over and wrapped my fingers around his shaft and rubbed him. With my other hand I cupped his sac and squeezed. He was heavy and full. He closed his eyes and I watched his breathing get faster. I could feel his mind swim in desire and lust mixed in with some sad emotion. I didn't stop what I was doing as I pulled him on to the bed. He laid before me and I picked up a vulnerability that was not there before. He was letting me into his mind. I trailed kisses down between his thighs in that special spot that made him plead for more. All the while I stayed in his mind exploring.

His cock was throbbing now and I knew I was going to have to give him his release soon. My wet mouth slid over his shaft making him grab the sheets ripping them with his talons.

His back arched and I firmly held him as he screamed my name and swore to get even. Elijah's mind was swimming with erotic emotions and emotions that seemed familiar from someone I used to know. Sudden images of Elijah coming towards me across the garden and the feelings of love and excitement flood me as he gets closer. Elijah bolted up erasing the image as if maybe he saw it too. I stared at him waiting to see what his reaction was going to be but instead he fell back. I watched his chest rise and fall letting my eyes follow his chest hair down to his cock that was still firm. I wasn't finished with him yet.

I rolled him over without any protest. I grabbed the oil off the night stand and smothered his buttocks. I massaged him making him moan. I got up and kneeled behind him lifting his hips up to me. He moaned a little waiting for what was to come. I thrust hard into him making him catch breath. I fucked him hard till I came all over his lower back. I rubbed my warm cream all over his hard sac and his hard cock. He was ready to come again.

I pulled over onto his back. He looked at me through his thick black eyelashes. I could barely see those black red eyes. "Come for me Elijah," I whispered close to his face. His eyes closed as I wrapped my hand around his shaft. He wasn't long until he came for me.

I kissed his temple like I was rewarding him for a job well done. He fell into a sleep and his mind drifted away from me along with any images that I might have stolen.

I got out of bed and went over to the book that was still open. The cautionary words about Hades were gone and replaced with a new words. *Nice fuck job.* I grunted as I closed the book. I grabbed some clothes and left the bedroom.

I met Zak in the kitchen. He looked like he had partied all night. He gazed up at me through half slit eyes. He let out a mournful greeting.

"Hard night, huh?" I grinned at him. As dangerous as he was, sitting there he looked like maybe he was someone I knew from my past. That thought made me stop pouring my blood drink. I looked back at him as if I was trying to place him. Was he a part of my past as well? There was no point in asking him. He wouldn't give me a straight answer anyway. I finished pouring my blood drink and decided to have my drink outside in the dead garden. Zak never stopped me. It was grey day which was perfect for me. I headed for the gazebo.

The grass crunched under my feet like brittle bone. How could it be this dry when it stormed last night? But I remembered what Elijah said, that this garden was special.

I made my way to the gazebo and noticed that the entire top step was gone. By the frayed fragments of wood it looked like it had been ripped off violently. It must of have been the storm last night. I easily leaped over the missing step and walked over to what was left of the built in bench. The dampness of the garden filled the old gazebo with a damp wood smell that tickled my nose. The paint was only barely there exposing the rotting wood. As I sat down and sipped my blood I gazed steadily at each flower bed trying to place it in my mind knowing that the three of us possibly lived another life here.

"You look like you need company."

I didn't look over at him until he was standing beside me. Zak had a glass of blood in his hand. I watched him look out over the yard.

I wondered if any of this rang a bell with him. Did he remember anything and how did he end up one of Hade's boys? I can only guess that Elijah had played a role.

Zak took a sip. His tongue ran across his bottom lip licking the blood. He grinned down at me. There was mischief in his black eyes.

Before he said anything, I spoke. "I don't want to play any of your games."

"You're no fun Avian. I was just going to suggest a little death witch fun." My nerves twitched when he said death witch.

"What death witch game? I thought we were to stay away from her," I said.

Zak just shrugged. "What would the fun be in that?"

Opportunities came in strange ways I thought. This was my chance to find some things out. "What do you know about her?"

"There is not much to know Avian. She Hade's little bitch. She's trapped here by him. She fights him every once in a while." He smirked. "Just like that little storm we had last night." He winked at me. "I guess she likes it rough sometimes."

I raised an eyebrow at Zak. "You mean Hades and the death witch are a couple?" Zak almost spit out his blood. "That's one way of putting it, I guess. They both love and hate each other which are about perfect for them."

"I see, well then this game that you want to play, does Hades knows about it?"

He smiled then. "He taught us." He then downed his drink. "Let's go love."

Chapter Eleven

WE STOOD IN FRONT OF THE cemetery with the fortress of snarly brambles daring us to touch. I looked over at Zak. "Now what?"

His brooding black eyes were scanning the brambles as if he was looking for the right place to scale them. Up close you could see the thorns, they were like sharp little fingers with claws ready to shred your skin and spill your blood. For all I knew maybe the brambles were alive and they drank your blood. They could have Zak's.

We both took a step back. As silent as a cat he leaped over leaving me by myself. There was no way I was going to do the same thing. Right away there was the sound of grunting following with a low growl. It was that thing that came after me when I ventured into the Death Witch's territory-her pet. I could hear it coming through the grass. It smelled Zak. Well if he was stupid enough to go in there then the gatekeeper as they called it could gnaw away at him.

Zak made a noise but then all was quiet. A shiver crept up my spine telling me that something had happened on the other side. A cold breeze blew around me sending the hairs on the back of my neck up.

I slowly turned around but there was no one there. A sudden flapping of raven wings startled me. The bird landed almost on top of me and squawked angrily.

"I had nothing to do with it, it was his idea." The raven ruffled up its feathers. I could also most hear mumblings coming from it. It was her. I swallowed hard. She looked at me with her blue black beady eyes. She knew now that I knew it was her. She smoothed out her feathers and threw her head in the air. The black magic rolled off of her like rain. I could hear foot steps behind me but I didn't dare take my eyes off of her. I could sense it was Elijah.

When he got closer her black feathers flew apart and flew over the brambles like a black cloud. Elijah wrapped his arms around me from behind. "Hey, your shaking love, what is it?"

A yowling sound from behind the brambles startled me. "Zak is behind there."

Elijah let go of me. He walked up to the brambles. The hedge appeared to almost cringe away from Elijah like he was poison to them. *Is that why the Death Witch left when Elijah came near?*

I thought he was going to leap over like Zak did but instead he just yelled. "Get the fuck out of there; you'll drive the gatekeeper crazy."

Within seconds Zak leaped over. He didn't seem any worse for wear. "How many times have I told you to stay out of there? That thing will eat you."

Zak just rolled his eyes. "That thing is too stupid to catch me. I think it's blind."

Elijah just shook his head. "You could have brought her out."

Zak looked back over the brambles. "She wasn't even there, I couldn't feel her."

I didn't say anything, I knew where she was.

"Well, you're lucky you didn't come to blows with her."

"You worry too much Elijah, my love." His voice was sweet and poisonous.

Elijah sighed. "What am I going to do with you?"

Zak immediately leaned into Elijah and whispered into his ear. Elijah chuckled. "Remind me love and I will make it a night that you won't soon forget."

Elijah led us both back into the house. Entering back into the study, the smell of vanilla candles with lavender filled my nostrils. A small cozy table was set up. Three place setting with tall crystal wine flutes sparkled off the flames of the candles. There was even a small bouquet of roses in the center of the table.

I glanced over at Zak who had become silent. I got a strange vibe off of him like Elijah had done this before. *What did the evening had in store for me?*

Elijah invited us to sit down at the table. He poured us some champagne that was chilling in a bucket of ice. *Where did he get all this?* The room we were in hadn't changed. The curtains were heavy with dust and everything was decayed and dead. But here we were in the corner about to have what?

There was a cart with a silver platter and cover. I shivered to what might be under that.

"Well, gentlemen I have a few things planned for us tonight and a surprise." Elijah looked down at me and those black red eyes were filled with desire and danger. I shifted slightly which I think only excited him. "This is an early celebration of Avian and my marriage to come. Yes love I have every intention of making you my husband." He bent down to me and in a low voice although I'm sure Zak could hear everything said, "You had a real fuck fest with me last night and this morning, you wait and see what I have in store for you." His breath was hot against my cheek. His red talon hand settled on my thigh rubbing me and getting closer, pulling my leg apart. I was getting hard and my face was getting hot. He massaged me for a moment. "That's what I like love." Then he casually went over to Zak and grabbed his hair and pulled back his head and bent down and kissed him hard. Zak didn't move.

With his other hand Elijah slid his hand inside Zak's pants making him gasp for air while still kissing him. When Elijah stopped he looked into Zak's eyes, Elijah was still massaging him. Elijah smiled so I guess Zak grew hard in his hand like he wanted. Zak's chest rose up and down in a fast even beat. Elijah sat down between us. He reached over and pulled the cart over. Under the lid were three steaks that were rare. "You boys get to enjoy some good meat. You're going to need your strength." He placed one in each of our plates. I could smell the blood.

All the while eating Elijah would reach over and massage me. He unzipped my pants finally releasing my throbbing cock. He was very pleased with what he saw. He was salivating. I knew he couldn't wait to slip his mouth over my hardness.

After we finished with our blood steaks he grabbed both our hands and led us to the large bed where he told us to undress in front of him. He sat in a chair and watched us get naked for him.

He told us to get into the bed and told us what position to take. Elijah threw Zak some oil. Zak rubbed my buttocks outside and inside.

"Bend over and rub his cock for a while." I felt Zak's hardness on my back as he grabbed my shaft and started stroking. "Now fuck him and fuck him hard."

I braced myself as Zak thrust inside me. I dug into the bed sheets as with each thrust his breathing sped up.

"Spill your cream all over his ass love." I soon felt Zak's release on my buttocks.

"Now massage that beautiful cream over his hard sac and cock." Zak did and I was soon wet.

"Lay on your back love." I did and Elijah came over and took all of me in. He spread my thighs apart slightly exposing me. He moaned as he leaned over and slid his mouth over my cock. Zak reached over and massaged my sac. Elijah must have told him in his mind to do that. I wanted to come so bad but Elijah wasn't letting me. It was pure agony. I begged him in his mind to let me fill his mouth.

He stopped for a moment and his black red eyes drifted up to meet mine. "You promise to stay faithful to me and give me many children?"

His words were muffled in my mind; I was so wanted to come. I nodded blindly. "Say it Avian, I want to hear you say the words love."

"I promise, I promise." I begged.

"Say what you promise me Avian, I want to hear your vow to me."

"I promise to be faithful and give you many children, I promise" I moaned.

He slid his mouth over my throbbing cock and Zak squeezed my sac encouraging me to empty. My body shook like a tremor when I finally released. Zak held on firmly to my sac while Elijah devoured what I gave him.

"I'm not done with you yet love; I want your ass too." He rolled me over with Zak's help and positioned himself behind me. He thrust hard into me. Zak laid underneath me sucking what was left of my come from my cock. Zak's magic touch made me come again. Elijah came hard and fast exploding inside me. I could feel the heat rush through me like it was straight from the fires of hell.

He collapsed pulling me down beside him. Zak went on the other side of me putting me in the middle. Sleep took all of us.

A clacking or clicking noise rattled inside my head. I tossed my head to the side as if that would shake it out but it came again. My eyes flew open and I listened. There was a presence in the room but not close by. The walls vibrated like there were mice scurrying inside them. Elijah and Zak were as still as the dead. The death witch was here, somewhere. She had cast a spell over them. But she left me alone for some reason. *What did she want?* I couldn't move as Elijah and Zak held me firmly in between them. Maybe she wanted it that way so she could set out to do what she wanted whatever that was.

I listened.

Above me something was going across the floor. She was upstairs. I think our bedroom was above. *What was she doing in there*? I tried to move again but I couldn't. It was like she was using Elijah and Zak to restrain me. *Damn her.*

I could hear drawers being opened and closed and paper being shoveled about.

What was her agenda? Something fell over with a hard knock to floor above. Zak stirred then and his arm fell away as he turned over. I was partly free now. I tried to move again and Elijah moved with me but instead of relaxing his arm tightened around me. He gently kissed my temple resting his lips against my cheek. I was still trapped as she stomped about upstairs. I tried to move one more time and this time I actually sat up without Elijah stirring. I looked back down at him and he was very still.

Everything was quiet now and that sent a shiver through me.

I could feel a cold rush of air descending down the stairs and a black mist flew past the entranceway to the study. The front door creaked open and was left open for the wind to play with.

She was gone.

That's when both guys stirred. Zak sat up holding his head. "Man, how much did I drink last night?"

Elijah sat up and rested his head on my shoulder.

"My eyes are burning," he moaned.

I sighed. *Gifts from the Death Witch.*

The morning came with a crack of thunder. It shook the bed waking us up. Zak's black eyes half opened. "Is he coming?"

I didn't know who Zak was talking about. Elijah sat up looking down at Zak. "Tonight we're getting married. Father will be here tonight."

Chapter Twelve

"HADES WILL BE HERE?"

Elijah smiled at me. "Of course love, he will witness our union into eternity together. It's the red moon tonight love."

My chest tightened when he said the red moon. I remembered a certain bedtime story that she'd told me.

Elijah kissed my temple. "I can't wait. You will be mine forever." His breath was fire on my cheek. Uneasiness settled inside my bones. The thought of the red moon and Hades made me shiver.

"Thanks for the warning," I said trying to sound like a tease. He just shrugged. "How much warning do you need, love? You want to be married as soon as possible, don't you?"

My voice caught in my throat. Zak slapped me on the back. "Of course he can't wait. The wedding night will be to die for," he laughed. I froze.

Elijah laughed too. "Oh come on Avian, it will be wonderful, you'll see and tonight will be very special, I promise." His silky voice glided over my skin making me flush.

Zak bounced out of bed. He didn't bother to cover himself up. He paraded around naked in front of us. Zak's black eyes shone and a wicked grin spread across his lips. "You like what you see Avian? Zak sauntered over to me. "You can have me one more time love before your married."

I shifted and Zak crawled onto the bed and without warning straddled me with Elijah right there. He stood up on his knees facing me. I stared right at his erection. He leaned over resting his hands on the headboard. "Take me love."

"This will be your last time for a while love as you and I will be together most of the time and only occasionally will you get to taste Zak." Elijah's voice filled my head. I took hold of Zak's swollen member. I put him deep in my mouth. I heard him gasp followed with a moan. It wasn't long before Zak filled my mouth.

"Well that didn't take long" Elijah joked. Zak frowned at him.

Zak threw himself off the bed nearly knocking Elijah over and grabbed his clothes. "I will see you later tonight." He marched out of the room leaving Elijah nibbling on my ear.

"Don't you have wedding plans to make?" I looked into his black red eyes and he smiled. "Yes I do. Tonight is going to be perfect love." He kissed me gently and sighed heavily. "Oh how I would love to make love to you right now." He gave his head a shake and leaped out of bed.

"You relax love and rest." He winked at me. "Because, you're going to need your strength for tonight." He kissed me again then left.

I fell on my back looking up at the decayed ceiling. I was about to be married. I loved Elijah but something was wrong with this world we were in. I thought of the Death Witch. She knew what was going on-if I could only talk to her somehow.

I wondered what she was looking for upstairs. She certainly didn't want anyone to interfere. I decided to tempt fate and go out to the cemetery.

I grabbed my clothes off the floor and as I pulled on my pants a strange voice wafted through the house. It was low and dark and made the room go cold.

"Where is he?"

"He's sleeping right now. He needs his rest for tonight." Elijah said.

"I want to see him anyway." The dark voice was pushing Elijah. "But..."

"Take me to him or I will find him on my own." My insides shivered. *Who the hell was it?*

"Father, please."

"Christ, it was Hades. I shook off my jeans and pulled my t-shirt over my head and threw it on the floor. I was barely back in bed when they both came in. Our eyes locked. Hades walked over to me without making a sound. I clung to the sheets. He stood over me and reached out with his hand and traced the outline of my jaw. Sharp black talons edged along my skin. His fingers were ice cold. Then he smiled, "Just like I remembered." Elijah was now right behind him. I didn't take my eyes off of Hades. He smelled like the garden-dead roses. He was certainly handsome with his dark hair and dark navy eyes. His skin was perfect. "I can't wait to see my boys married and united in eternity." There was fire in his eyes and danger. "We will have a celebration tonight that will light the fires of hell." I swallowed hard. His delicate fingers once again traced the outline of my jaw. His thumb rested on my bottom lip. I froze. Then quietly he dropped his hand. "We'll see you boys tonight." His long coat tails swirled around and he silently disappeared like black mist.

I caught my breath as Elijah sat down beside me. "I'm sorry, father can be persistent."

"You think?"

Elijah sighed. "He wanted to see you; he just couldn't believe that I found you again."

My eyes widened. "What do you mean, 'found me again'?" This was a moment to grab to get information out of him about the past.

His dark lashes cast down a shadow of coldness. Then his eyes fluttered. "There is much to do for tonight. I want it to be perfect. I can't wait to call you my husband." He smiled with a slight flush in his face. He leaned over and gently kissed me. "Get some rest."

He left me to gather my thoughts. In a few hours I would be married and be one of Hade's boys-something I had avoided all these years.

I looked over at the large windows facing the garden. The grayness from outside clung to the window panes making them look like the dust was etched into the glass. I got up not bothering to cover myself and walked to the window. I could barely make out the garden. I followed the path that led to the cemetery. I still wanted to go to her but how would I get there without Elijah or Hades knowing. There would consequences if I got caught.

"Avian, why aren't you resting"? I startled and turned to watch Elijah walking up to me. He slid his arms around me and pulled me close into him.

"Oh Avian, I love you so much and you will be all mine in mere hours. I can't wait."

I looked into his eyes, searching for the chestnut color that was in my past dreams.

All I saw was the black red that fluttered through his dark thick eye lashes. They were drunk with love and lust. He kissed me and I could taste every desire that ran through him. He was a storm waiting to be unleashed.

Elijah cupped my sac giving me a firm squeeze. I grew hard for him as he ran his tongue along his bottom lip salivating. Finally Elijah bent down and took all of me in his mouth. His tongue flicked and sucked sending me into a need for him that only he could fill. I wanted him to take me and make me his now. I was willing to submit to his every need and I knew Elijah could taste my willingness. Elijah let out a low growl that was predatory. I moaned. Elijah sucked in air and in a blur had me on the bed on my back. His eyes glazed over my body making me beg for his touch. Elijah took off his shirt and slid off his jeans. He was now naked and he carefully laid on top of me letting our skin touch, lighting a fuse that now crackled and sizzled. I felt every muscle of his chest and stomach and his hardness pushed against my thigh. He lifted himself up. He pushed down on my chin with his thumb to open my mouth. He pushed the tip of his penis just inside and slid against my tongue in a slow movement. Then he pushed deeper and I took all of him in. I opened my eyes and he was watching me. He pulled out of my mouth and I let out a moan of resistance. He slid down and took hold of my hard member and started and rubbing me. I wanted to let go.

"Not yet love" he cooed. He reached into the drawer of the night stand and pulled out a black ribbon. I wondered what he was going to do with that. He spread my legs apart and slid the ribbon under my sac and tied the ribbon into a bow. He pulled very tightly. "That will hold you back love."

He then left a trail of kisses down my throat to down across my chest. His tongue briefly licked and flicked at my throbbing head. I so wanted to fill his mouth. The fire in me was a back draft waiting to be extinguished. I moaned and begged him.

"You're moving too much love; we have to do something about that." He threaded his fingers through mine and pulled them above my head. He tied my hands to one of the rungs on the headboard with a pillow case. He did the same with my ankles tying each ankle to the bottom headboard with a bed sheet.

"That's better". He firmly squeezed my sac again and gave his bow a tug making me gasp. He took me in his mouth and worked magic with his tongue, sucking quite hard. I so badly wanted to fill his mouth. I pleaded with him to let me.

He smiled down at me. "Listen to me. I'm going to sit on your cock and let you slide in between my ass." I nodded.

"Good." He grabbed some oil and rubbed it all over himself and on me. He eased himself on me slowly and very slowly did this slow rhythmic movement that sent me into overdrive. I was going to pass out. He finally undid the bow. "Now, I'm going to fuck you real hard and I want you to fill me. Look at me with those beautiful eyes and never take them away from me. I want to see you come."

I did as I was told. I couldn't move my arms or legs as he thrummed against me. He was getting great pleasure out of this. "Come for me Avian, come now." I exploded screaming his name, damning him. I gasped for air.

He reached over and untied my hands. "Sit up Avian and I'll give you a taste."

He was ready to come. I was still inside him but I wrapped my arms around his waist and took him in my mouth and he moaned in response. I sucked hard making him fill my mouth as he cried out my name.

He untied my ankles and he took me in his arms and wrapped his body around me. "You are all mine, for all eternity."

I let my cheek lay against his warm skin. I fell into a darkness that was a black endless pool.

Chapter Thirteen

A COLDNESS SWEPT ACROSS my forehead. I think I blindly tried to wipe it a way only to have my hand caught by another hand. They were ice cold.

My eyes flew open and I was looking into blackness. Dirty blond hair fell into my face. It was Zak, "Time to wake up my prince."

I moaned in protest. "No, no, no my love. It's your wedding night," he whispered into my ear. My insides shivered.

"Come, we have to get you ready." Zak pulled me up into sitting position. "Follow me upstairs." He held out his hand. I took his hand and he pulled me up onto my feet. Instead of letting go of my hand he firmly weaved his fingers through mine. His fingers were cold; I don't recall them being that way before.

We went upstairs into our bedroom and through to the bathroom where the scent of jasmine and sandalwood greeted me. Zak had drawn me a bath. The frothy bubbles looked inviting.

He helped me into the tub where I sank into the very warm water. Zak didn't leave as he proceeded to grab a large sponge and lathered it up with soap that smelled of musk with a hint of jasmine. He swept across my chest with the sponge leaving a trail of frothy bubbles.

I grinned. "You know I could wash myself."

He raised an eyebrow at me. "Give me your arm and don't roll your pretty dark eyes at me."

I sighed as I handed him my arm. He just smirked. Zak was being very thorough. Then he reached down into the water and cupped me.

"Hey, that's tender."

"I know, you two should not have gotten carried away earlier but Hades was pleased with your lust." My eyes widened at Zak. He just shrugged. "He knows everything" he said quietly.

He massaged me and it felt soothing. "Stand up on your knees." I did and the first thing I knew Zak is bent over guiding me into his mouth. I didn't realize I had gone hard under his touch. I closed my eyes and let him suck. He was gentle and I released into his mouth with a light shudder. He pushed me back down in the water. "Relax."

I felt warm water over my hair. A massage over my scalp felt amazing. He kissed me on the forehead and over each closed eyelid. I seeped into a slumber that numbed my body. Then I felt the warm water again over my head. My eyes opened. Zak smiled and gestured with his hands, "Time to get out."

He helped me out and started to dry me with a towel. I was about to say that I could do that but I stopped myself. Zak was obviously given a mission and he was enjoying every minute of it.

He followed the drying with taking a lotion and started to rub all over my chest and arms massaging me with his fingers. He reached into my inner thigh and I sucked in air.

"You like being touched there, love?"

I nodded.

He made me spread my legs apart slightly so he could get to every part of my inner thigh and squeezed my buttocks slipping one of his fingers slightly inside.

I could feel myself getting hard again. Zak smiled. "Not now love, you have a night to prepare for." He finished up but it was hard not get aroused. He knew it too.

He opened the door and gestured for me to go first. As I went by his eyes took all me in.

My clothes were laid out on the bed for me. A black tux complete with tails and a crisp white shirt was waiting for me. Zak looked over everything on the bed making sure everything was just right. "Okay, we can get you dressed now."

Zak grabbed the pants and I looked at him. "What," he asked.

"Aren't you forgetting the underwear?"

A small smile spread across his face. "If you insist, but it's less to take off after the ceremony, you know." I just shook my head.

Of course he pulled out some shorts that were snug fitting. He liked what he saw. "I think you were right. Elijah will love to 'unwrap' you."

Zak stood back to admire his work, "just one more adjustment." My tie got fussed over.

"Perfect." He stepped back pleased with himself. Then out of the blue he comes in close to me and kissed me deeply. A sigh escaped him when he pulled away. "I won't be able to do that for a while until Elijah invites me back into your bed."

"It won't be long now and you will be Elijah's husband and another lover for me." His lips ran over sharp teeth. "Just make sure you don't give Elijah any doubt about your love for him. Tell him and show him that you love him and he will reward you with and an eternity of blissfulness or otherwise it could be an eternity of hell." He smiled at me with those sharp teeth, just to remind me which side I should choose.

I nodded.

"I know you love him, I'm not worried." His black eyes shimmered.

"Now, just wait here for a moment and I will get dressed and then I will come get you, okay?"

"Okay," I said.

So, here I was alone dressed for my wedding about to take a husband that I knew I was supposed to have married in another life time, I could feel it. Elijah had asked me to marry him and I said yes but what happened and how did we arrive here in this world, the underworld?

I thought of the Death Witch, I think she had answers and I made a decision right there and then that I would seek her out somehow and try and find answers.

The door opened without a knock so I knew it was Zak back. He was in a black tux as well. He looked more foreboding than he usually did. He held out his arm to me, "time to take you down stairs, love." His voice was velvet smooth. I slipped my arm though his and he led me out the door.

As we descended the stairs a quiet thrum settled into my chest. I had anticipated I would see Hades at the bottom of the stairs but was thankfully greeted by Elijah who beamed when he saw me.

"You look so handsome; you take my breath away love." He didn't come near me; I think he was holding himself back. I think he was also a very nervous groom.

"Are you as anxious as I am Avian, love?" Zak came up beside him and slapped him on the back. He winked at me. "Of course he is he can't wait to become your husband." Elijah smiled.

Zak kissed Elijah on the cheek softly. "It's time for you to go out there and join Father." Elijah nodded. His black red eyes drank all of me in before he went out the door. Zak chuckled as his black eyes settled on me. "He can't wait to get you naked." I rolled my eyes at him.

"Hey, don't do that." Then he laughed. "Come love, it is time for you to be wedded into eternity." He wore a wicked grin.

He escorted me out side. The air outside was electric and a reddish glow glowed over the garden. I looked up into the sky. The moon was almost completely red- the blood moon.

The old path was lit up with torches that created a heated glow.

"What is all this," I asked Zak.

"This is the path we follow to the gazebo where you and Elijah will be married." I silently walked beside Zak taking this path that gave off an eerie glow. The tall grasses created shadows. It seemed as if the monsters that hid in the garden where coming to this affair as well.

The gazebo came into site. The entire area was lit up with candles. Some of the candles floated in the air and even though there was a cold breeze they never wavered. Everything around the gazebo glowed–reminiscent of hell.

Behind the gazebo I caught a glimpse of the cemetery. I wondered if the Death Witch knew what was going on. I wanted to see her.

"Does the Death Witch know what's going on tonight?"

Zak glanced toward the cemetery. The glow from the candles reflected in his black eyes. He looked deep in thought like he was remembering her. Then he lazily shrugged. "I don't know."

"Can I meet her?"

Zak chuckled softly. "Not in this life time." Then he laughed at his own joke. That meant never.

The gazebo was getting closer and I could make out Elijah. There were others behind him standing just inside the gazebo. The candle glow reflected a tall slender figure-a lady. Her long dress billowed gently in the breeze. The memory of the story the Death Witch told me entered into my mind making me shiver.

Behind her was a large dark figure and all I could see was the glow of its eyes. It moved blocking the candle light making them all disappear into the dark. What was that? Then it moved again and they were back.

"It's time Avian." Zak's voice was soft and gentle. He squeezed my hand as Elijah met us half way. Zak stepped aside and Elijah took his place. Elijah's red black eyes seeped into me that sent a chill through me. We walked silently the rest of the way to the gazebo where the tall lady was now waiting. As we got closer the glow from the candles danced off of her reflecting her sharp features. She had a long face and pointed nose. Her lips formed a thin blood red line and her eyes resembled hollow holes. A lump caught in my throat. I took a tighter hold of Elijah who whispered in my ear. "It's okay love, I'm with you."

I let his words settle into the crevices of my bones. As we got closer to the lady, coldness wrapped around me. Despite the heat from the torches and candles, all I could feel was coldness.

We stopped right in front of her. She stood on the entranceway into the gazebo and towered over us casting an eerie shadow over us. In her hands she clasped a book that draped a black velvet ribbon. Behind her was Hades. His navy eyes were now softly burning embers. His presence terrified me. I wondered what part he would play in this ceremony.

When she spoke her voice was ice cold. Hades stayed behind her and remained perfectly still. She made us face each other to take our vows. She stepped down to get closer to us. I jumped. She paid no heed to me. Her bone like fingers wrapped all the way around the book liked hooked claws.

Her thin red lips formed a straight smile and when she opened her mouth she revealed a row of sharp jagged teeth. I took a tighter grip of Elijah. His hand went over top of mine for reassurance but I couldn't take my eyes off of her.

She made us recite ancient vows that were deep in black magic and with every word that I said my mouth tasted more of acid.

The black velvet ribbon now was a gleaming blade. The fires reflected in the steel of the blade. She instructed us to hold out our hands. The image of the two lovers played over in my mind. I was going to die again. I closed my eyes.

Without warning she sliced through both our hands. The sting from the blade was intense and my eyes flew open to see both our hands drenched in blood. My hand felt like it had been touched by fire. Her boney fingers wrapped around both our blood soaked hands and clasped them together. When our hands touched it was like pure acid, I thought my hand would burn off. Even Elijah could feel the pain. The fire from the torches went out and the floating candles extinguished themselves. The only light to cast over us now was the red moons glow. The garden took on an eerie redness. You could feel death everywhere. A howl erupted from the lady followed by Hades. His eyes were fire now. My wide eyes focused on Elijah whose red black eyes cast a wicked glow. He smiled at me sending a shiver through me. My love looked as dangerous as when I met him on that night.

Then abruptly, the fires from the torches and candles came back to life. Our blood soaked hands were still holding onto each other. The lady stepped to the side while Hades came forth before us. The glow from the fires showed his perfect skin.

Hades reached into his pocket and pulled out two rings. They looked like silver with a ruby stone set in each one. The stone flickered like fire. He held out the rings on the palm of his hand and the lady waved her hands over them making them shake. My chest was alive with fright and my aching blood soaked hand hung on to Elijah's.

The deed was about to be finished. Then he held the first ring out in front of Elijah. He said some strange words and then Elijah took the ring with his uncut hand and slid the ring onto my bloodied finger. I gasped as I felt this wave of energy run through me. I thought I would faint.

Now it was my turn. He handed a ring out to me. I shook as I tried with my uncut hand to take the ring. I could feel his eyes on me. I was ready to crumble. The ring felt heavy and cold but I managed to slide the ring onto Elijah's bloodied finger. He flinched once. I glanced at the ground; the dead grass was red with our blood. I wanted to be sick but I was too numb. I wanted this over.

Hades stepped aside and the lady once again was in front of us. She placed out cut hands over the book and said a little chant. The wind got up and it was cold and the red moon shone brightly now casting an eerie blood stained glow on us.

It was over.

Zak came up to us smiling. He placed his hand on Elijah's shoulder. "Now you can kiss the groom."

Elijah pulled me close, cupping me with his hands and he kissed me. His lips were cold, and then they turned to fire. Zak laughed out loud. "Now we can celebrate."

Chapter Fourteen

THE DARKNESS came to life around us. There were others around us now. I recognized them from the hunt. They were Hade's boys. These were the ones I spent an eternity staying away from. Zak went and joined them and so did Hades. I was thankful to have distance from them all.

Elijah took my hand and led me away from everybody. I can't say that I didn't mind. He was leading me back to the house. He never said a word.

We went up the stairs to our bedroom. He took me past the bed through to the bathroom. He was drawing a bath. "This will relax you, love." He poured some salts into the water. I could smell lavender.

"Give me your hand." I knew he meant the cut one. He filled the sink with warm water and placed my hand in it. The water stained pink. He put his own hand in as well. After a minute he took my hand out. The wounds were almost sealed now.

"We're blood bound now love and we're together for eternity." He leaned in and kissed me.

He sighed contently. "You are actually all mine." He grinned mischievously at me. "It's time to get you out of these clothes love." He undid my bowtie. He grinned at me. "We'll use this later."

He slid off my jacket and then undid each button while sliding his fingers along my skin. Elijah pulled the shirt over my shoulders and kissed along my shoulder up to my neck. Then he let the shirt drop to the floor. My breathing was getting faster.

He undid my pants and got a glimpse of Zak's choice of underwear. His tongue ran along the bottom of his lip. He pulled my pants down and knelt down and took off my shoes and socks. All that remained was the underwear which he left for now.

He got rid of his own jacket and threaded his fingers through his own bow tie and quickly undid it. I started to undo his buttons. He watched me but I never touched him. His chest was rising and falling. I wanted so badly to touch his skin and I knew he wanted me to but I held back.

When his pants fell to the floor he was naked. He led me over to the tub and told me to get in. I still had my underwear on but got in the tub anyway. The material even though was snug, clung to me even more and made my hardness more pronounced. He groaned as he looked down at me.

Elijah got in the tub and slid in behind me. I leaned back into him and he started a trail of kisses across my shoulder up to my neck. He nipped me and sucked my blood for a moment.

"You taste like heaven, if that's possible."

His hand slid down and cupped me making me moan. "We have to get you out of these. Stand on your knees and face me." I did as I was told. He looked up at me and his black red eyes were smoldering embers. He kissed the wet fabric where I was ready to burst. With his fingers he slid the underwear down finally freeing me.

Elijah massaged my sac. "You're full and ready."

I thought he was going to take me in his mouth but he didn't. Instead he took the sponge and lathered me up and proceeded to rub my thighs and slowly worked his way to the inside of my thighs where he was on his way to driving me into a frenzy. His fingers squeezed my inner thighs. A deep moan from the back of my throat escaped. He tickled the back of my sac. Elijah got up on his knees and now was facing me. His hands slid around my waist pulling me close so our skin was touching making our erections push against each other. I wanted him so bad that I pushed harder against him. He smiled. His hand slid down my buttocks and squeezed them. Elijah parted my cheeks and slid his finger in. I caught my breath. He pushed his finger in and explored finding that special spot.

"I'm going to come," I breathed.

"Oh no, not yet love." His voice was so seductive that I didn't think I could hang on any longer.

"Let's get you to the bed. I want to give you a little more pleasure first." I shook my head.

Elijah got out of the bathtub and I took his hand and let him lead me out to the bedroom. He grabbed the bow tie on the way out.

He laid me on my back on the bed and he spread my legs. I just wanted his wet tongue on me-now.

He went back to his massaging and trails of kisses. He finally paid attention to my throbbing cock. He devoured me. He sucked hard but oh it felt so good and finally I let go.

"Mmm, you taste so good."

I knew this was only the beginning. He was over top of me now. His red black eyes were searing hot. He pulled up my legs and placed a pillow underneath holding me up. Elijah took his favorite oil and massaged all around my hole sliding his fingers in and out.

"Are you ready?"

I nodded. He eased himself into me all the while keeping his eye contact with me. He filled me.

"Relax love, you'll love this." He got into a rhythm that got both our breathing going fast. Elijah was about to let go. He pulled out and smothered my cock and balls with his sweet warm cream.

He massaged his cream over my cock and balls and into my hole. "Come all over me love." I did what he said. He rubbed my cream over his cock.

"Taste yourself and me together."

I took his cock in my mouth and tasted myself and soon I tasted Elijah too. Together the taste was rich and seductive.

I laid back exhausted. Elijah laid beside me. He folded his arms over me and held me. "I love you so much and you are mine forever. Forever love."

"I love you too, more than anything." We kissed letting our tongues explore each other's mouths still tasting what our sweet cream together was like-intoxicating.

I woke to a sensation. I was lying on my stomach and felt this probing between my cheeks. Then I felt my hips being held and Elijah pushing his erection through my cheeks filling me.

I held still while he thrust into me and finally with one cry he filled me. He pulled out still letting go. My sac was warm with his cream. His fingers slipped into me and found that little place that made me groan.

He rolled me over spreading my legs. His fingers were back inside me and with his other hand he held my hard cock. The two sensations were almost too much. I didn't think I could let this much go but I just kept coming and Elijah didn't let go of me. He was in my mind telling me not to stop. I didn't realize it but there was something over top of my penis. I was coming inside a metal object.

"You did good love."

"What is that?"

Elijah massaged my penis instead of answering me. He squeezed the head of my cock making me come a little bit more.

He held up this metal vessel with ancient scroll markings on it.

"What is that," I asked again.

"This is the start of our family. Suck on me so I can put my seed with yours."

"But..."

"Do it Avian."

I sucked on his cock and it wasn't long when he pulled out of my mouth and emptied into this silver vessel. He gave me an exhausted smile.

"What are you doing?"

"This is the start of our family love. I want to have many children with you."

I was stunned. I sat up and watched Elijah go over to the drawer and pull out a small silver dagger. The handle had the same ancient scrolls that the vessel did.

"There is one more thing we have to do." His black red eyes held me. "You trust me love right?"

I nodded but I wasn't sure if I should trust him. Elijah took hold of my hand with my palm facing up and with a blink he slashed the knife across my palm. There was a searing heated pain. His grip on my hand tightened as I looked at him with hurt.

"It's okay love, it will be fine. I just need your blood to go inside this vessel." He held my hand over it and my blood dripped into the vessel. "It's okay love," he said again. His voice was soothing and comforting. He brought my hand up to his mouth and licked the wound savoring the taste of my blood. My wound was starting to heal but I could still feel the sting of heat from the knife.

Elijah held the knife in front of me with my blood still on it. He licked both sides with his tongue. I could see the blood on his tongue.

"Open your mouth love." I only slightly opened my mouth but it was enough for Elijah to slip is tongue into my mouth. His blood soaked tongue filled my mouth with the heavy iron taste of my vampire blood. He kissed me. The knife was still in his hand.

A creepy feeling slithered over my chest waiting for Elijah's next move. I watched him turn his own hand around with the palm facing up. The silver blade laid across his palm. In a flash he sliced across his own palm. He winced but never wavered at the task at hand. Elijah held his cut hand over the vessel and let his own blood drop in all the while saying some ancient demon chant.

The room became very cold and it felt like there was another presence. Standing at the foot of the bed was Hades. His claw like hands wrapped around the bed posts and his eyes burned like embers. Elijah handed the vessel over to him. The vessel almost disappeared in his hand. Hades brought it up to his mouth and kissed the vessel as if it was some kind of blessing. He then motioned for us both to come over to the window. We each wrapped ourselves in a sheet.

The red moon that shone on our wedding was now back to its ghostly silver. Hades hung the vessel in front of the window letting the light from the moon bathe it. It glistened in the white light hanging there like an omen. All I could think of was demons pouring out of that thing. I shivered.

Elijah led me back to our bed. Hades was still in the room. I was waiting for him to leave but it seemed he was waiting for something.

Elijah knew what it was. Elijah pulled back the covers of the bed and dropped the sheet that he had covered himself. He stood there naked in front of Hades and Elijah did not wait for me to do the same, he undid the sheet that was around me. Now I was naked in front of Hades.

Elijah gently pushed me onto the bed and laid beside me. He started to kiss me driving his tongue deep into my mouth.

It was like he was hungry for my taste. His hand pulled my leg apart so he could cup my sac. He squeezed and massaged urging me in my mind to get hard. His tongue went down my neck flicking and when he found my nipple he sucked hard. Elijah took hold of my cock. He told me in my mind to get hard in his hand. I could still feel the coldness of Hades in the room. He was watching all of this.

I grew hard in Elijah's hand. That made Elijah smile, "Very good my love."

He slid down and slipped mouth over my cock. He slipped up and down my shaft making me groan. Then he sucked real hard and I knew I was going to come. It wasn't long till I filled Elijah's mouth. Elijah moaned and took in every drop of me.

I laid there a moment trying to catch my breath when I heard a deep voice. It was Hades.

"Fuck him now Elijah. Fuck him hard."

Elijah did as he was told. He spread my legs apart. He took his oil and massaged it over his own swollen cock and then all around my hole slipping his fingers inside and out. "Relax love."

That was rather hard to do when there was this demon in the room expecting a show.

Elijah eased his way inside me filling me. He started off slow until I got use to him and then he started thrusting shaking the bed. He was so deep inside me.

"Change positions Elijah and fuck him from behind." Elijah changed me around being on all fours. He spread my legs and my cheeks apart and thrust back inside me making me gasp. Elijah slowed down to an even rhythm. He bent over for a moment and grabbed my cock.

He squeezed and rubbed my tip trying to bring my wetness to the surface. He whispered in my ear. "Hades wants to see you erect love. He wants to see your precious cream come flowing out of you."

Elijah slid his hand up and down my shaft all the while deep inside me. I came for him and I emptied and emptied until I thought I was going to pass out.

I could hear a moan in the room. Elijah grabbed me by the hips and started his own trusting into me again. He was coming near. He filled me with his heat and pulled out covering my balls with his cream.

"Rub your cum all over his balls and cock and rub his own cum into his hole then lick him."

I went still as Elijah with his fingers scooped my cream off the bed sheet and rubbed it all over me and in my hole mixing it with his own. I felt his tongue go deep inside me licking and sucking. I felt this arousal go through me. I wanted more of this and I didn't care if he was in the room or not. I liked what Elijah was doing. I went hard again moaning and pushing my buttocks into Elijah's face making his tongue go deeper. Finally, I couldn't take it any longer.

"Fuck me Elijah, now, please."

Elijah didn't need any more encouragement. He thrust inside me with a force that made me dizzy. He filled me so good and I loved it. His balls were slapping me. I was going to come soon. He knew it. Hades made us roll over and he stayed inside me. He held up my one leg keeping my legs apart. My swollen cock was fully exposed to the open. Elijah still was still fucking me, just in long even strokes that pushed in as far as he could. I was going to explode at any moment.

Elijah pulled me more toward him and he filled me. He was letting go so much I could feel his cum dripping out of my hole. Elijah was still inside me as he took hold of my cock and rubbed till I let go. Elijah's hand was covered with my cream.

Hades was now at the edge of the bed again. "That's how I like to see my boys."

Elijah had pulled out and laid beside me on his side and I was still on my side. All I wanted was for him to be gone and I could sleep with Elijah.

But before he went he took hold of Elijah's hand and licked our seed off, savoring it. Then he reached behind me and slipped his hand in between my cheeks to get some of Elijah's cream. He almost slid his fingers in but didn't. He tasted Elijah and me. "My beautiful boys, you're both such lovely treats. I'll leave now but I expect you two to spend most of your time in this bed fucking as I want many children from both of you." The coldness in the room disappeared.

"Hold me Elijah." Elijah slid up behind me and held me tightly whispering in my ear that everything was okay.

If only I could believe him.

Chapter Fifteen

THE NEXT MORNING CAME to me in sounds. Something was hitting the window. My half opened eyes focused on the window where the sound was coming from. Of course the vessel was hanging there flooding me with memories of last night. My eyes instantly flew around the room. He was not here. The grey light from the window cast a dull glow over the room. Dusty webs hung in corners and dust etched its ways into every crevice in the room.

My attention went back to the window. I looked back at Elijah and resisted the urge to kiss him. Instead, I got up not bothering to cover up and walked over to the window to see what was hitting the window. It was small pellets of ice-hail. The garden had a thin layer of ice pellets on the ground giving it an almost wintery look. I stood there and gazed at the sight.

With my eyes I followed the path to the gazebo where the ceremony had taken place. I remembered the hot acid air and thing that tied Elijah and I for eternity. Now the site outside was cold like death. I shivered as if the ice pellets were touching me.

I felt hands slide around my waist and kisses on my shoulder going up to my neck. I closed my eyes and let my head fall on his shoulder exposing my throat. I put the outside world out of my head. He kissed and lightly sucked.

My eyes flew open and my body tensed. Elijah had sunk his teeth into my neck. He sucked and moaned. I could hear the word relax in my mind. I tried but it was hard when his hand slid down and took my cock in his hand, squeezing and rubbing me to get me hard. I could feel his erection prodding to get between my cheeks. I grew hard in his hand.

He licked my wound and it healed. "You taste so good love and I can't wait to taste that sweet cream again." He took my hand and led me back to the bed. All the while the ice pellets hit the window.

"Does that bother you love?" He snapped his fingers and the curtain shut although the dull light still shone through some of the bare threads of the curtains. We weren't in total darkness.

I laid back on the bed facing him. His red black eyes shone through the dimness in the room as he peered down at me. "You are so beautiful love. I can't believe you are my husband and we are going to have our first child."

My eyes glanced over at the vessel. I could see the outline of it behind the bare threaded curtain. I wanted to forget that thing. I kept quiet as I liked seeing Elijah with so much love in his eyes. We shared a deep kiss. He was taking his time this morning, savoring every taste of me and I savored him. His tongue went to that special place inside my thighs that made me groan in pleasure. He sucked at my sac making me squirm. He slid himself up next to me. "Love, I want you to fuck me first. I had sex dreams about you fucking me."

"Sex dreams, really?" He gave me a wicked grin.

"Of course, the best kind of dreams to have is of your new husband." He grabbed the oil and rubbed all over my hard cock. He spread my legs and rubbed oil over my hard balls giving them a good squeeze and of course couldn't resist sliding his fingers in my hole catching me off guard. He shoved his fingers in deep finding my weak spot. I thought I was going to come.

With his other hand he took hold of my cock and started to lick off the wetness that was already coming. He stopped.

I thrust inside him and he groaned. "Oh baby, don't stop. You feel like heaven."

Elijah screamed when he let go and that made me fill him. I collapsed on the bed panting and when I looked at Elijah's half sedated eyes he smiled. "That's a good way to start the morning."

He laid on top of me kissing me and I knew round two was coming.

"You know love, you haven't fed. I want you to feed off of me. You can feed off anywhere you please." His eyes were full of mischief.

I chose the inside of his thigh right next to his sac. He laid back willingly while I sunk my teeth into his thigh. I took him by surprise. He let out a gasp followed by a laugh that would chill you. I savored him as his blood hit the back of my throat. Elijah was rich tasting and like a drug -addictive.

I fed well. He sat up and looked down at me. "You were a hungry boy." He was wearing a mischief grin that told me his mind was full of naughty thoughts. "This will make you even feel better." He took hold of his cock and showed me the drop of pearly white cream. "Suck me love and let me fill your mouth."

I licked the cream of his bulging head and then slipped him into my mouth devouring him like he was candy. He moaned and threaded his fingers through my hair holding me firmly in place while I begged him for his release which he gave. His rich cum poured into the back of my throat.

I swallowed everything that he gave me. Elijah fell back and rested while I licked what was left of his sweet cream. I rubbed my hard cock along his stomach leaving a wet trail.

"Come closer love; let me savor that cock in my mouth."

Before I got to him he shoved me over onto my back and he grabbed something black. It was his bow tie from last night. In fact he had two which made me nervous and aroused at the same time. He tied both my hands up to the bed rail with one tie and the other…I knew where it was going. This was going to be agony. Elijah very carefully tied the other one around the base of my sac snuggling it up pretty good. He was going to work me up into a real good frenzy.

Wetness was starting to come more and Elijah quickly licked the head of my cock all up squeezing my head to make more. He held my cock while he dribbled oil on me. The oil slid all over down my shaft. It was warm and a musk smell filled the room. Elijah straddled himself over me and lowered himself. I was inside him as far as I could go. Elijah was enjoying the sensation as he rocked and moved his hips from side to side. Then he started bouncing and between the warm oil and the pressure he was applying to me I was ready to explode. "Please, Elijah undo the tie so I can fill you."

"Ah, I just came in time." Zak was on the bed before I knew it and noticed what Elijah had done.

"I like this Elijah. Let me play with you." Elijah didn't say anything so Zak laid right next to me whispering in my ear, "I don't think I gave you a congratulations kiss." His black eyes were on me and his tongue slipped across my bottom lip. He pushed his tongue into my mouth and kissed me all the while letting his tongue explore my mouth. "Hmm, I taste Elijah."

Zak still had his white shirt on from last night. It was half undone. I could see his nipples all the way down to the bulge in his pants.

"Can I untie the bow tie when you're ready to let him come?" Elijah nodded and then finally with my pleas he let Zak untie the tie. It felt good to release.

"He filled your ass good." Elijah laid on top of me. Zak scooted down to behind Elijah and started to lick Elijah. He spread Elijah's cheeks apart and probed Elijah's hole with his tongue licking all my cream.

Zak quickly undid his pants freeing his throbbing cock and thrust himself into Elijah. Then Zak leaned over and whispered into Elijah's ear. Zak let Elijah lift himself up and spread my legs and pushed my knees up. He poured some that warm oil over my hole. He slipped his fingers in lubing me up. Zak guided Elijah's cock into my hole. Both Elijah and Zak then got into a rhythm that pounded me. They both came and Elijah filled me. After Elijah pulled away Zak bent down and started to lick the cream off my hole. He sucked and probed with his tongue. He was enjoying every bit of it. Elijah massaged my balls while Zak was helping himself.

I couldn't believe it but the more Zak played with his tongue in my hole I was getting hard. Elijah with his other hand started to massage my cock. The two sensations from both ends felt so good. I laid there with my eyes closed enjoying it. They took turns. Elijah's tongue was playing in my hole while Zak was enjoying sucking on my cock. Just before I let go Elijah stuck his fingers up my hole and they both shared my cream when I let go. They both licked me clean.

Elijah untied me. "I think we should let him rest. We've had a busy morning." Zak reached over and kissed me. "Sleep tight love so we can do this again."

My eyes shut into darkness.

Chapter Sixteen

THE WORLD WAS A BLUR and it felt like the cobwebs off the ceiling had crept into my head. I felt like I had been drinking all night but the only toxic drink I had was Elijah's blood which was worse than what any alcohol hang over could leave you. I forced my eyes to open. The curtains were open and the dull sun was shining through.

I managed to sit up and I looked for Elijah or Zak but everything was quiet-too quiet. My legs against their will swung over the bed and stood me up. I walked over to the window. The ice cold world of yesterday was gone. The garden looked its usual dead self. I sat down on the chair by the window and that thing caught my eye-the vessel. I shut the curtain to hide it. I didn't want to think about it.

I blinked at it-the black velvet book. I was tempted but instead I had another idea. I grabbed some jeans and t-shirt. I didn't bother with any underwear. I got out the room okay and down the stairs. There was no sign of Elijah, my new husband or Zak. I slipped out the door.

The bright light took me back. It didn't burn but there was something about it that made my skin irritated. I took to the shade and made my way around the yard by sticking to the trees that outlined the yard. I knew the cemetery was at the end of this row of trees. An old oak tree leaned over in the direction of the small chapel.

I never noticed before but there was an opening on this side that I missed before. I stared right through to the chapel. All the windows were gone and the back of the chapel was caved in. The trail I seen was used probably by foxes, coyotes and coons. So, I figured I could use it as well. The only problem was it was open between me and the cemetery. My skin would get irritated. I went for it anyway. In a blink I was under another gnarled up oak where the path was.

My skin went only slightly pink. My speediness wasn't as fast here as in the human world. I stood there staring waiting for something to jump out of the tall grass like the troll that attacked me before but nothing.

"Hello," I said but my voice just fell silently into the grass. I edged a bit closer to the chapel.

"Hello, anyone here," I asked into nothingness. There was no response. All I could see was the stones that leaned over and just peaked through the long grass. I walked over to them. The names were nothing but outlines in the stone. I could make out one name-Zachary James. The name seeped into my head but found no meaning.

"What are you doing?"

I turned around and saw Zak who was sauntering up to me. He stood beside me and looked down at the crumbled stone. "Why are you hanging out with the dead?"

Zak took my hand. "Let's leave here." It was like Zak got very nervous and was almost-scared. We left the cemetery. "Don't worry about the sun; your ring will protect you from this sun."

I was going to say something to tell him otherwise but when I let him lead me out, my skin was okay. What happened?

We walked back hand in hand back to the house. Zak was totally silent which was not like him. I wanted to ask him what was up but I didn't have to as I got my answer when we got to the house. The air was cold which meant only one thing-Hades was here.

"There you are love." Elijah came up to me and took me in his arms and kissed me. "You must tell me where you are."

"There was no one here…" I couldn't finish as my eyes fell on him-Hades.

Hades was expressionless as we all walked into the kitchen. I averted my eyes away from him and stayed close to Elijah who took my hand, firmly squeezing me.

Elijah glanced down at me and grinned. "Father is throwing us a party." Zak seemed to come to life then when he mentioned the word "party."

"Yes, tonight we will celebrate with a few close friends and celebrate the upcoming additions to our family."

My eyes shot up to Elijah. "Additions?"

Elijah's face lit up, "Yes love we are going to have twins. There are two life forms in that vessel. Our love created them." Elijah was over the moon and so in love that he was blind to the evil that stood two feet from him. All I could do was rest my cheek against his arm. What was I doing? There had to be a way out of all this and keep Elijah? I sighed.

"Come my children, we will celebrate in style tonight as the sun goes down and darkness brings its pleasures. I will see you all then." His eyes fell on me and I got the message that I was warned. The door shut and Elijah took my hand. "Let's go upstairs. I so want to show you how much I love you."

Zak chuckled. "Be easy on him, Father will be expecting you both there-in fine form."

I laid naked on my back with Elijah lying naked beside me. He wrapped his arms and legs around me enjoyed the touch of our skins. He kissed me and his hot tongue searched inside my mouth. We kissed for a while before he pulled away and looked me in the eyes.

"Are you happy?"

That was a question I didn't expect. "Of course I am. Why would you ask that?"

"I don't know. You didn't react to the news of our twins. You didn't say anything."

"It is a bit overwhelming all of sudden to become a father."

"You will be a wonderful father."

"When will these children be here?"

"I'm not sure but it will be fewer months than a female pregnancy."

"Are they going to be demons like you?" This was a question that just came out before I thought about it but it was too late now. Elijah just stared into my eyes.

"Our children will be demons who will carry the blood lust with them." Elijah kissed me sending a chill through me.

These children were monsters. What have I done?

"Now enough talk about our children of which we will make many more." His hand slid down and took a firm hold of my cock that grew hard in his hand. He meant business.

I closed my eyes and let him pleasure himself on me. He sucked hard making me dizzy.

Just as I thought I was going to fill his mouth he stopped and spread my legs apart so he could massage my sac that was so full and ready. He kissed each side and sucked and tickled with his tongue. I so badly wanted to come.

He scoots up to me and offers me his hard throbbing cock. I eagerly took him and savored him. He moaned and started moving slowly in and out of mouth and going deep. I had no problem taking him all in. I thought I was soon going to taste him but he held back and pulled out of my mouth. He was going to drive both of us crazy with this teasing game.

"Lift your legs up and show me your pretty little ass."

He wetted his fingers in his mouth and then shoved them up me as far as he could go. "I love fucking you." He continued to play in my hole while massaging my sac with his other hand.

"You're so ready, aren't you?" I nodded with a plea in my eyes.

"Okay love, I'll let you come." He bent over and took hold my cock. He first teased my head with his tongue licking off my wetness. Finally after I thought I was going to burst, he took all me in his mouth and sucked hard stroking my shaft with his tongue. I grabbed onto the sheets and released filling his mouth. I didn't think I would ever stop. It was like having one orgasm after another. Elijah just kept his mouth over me swallowing everything I could give him."

He grinned as he licked the cream off his bottom lip. "Now that was a load love. We will definitely do this again." He kissed my head and licked off what was left. Everything was so sensitive.

"Your ass is next love." I held my breath as he eased into me filling me. "I'm going to fill you love, hold on."

Elijah started out slow, easing in and out. His breaths were catching fast and his thrusts where too. I could feel his sac hitting me. He was going to come soon.

Elijah cried out my name as he emptied inside me and pulled out and continues to come over my balls and cock. I was smothered in his thick white cum.

"Hmm, you look so good this way covered in my semen." There was semen coming out my ass and it was so warm, demon warm. He shoved his fingers up pushing more inside me. The heat was racing through me. "That's warm Elijah."

"I know love, I'll lick you clean and make it better." He did just that but the warmth inside me stayed.

Elijah cuddled up beside me. "You do feel warm love. That will stay with you for a while. That's good, I'm glad my cream does that to you. I want you to feel my heat for you."

We shared a deep kiss that sent me into a sleepy slumber.

A hot breath on my cheek made me moan, I thought I was having a sex dream but my eyes opened and looking down at me was Elijah.

"Dreaming my love?"

I moaned again. "Ahh love we'll fix that for you." He started rubbing my hard member and I kept pushing myself into his hand. "Take it easy love." I was so on fire and Elijah was the only one who could put it out.

He finally took me in his hot mouth and he worked his magic giving me the release I wanted so badly.

Elijah grinned. "Now that is how I like you waking up. The desire and lust in your face was out of this world love." He deeply kissed me. "We're going to have a wonderful eternity together."

I took a deep breath and just let Elijah's words seep into some dark place in my mind.

"Come, we have to get up and get ready."

"Get ready?"

"The party, remember?"

"Oh, that." My insides fell flat at the prospect of mingling with Hades and his friends.

"Don't sound so enthused love. The party is already started."

I glanced over at the window and it was dark so that meant that downstairs was filled with monsters.

"I have a surprise for you first before we go down. Follow me."

I followed Elijah into the bathroom where candles were lit everywhere giving the room a soft golden glow. The smell of jasmine with a hint of sandalwood filled the room. Well, this was more inviting than what was downstairs. I kissed Elijah. "This is very nice."

We both slipped into the tub and it was heavenly. After a while Elijah told me to turn and rest against him. I knew he wanted to touch me but that was okay. I leaned against his warmth and instantly felt his erection against my lower back. He sent a trail of kisses down my neck to my shoulder.

"You need to feed again love."

I looked around for a pitcher but there was none. "I don't see any…" Before I could finish his arm was in front of me offering his wrist.

"I can't…" I didn't want to go on that kind of high.

"Oh come on, you know you want to. I like what my blood does to you."

He brought his wrist up to my lips. "Go ahead Avian."

I sunk my teeth in and instantly had warm blood shoot to the back of my throat. Once I had his taste in my mouth I couldn't stop. The blood beast was awake and alive.

I finally let his arm go and the buzz hit me. He spread my legs apart and slipped his finger up my hole. Then he guided his swollen member and lowered me on top of him. He moaned as he pulled me back. He was just enjoying being in my ass. His hand came around and started rubbing my own hard cock. I was getting high with his blood soaking into my veins. Everything felt so much more sensitive.

He finally positioned me doggy style and started to give a major fuck. His fiery cream sent me into an orgasm. We both cried out. Elijah pulled me back in the water against him. "That was worth the price of admission."

"Was it now? You have to stop giving me your blood. I'm light headed."

He chuckled. "That's okay; it will let up in a short while. You will be alert when we go down and join the others."

My head fell back against Elijah's chest. "Do we have to go?"

"Father is expecting us and besides we are already extremely late."

I turned to face him. "Then what does it matter if we are a little later." I was thinking of just letting them celebrate without us. I kissed Elijah before he could say anything and that is when the door opened.

Chapter Seventeen

ZAK WAS LEANING AGAINST the door jam. "Are you two done fucking yet? We've heard all your orgasms and sex dreams Avian. Man, do you like being fucked. Get out of there or father will come up here and take you both down naked and parade you around the room. Then you'll have to perform in front of everybody sucking each other's cock till you both come and some of the guests may want a taste." His grin was wicked and it was enough for both of us to get out.

Of course, Zak stayed and helped us get dressed all the while teasing and touching us trying to get us to play. Elijah knew better than to do that or else Hades would be up here or better yet he would bring everybody up here for a show. That thought was enough to bring me out of this room.

Zak escorted us down stairs. I could hear voices and other noises that didn't sound like the others but more animal like. I held onto Elijah's hand-tightly. He passed me a reassuring smile that it would be okay.

Zak announced us. "Here are the newlyweds Elijah and Avian." Everyone clapped and I tried not to make eye contact with any of them. I didn't want to actually see them but that was impossible as they all started to come toward us.

The first ones up where the rest of the boys from the hunt. They shook Elijah's hand making remarks about the sex we had. Some wanted us to perform for them later but Elijah said no. Their greeting weren't too hard to take but it was the rest of the guests that gave me the creeps. Demons with horns and burnt skin came up to us along with things that looked like dogs but they were something else. They sniffed at my feet making a growling noise.

Towering over us was this thin creature. She looked down at us with hollow eyes. A lump grew in my throat. It was the creature who married us. A thin straight smile formed across her pale lips. "I see you two have been very much…busy. Hades tells me that you are about to have twins. That is wonderful news. We all encourage you to keep that up." Her breath could form ice. I leaned in closer to Elijah and she seen it. She looked over at Elijah. "I could give you another vessel dear."

"There is no need for that." Hades joined us. "I will give them all the vessels they need…for their pleasures." His navy eyes rested on me as his grin formed a full smile. "Isn't that right Avian? You love nothing more than filling the vessels with your life with Elijah and making more children. In fact maybe I will present Elijah and Avian with a special vessel and tonight they can have the pleasure of creating another life." The tall creature's eyes widened.

My insides flipped. What did he have in mind?

Hades left us alone and he mingled with his guests. I was so hoping he would forget about that vessel. I stayed close by Elijah and he didn't mind keeping me close by. He would kiss me every once in a while and I would kiss him back. What we shouldn't have done was massage each other in the crotch. We both started to get heated when Hades came up to us an instructed us to follow him. My chest vibrated.

Hades led us into a small room and closed the doors behind us. He smiled at us both. "I'm so happy to see you both so happy and active." We both knew what he meant by that. "You two will fill the house with your children and that makes me happy. I want to give you two a special gift." My gut sank.

It was like magic as he pulled out this red vessel from his long black coat. The thing seemed to materialize in his hands. Elijah stared at it. He was taken back by it and by the look on his face he knew what it was.

"You know what this is Elijah, don't you?"

He just nodded and I could tell by the look on his face that he would rather not have anything to do with this thing and that made me very uneasy.

"I will pick a special night for you two to bless this vessel with your lives and blood. Together with the black magic that this vessel holds you will create a powerful demon that will be by my side." Hades was quite excited by that prospect.

"Father, I'm not sure that I want to do this. I love Avian very much and I don't want to…"

Elijah started to choke and he fell to his knees.

"You will obey me," his words were meant for Elijah but his eyes were on me.

"Please let him go." I locked eyes with Hades. And at that he stopped. He smiled at me.

"I knew you wouldn't disappoint me."

I bent down to Elijah and held him. "You two will complete this task in two days. I suggest you spend your time in your bed-practicing. Take Zak with you to help keep you get motivated." He left us on the floor.

"Are you okay?" He nodded and before I could help him, Zak entered into the room, no doubt sent by Hades.

"He wants us to go upstairs."

Zak looked at Elijah who then came over to us. "Let's go upstairs where we can be alone." Zak for a moment when he saw Elijah on the floor showed emotion in those black eyes. They looked almost-hurt.

We all laid on the bed fully dressed being totally silent. Zak finally took out a bottle of old whiskey. He popped off the top and took a swig. I could smell the stuff. He passed it to Elijah who threw back a good swig. It burned by the look on his face. Then he passed it to me. I took a swig. It burned all the way down but I didn't' care as it burned away the night we had. I passed it back to Zak.

"Are you two going to go through with it?"

Elijah shrugged. "I guess we have no choice."

"You two want to explain to me what that thing is all about?"

Elijah took my hand. "That thing is the very meaning of black magic. Our bond is very tight and strong and our blood and semen would produce a very powerful demon that could help Hades in his quest for more power."

"I'm not touching that thing," Zak announced to us. "That thing is more evil that the combination of all those guests downstairs." That didn't make me feel any better.

Zak looked at me. "It also can take a lot out of you. That thing can possess you into doing its bidding when it is set free. You could be filling it with your sweet cream all night, it can get very greedy if you taste good and you do love." He took another swig and passed it on to me. I took a good gulp. There had to be a way out of this.

Thoughts of the death witch came into my mind. "Do you think the death witch could help us?"

Zak just about spit out his whiskey. "Why would that bitch help us, she hates us."

"Why does Hades keep her here anyway?"

"The death witch was his love and now they are bittersweet lovers who fight always. He won't let her go so he keeps her here. She tolerates us," explained Elijah.

"Barely," sniffed Zak.

"I think she would talk to me," I said.

"Why would she talk to you, you are Elijah's husband."

I shrugged. "I think she would. Would you take me to see her?"

"She won't come out while Hades is here love," said Elijah. That would explain why I had the silence in the cemetery I thought.

"After he leaves then?" I asked. Neither one of them said anything. Elijah looked over at Zak who just shrugged.

Elijah sighed, "After Hades leaves then."

I leaned over and kissed him.

"Hey what about me?"

I pushed Zak off the bed.

When the morning arrived, I woke in the middle of a tangle of bodies. We were all naked but we didn't do anything. We just wanted to feel each other's skin for comfort. They were both hard. I decided to do something. I took Elijah's cock in one hand and Zak's in the other hand. I went back and forth sucking their cocks. They both stirred and Zak looked down at what I was doing. He closed his eyes to let me continue. Elijah moaned wanting more. I sucked him hard for a little while then stopped just as he was starting to arch his back. I turned my attention to Zak and did the same and stopped.

"He's going to drive us crazy Elijah. This boy needs a good fucking by both of us."

They pulled me down between then and started rubbing my ass. "Rub oil on me Elijah."

Zak started working me and soon pushed his way inside me. "Ah that feels good. Your ass is fantastic."

Elijah continued to let me suck on his cock some more. Both guys were enjoying it.

Zak thrusts were getting more urgent and soon he filled me and pulled out still coming smothering my ass with his very warm cream.

"It's your turn Elijah." He traded places with him and turned me on my back. Zak held my legs up.

"Look at all that sweet cream." He started rubbing it over my sac. Then he went down and licked my hole. "Push out more cream love." As I did he licked it all up.

"Now, it is my turn." He pushed his way deep inside me. Zak stroked me licking my wetness.

The sensation that both of them were giving me was driving me to explode. Elijah started hitting me with his sac all the while stopping occasionally to cup my sac and give them a squeeze. Zak started to suck hard.

Elijah filled me first. Then I came and both Elijah and Zak enjoyed my endless stream of cream.

My balls and ass were covered in both their seed. I laid between them while they kissed my nipples and massaged my wet sac. Zak slid his fingers up my hole shoving more of their thick cream up my ass.

All I could do was lay there and let them play. I knew I would probably get fucked by both of them again.

I was right. They played with different positions. Zak was full of kinky ideas. They took me twice more before they collapsed totally satisfied.

I was all wet and sticky as I walked around the room.

"He looks good wearing our seed," said Zak in a smug tone.

"Of course he does, he's got a beautiful cock," cooed Elijah.

"He's got a nice ass too, especially when his legs are spread apart showing us that sweet spot of his," Zak added.

I rolled my eyes. "I'm going to soak in the tub-without you two."

Zak made a pout. Elijah grabbed Zak and pinned him down. "I'll make you feel better." He started to tie Zak up in such a way that he couldn't move. Elijah then got out some sex toys.

Chapter Eighteen

I SLIPPED INTO THE soapy water and let my lower half recover. I could hear Elijah playing with the sex toys. Zak was begging for relief but Elijah wasn't giving it. Their rough game was not for me. I soon shut them out.

I laid back in the water and let the scent of the lavender crystals drift into the crevices in my head. I was happy about one thing-I was now going to get to meet the death witch which I believed held answers.

I wish I had bought the black velvet book in here but then again she might not tell me anything but the thought pulled at me. I finally got out of the tub and went out.

Elijah was still teasing Zak. "Hey, my sweet little ass, come here and give me some relief. Your husband is being a bastard."

I ignored them. I grabbed the book and Elijah watched me intently as I went back. I closed the door to Zak's pleas. I just sat down on a rug near the tub. I placed the book a little ways from me as if it might jump to life. My fingers were a hairs breath away when it flipped open and the pages turned madly until they came to an abrupt stop. I stayed back.

The candles in the room came to life. The flames soared for a second till they died down to normal. I was waiting for her to appear but instead ink started spewing out the middle and running over the pages seeping and smearing on the paper and not making any words.

The flames shook. Was she mad? Then the ink started to clear and form words.

"So, you want to talk to me. Well not with those two little bastards with you-even if one of them is your husband. I was not invited to the party. That evil bastard down stairs did not include me in your celebration of going to hell."

She was mad about not being invited to the party?

They were lovers at one time, I wondered what happened. I took a deep breath and spoke out into the room listening to my own voice. "I'm sorry that you didn't get asked. I would have asked you." My voice seemed to settle in the room.

Suddenly, vibrant writing leaped across the page. *"I knew you were different. I like you and we will meet-just the two of us-real soon."* Then the book went quiet and the candles were snuffed out.

"Wait, when are we going to meet?"

"Who are you going to meet love?" Elijah came straight for me offering me his hand. I took it has he pulled me into his arms. He had bite marks across his chest with blood smeared across his lower abdomen. The smell of the rich blood made my throat tighten.

I could see Zak laid out on the bed through the bathroom door and he looked like he was lying in blood stained sheets.

"What the hell were you two doing?"

"Just a little demon love Avian, that's all. Zak likes it rough sometimes."

He looked back at him and then me. "Don't worry love, he'll be just fine. Now let's get into the tub and you can tell me about whom you are going to meet."

I leaned back into Elijah. "You're not going to get rough with me are you?" I didn't want to talk about the death witch.

He nuzzled into my neck. "No, love never. You are different to Zak. You are my husband and I will treat you like a fragile piece of crystal. Keeping you happy and safe are the most important things."

I didn't respond to him I just enjoyed Elijah's kisses.

I washed Elijah up and washed his hair. He liked that. We kissed for a while and I whispered in Elijah's ear-"make love to me."

Elijah helped me out of the water.

The bed was a mess and Zak was still there.

Elijah grinned. "I know another place." He led me down a hallway that I had not been down. At the end of the hall way, two massive doors stood there like guards. There were intricate patterns and carvings on the both doors.

"Should we be here," I asked Elijah.

"Trust me," whispered Elijah.

I held my breath when Elijah opened the doors.

They only made a slight creek. Of course the room was in complete darkness. Elijah with a flick of his wrist opened the curtains bathing the room in the white ghost light of the garden's moon. A massive four poster bed took control of the room. The carvings that were on the door were also on this bed. Each spindle had a dragon twined around it. The canopy on top drooped slightly and looked worn. The room gave off an eerie presence like something lived in the room.

The bedding on the bed looked decayed. Elijah once again threw out his magic and the bedding was instantly changed into clear white soft linens.

He offered me his hand. "Shall we love?"

I let him take my hand and lead me to this massive bed that felt like it would swallow us up. I laid under the canopy that was quite taunt now. Elijah slid in beside me and took me in his arms. His hot breath covered my lips and his tongue went deep exploring and tasting me. We kissed for a while until Elijah made a suggestion. "Let me give you a massage love."

Where the oil came from I don't know. He pulled back the covers so he could see all of me. "I love your naked body love and you are all mine to enjoy." His red black eyes reflected in the pale moon's light.

The oil was even warm as he dripped it on each of my nipples letting the oil run over the rest of my chest. Elijah then started his massage. He teased my nipples with his fingertips running the base of his thumb down my stomach to the tip of my erection just brushing up against my head. He massaged my hips and slid to the inside of my thigh getting close to my aching sac but only barely brushed his hand up against me. He worked his way down my legs to my feet.

He was a good foot massager. My eyes were closed enjoying it when I felt my legs being pulled up and spread. Elijah pulled out a silk rope out of the night stand drawer next to the bed. He tied it around my ankles and then to one of the post above my head. It suspended my leg up. He did the same to the other leg. Then he tied my wrists to another post behind my head. This bed was equipped for this. I wondered what had gone on in this bed. I pushed all thoughts out and just focused on my husband.

I was fully exposed to Elijah now and I could not move. He looked down at me and his eyes were smoldering. He was full of lust and desire. He first kissed me biting my lower lip but no blood-for now.

"I want to fuck you so bad Avian. You're my heaven in this hell."

He poured warm oil over my erection that ran down over my sac over my hole. I could smell peppermint. Elijah took all of my cock in his mouth moaning and savoring as he sucked and teased with his tongue. I could feel myself losing it.

"If you have to come Avian go ahead. I want to see lots of that sweet cream of yours. I'll just make you come again and again."

I moaned and twisted my body to his touch. His own cock slid deep into me holding me in place. He took his fucking slow teasing me and watching my cock leak. "Take me Elijah, please."

He moaned, "With pleasure love." His onslaught came. He fucked me hard slapping his sac up against me. Every once in a while he'd stop and massage my sac encouraging me to come.

He picked up his speed shuddering on top of me as he filled me. His heat ran through me setting me on fire with desire. He slid out of me and bent over and took my cock in his mouth. I instantly let go for him filling his mouth with what he wanted so badly. The orgasm he gave me sent my body into over drive. One wave after another hit me making for an endless stream of cum. Elijah's face was covered and he loved it.

He pulled out of me leaving me panting. He untied me and wiped his face with a towel that was conveniently on the night stand. "That's my boy. Keep your legs apart so I can hold you." I let my legs flop open. He pulled up beside me sliding his hand over my tender sac and slipping his finger in my hole a bit. "Just relax love."

"What a beautiful site." Elijah instantly threw his body over me as if protecting me. It wasn't Zak and not Hades either. But Hade's voice soon followed. He chuckled. "Oh you are right, my friend, this is a beautiful site." They both came up to the bed. Hade's friend smelled the air. "I can smell their seed. What a rich scent."

I stayed perfectly still and I could feel every tense muscle in Elijah. I didn't recognize this friend of Hades. His dark sharp features were framed by large black red eyes that looked through thick black eyelashes. He was tall and muscular and completely dressed in a black navy suit. He came around to the edge of the bed with hungry eyes. Elijah moved over a bit more over me. He laughed softly. "Come Elijah let me have a look." Elijah very slowly moved his body away.

I noticed right away, the long claws similar to Elijah. He ran his clawed finger down my chest and never stopped until he got to my seed covered parts. Elijah growled.

He pulled away. "Hmm, you are protective of your mate. That is good. You've claimed him well and together you two will make lots of children for our family."

Hades was pleased and paraded around the room like a proud poppa. "I think this room will be perfect for them. They can spend all their nights in here making love each night and filling this room with their cries of lust."

His friend nodded in agreement. "I could decorate the room for them-my gift to the newlyweds." Elijah's eyes narrowed at the guest and the red in his eyes deepened. The vibe I got off Elijah was that he did not like him. He pulled the sheet over me covering me and pulled me close to him. I laid my head against his chest and prayed that they would leave.

"Okay, Elijah, I get the message. You want to be alone with your husband. I'll leave you for now but when I come back for a visit, I expect to see the red vessel hanging in the window proudly."

He walked over to Hades who had taken a wooden box out of a desk drawer. He placed his talon hand on Hade's shoulder. "Ahh, we have what we came for, good." He whirled around with a grin on his face. "You two can go back to what you were doing. Welcome to our family Avian, I hope next time I see you holding your first born. You two certainly didn't waste any time. That's good, so Elijah, I expect to see the other vessel hanging, okay?" He chuckled and

Hades followed. "Let us go my friend. I'm sure their lust is simmering under those sheets."

"I certainly hope so Hades, I certainly hope so."

Chapter Nineteen

I SHIVERED IN ELIJAH'S ARMS. He cradled me for some time before lifting my chin up with his finger. "Look at me Avian."

I peered into a sea of black and red. "I love you Avian and will not let anything happen to you. You and I are expected to have a big family. They want us to fill vessel after vessel. They both want an army of demons to take control over the underworld. Our bond is so strong and that would go through to our children. They would be very strong demons."

I couldn't say anything and I don't think he expected me to say anything, just listen to him. "My love, I will make love to you every night in this bed and when I choose we will make more children. You have to comply love, alright? You are mine and will be well taken care of as long as you give yourself to me completely. I want you to understand that my love. You understand right? Tell me. I want to hear your words."

"I understand you," I said.

He held my chin as I looked him in the eyes. "I understand, completely. I love you Elijah."

He smiled. "Ahh, my love, I know you love me and I love you oh so much and right now I want to show you my love." He kissed me deeply pushing his tongue into my mouth. We both moaned while his hand slid down to my cock. He started to stroke me. I grew hard in his hand and that gave way to a night of Elijah's passion. I was totally consumed by my husband's love for me albeit possessive.

A thumbing sound from below the bed woke me. I moved Elijah and he stirred. "Good morning love." He leaned into me and kissed me. Then the thumping noise started up again.

"What is that?"

"The party," said Elijah.

"It still going on?" I breathed out.

"They've only just begun love."

"When are they going to leave?"

"Within the hour, they will move the party over to Hades or Sebastian's."

"Who is Sebastian?"

"The one you met in here, last night."

"Oh, I see, you don't like him do you?"

"No, I don't love and I don't want you going near him, understand?"

"Yes, I understand but …"

"Promise me Avian." His voice was stern.

"Yes, I will stay away from him." I wouldn't have too much trouble obeying that order as I didn't like him either.

"Good, now let's get you fed." Elijah sat up and on the nightstand there was a pitcher. He poured me a glass and handed it to me. "Drink up love and there is much more for you." I sat up and drank. As I was drinking Elijah pulled away the sheet. "I just want to admire you."

"Would you like some food with your next drink?"

I nodded. That was something I hadn't had in a long time. Food wasn't necessary anymore but I still enjoyed the textures of food and the smells.

"Then let's go down to the kitchen and I will make you something to enjoy."

We walked arm in arm down the hallway and walked past our room. "Are we going to get something to wear?"

Elijah shook his head. "No love I enjoy being naked with you. We'll eat naked together. Maybe we'll have sex in the kitchen…with any luck." He winked at me.

We continued on and when we went into the kitchen Zak was sitting at the table with his head resting on the table.

Elijah smirked, "Rough night Zak?" Elijah went over to him and grabbed him by the hair. His eyes were shut and he was unresponsive. "The boys from the hunt must have found you."

"Is he okay?"

Elijah chuckled. "He's fine love, he's been in far worse shape before but he always bounces back."

Elijah filled up a large tray with breads, cheeses and some meats. He also found some fruit. "Take the pitcher love and follow me."

We went down to the large study with the big bed in it and he laid out the food on the table beside the bed. He pulled out a chair for me.

"Really?"

"Of course," he smiled. He rested his hands on the back of the chair waiting for me to sit. "For you my love." I sat in the chair and I should have known. He slid his hands over my shoulders around my shoulders and leaned over and kissed my shoulder and slid his hand down to my cock. He teased me.

"I thought we were going to eat."

"Oh, I forgot, you're right." He nipped me before he left.

We ate the food and forgot about everything but us. The world revolved around us for a moment and that felt great. I loved my husband and I wished I knew our story from the past and what happened. This whole house had a story to tell. Thoughts of the death witch crept into my mind. I was hoping she could tell some story but I don't know if she was trust worthy or not. I would bet on the "not."

"Come my love, the bed awaits."

We slipped into the big bed. He was hard already. I took his cock in my hand and started to stroke and rub his head. He closed his eyes and savored my touch. I massaged his sac and inside his thighs where his weak spot was.

He moaned along with his breathing getting faster. His eyes were half shut. All I could see was a hint of red through those lashes of his. I kissed each eyelid and then his lips. I pushed my tongue deep into his mouth and savored his taste.

He responded by taking my hand and going to his sac. I took hold of his sac and squeezed and massaged him, getting him harder. I could feel his wetness on my arm. "Oh Avian, I can't live without your touch. Fuck me Avian, now, please." He had started to spread his legs and pulled me on top of him. I let my full weight fall on him. I rubbed our cocks together for little while letting out wetness smother each other's throbbing heads.

Elijah wrapped his legs around my waist. I shoved deep inside of him. He gasped. I didn't take it easy on him. I fucked him hard and he loved every minute of it. When I filled him he held onto my buttocks and pushed me in farther. Then he let go. His cream was sandwiched in between us. I could feel his heat on my skin.

We shared a kiss before I rolled off of him. "You're a bad boy" he breathed.

"You wouldn't have it any other way."

"You're right love, I wouldn't."

"Ah, what have I been missing?" Zak came rushing into the room. "I could smell your sex a mile away." He drooled over the thick cream on Elijah's stomach. Zak took his black lacquered finger nailed finger and scooped up some of Elijah's cream and popped his finger into his mouth.

"You taste better than candy." He hopped onto the bed stretching out. "So are you two going to fuck all day-or should we say practice for your little task."

Elijah just moaned. "I don't want anything to do with that task that was given to us."

"What are you going to do about it then?" Zak's eyes were searching.

Elijah stared up at the ceiling before averting his eyes to Zak. "Do you have something in mind?"

Zak's grin was wicked and I could tell Zak has been contemplating this little situation.

"We can fool them. You know that can be done. Trickery is easy to pull off." He bent down to Elijah's ear. "Even in front of *daddy.*"

Elijah slowly grinned. "That is true my sweet and we know things that he doesn't."

Zak flashed a smile. "Now you're talking."

My insides were flip flopping. These two were considering to do a fowl deed behind Hade's back and I don't think these two thought of the consequences of being caught.

"What are you going to do?" I asked my question to the both of them.

Zak's black eyes smoldered. "You just stay in bed with your husband and fuck for the rest of the day and I will do a little "shopping." He bounced off the bed sending his long black coat flopping off the bed.

"Give me a kiss?" He was full of mischief today.

Elijah sat up. "Come get it."

Zak licked his lips. He sauntered up to Elijah and bent over and just as they were going to kiss, Elijah threw him into the air. He landed in a heap near the doorway. Elijah laughed.

"You son of a bitch…you're asking for it love."

Elijah just laughed again. "You're going to punish me or something?"

Zak got up and dusted himself off and gave him the finger before he whirled around and left us.

As if he wasn't even in the room he turned to me. "Now my love what shall we do now?" His black red eyes burned through me.

"What are you and Zak going to do?"

He kissed me instead of answering me. I asked again, "What are you and Zak going to do?"

This time I put some space between us. In fact I went to get out of bed but I was pulled back.

"Where do you think you're going?" He pulled me effortlessly back up onto the bed. "I have plans for you love." He kissed me again. "Let's go up to the bedroom."

I wondered which bedroom he was talking about but I guess I would find out.

We ended up in the large bedroom again. I wondered if Elijah had a change of heart about this room. I watched him look around the room as if he was sensing something.

"What is it?"

He smiled. "Nothing love, we're okay. Now let's get your naked little self onto the bed. Position yourself on all fours. I have a few surprises for you."

He could tell by the look on my face that I was hesitant. "Don't worry love you will enjoy this."

I climbed onto the bed but instead I laid on my back and watched Elijah go over to an armoire. It was a beautiful oak cupboard. There were drawers on the inside. He slid one drawer open and wrapped in toweling he took out two objects. He brought them to the bed as I sat up to see what he had.

"This is a nice soft gel toy." He put it in my hand. It looked like two penises joined together. "We can use it on each other or together."

The other one was a string of glass beads that were all connected with a loop at the end. The glass beads was a clear blue.

"These beads are an anal toy. I start off with the small bead and keep going until we get to the large bead. Let me show you."

He spread my legs apart and pushed up my legs. Those silk ropes were still here so he used them to secure my legs up. Next he took some oil that smelled exotic, like some tropical fruit. He put some of the oil on his fingers and started to play with my hole. His fingers were magic as they stretched and pulled my hole to relax.

I watched Elijah drop a bit of oil on the glass beads. Starting with the small one he popped it into my hole. It felt strange at first. Elijah pushed the second largest one into me and kept going until he inserted the largest. I could feel the glass ball rubbing against my gland. It was a different sensation. Elijah started stroking my cock. I moaned. He shifted the beads around with his fingers. "You like that love?"

I couldn't answer him. He sucked at my nipples getting them hard then back down to my cock. He sucked me for a moment enjoying the wetness. "Now let's try the other toy." He pulled the beads out which made me dribble out some cum. "Hey that was a bonus." Elijah licked my cock clean. "We'll see what this does for you."

He lubed the gel cock and then he eased it into me. It almost filled me as much as Elijah did. He moved it back and forth making sure he was reaching my gland. He rubbed oil on the other end and got in front of me and inserted the other end into himself. He rocked back and forth making the gel cock move in and out of himself and me.

Both our cocks were leaking over each other. I think we were both ready to come. "Let's make it happen." Elijah picked up speed.

Zak entered into room. "I see I arrived just in time, this time." He climbed onto the bed and his dark eyes went wide. "Sex toys and look at that cum from both of you." Zak wrapped his hand around both our cocks and put us into his mouth. He had no problem sliding ours heads into his mouth. He sucked all the seed off. "Now give me a full load boys."

His mouth went over our heads again. He sucked hard while stroking with his hand down our shafts.

We both arched as we filled Zak's mouth. He licked cum off his bottom lip. "That was most delicious." Elijah pulled himself away from the gel cock.

"Avian you got a beautiful ass. That cock looks good in your ass," said Zak. He started moving it back and forth shoving it farther and really pushing into my gland. I was still sensitive from my orgasm.

I sucked in air. He pulled it out and I was relieved. But he wanted to play. He bent down and held my hole open while he flicked his tongue in and out. His wet tongue did feel good. I just laid there and let him probe with his tongue inside.

"Now, you're going to get my toy." I opened my eyes to see that Zak had his pants off. He was hard and ready. He smothered his cock in that oil and eased his head into me pushing in and out with just his head. It felt good. Then he slid right in. His eyes shut to take the moment in.

Now Elijah was behind him massaging his balls. Zak moaned.

"Fuck him hard or I'll fuck you so hard."

Zak grinned. "Is that a promise?"

Zak yelped. He was pinned against me and Elijah was giving it to him. Zak laid his head against my shoulder. Zak was buried in me. Finally, Elijah released making Zak come filling me.

We all laid on the large bed exhausted. I snuggled up to Elijah. "Hold me." I needed his comfort.

"Of course love, I will hold you as long as you want me."

Zak came closer and both of them shared whispers. It sounded like Zak had accomplished what he had talked about earlier. Whatever it was, the best or worst was yet to come.

Chapter Twenty

I STARED UP AT THE SNOW WHITE ceiling medallions. The snow white color looked too pure and innocent to be in this room. This whole room was an elegant room furnished with antique furnishings like this large bed that had these elaborate carving of dragons on them. Maybe this bed was suited for demons but the rest of the room didn't.

There were white lace curtains behind the heavy navy velvet ones. The walls were wallpapered in pale blue toile. The rugs in the room were rich burgundies and navies with ivory. The massive armoire made from oak, where Elijah got the sex toys from, stood strong in the corner. A dresser wasn't far from it but the mirror was tarnished. The wood looked like a cherry wood. It had some carvings on it too but small.

I got up out of bed and walked around the room. I didn't bother to cover myself up. Being naked was second nature here. There was a door off this bedroom. I decided to open it and it was an elaborate bath. Light flowed into this room. A large tub with gold feet sat in the middle of the room. There was a floral design on the porcelain. Tall gold taps stood behind it ready to fill the tub. A white stained glass cabinet rested against the wall. It was filled with bath salts. It also had a few drawers in it.

"Would you like to have a bath love?"

I startled.

"I didn't mean to scare you love." He came up to me and wrapped his arms around me. I rested my head against his chest. "I love you," I whispered into his chest.

"I love you too. What is this about? You sound empty." He lifted my chin with his fingers and cupped my face.

"I don't know. Sometimes I feel confused by all this. I love being married to you but Hades…doesn't feel right in our lives."

Elijah took a deep breath. His forehead touched mine. "Don't worry about it love. Hades will not bother us. After we have done this task for him then we will be left alone for the most part."

"You and Zak were talking about something to do with that. Are you still doing something?"

"Oh Avian, please don't worry about this okay. I want you safe and that is the main thing. You're everything to me. You belong to me and I love you more than you will ever know. You're more precious to me than anything this world could offer." He held onto me tightly and then kissed me deeply to let me know that he meant every word of what he just said.

"Come, let's bath you."

Of course, Elijah's idea of bath would be sexual. He washed every part of me. By the time he was done my cock was so hard that I thought I would explode. He wouldn't let that happen until we were in bed. He took all of my hard cock in his mouth and soon I was rewarded with a sweet wonderful release. He licked every bit of my cream off my cock.

"Now it's my turn."

Elijah laid back. "I'm all yours love."

I smiled. "I know you are."

I showed him I could bring him into an ecstasy that he never dreamed of. I secured his wrists to the headboard. His black red eyes were electric. I left a trail of kisses across his chest and stopped at one of his nipples to tease and bite. He moaned.

"I'm going to go get something love." I went over to the armoire and pulled out the drawer where the sex toys were. I made my selection. I was half way back when the door flew open. I froze.

It was Hades and he was not smiling.

My eyes flew instantly to Elijah. He was trying to release his hands. The air in the room went to ice. Hade's eyes looked me over.

He grinned at me. "Go over to the bed Avian and untie Elijah. You two have work to do."

In a blur I was with Elijah and untied his wrists. He wrapped his arms around me. He was protecting me. The question was why?

Hades narrowed his gaze at Elijah. "You know son. You were always the one who always listened. What happened?"

"What do you mean father?" Elijah was being very coy.

"I gave you a most enjoyable task to complete for me and you did this?" Hades held up a red vessel. My eyes widened. Thoughts of Elijah and Zak having a certain conversation made me shiver. What had they done?

Elijah was very quiet. I could feel a raw energy vibrate off of him. He was scared.

"Now, my sons you two will fulfill this little task right now in front of me. If I have to "help" you I will. He came over to the bed and laid the red vessel down on the bed in front of us. He sat himself down at the end of the bed as well. "I suggest you better get started."

"But…" Elijah was cut off by the raised hand of Hades. "Make love in front of me and I want to see lots of that sweet cream from the two of you."

His voice was cruel and deadly. Elijah pulled the sheet over us but Hades pulled it back. "I want to see everything."

Hades gestured at Elijah. "Make Avian hard in front of me. I want to see his cream."

Elijah laid me on the bed and spread my legs apart fully exposing me. Elijah started to massage my sac and then he took hold of me and started to rub me and encouraged me to get hard for him. I did for him. Hades was watching intently. Elijah took my hard cock in his mouth and sucked hard. When he let me go I was starting to leak out the cream that Hades wanted to see. That made Hades happy. I could feel Elijah's hardness against my thigh.

"Come here boys." Elijah took my hand and we went to the end of the bed where Hades was. "Go on your knees and face each other."

When we did he took hold of both our cocks and rubbed them until we were both wet with our wetness. He took the vessel and brought it closer to us. "Okay my two sons; it's time to fill this vessel." He bent down and took both of us in his mouth. His mouth was hot as fire. He sucked so hard. Then he finally let go. He continued to rub us. He felt our hard sacs that were ready to release. "Both of you come for me now. Fill this vessel."

As we both came Hades pushed our penises into the vessel. Elijah took me into his arms. He was shaking.

"We're not done yet. I need blood from both of you." He pulled out a silver dagger out of his jacket. He took Elijah's hand and as quick as blinking he slashed his wrist. I gasped. Hades paid no attention to me. Elijah gritted teeth as Hades took hold of his wrist and squeezed out his blood. It poured black into the vessel.

I was anticipating him doing the same thing to me but instead he slashed the palm of my hand and dropped my blood into the vessel very carefully like he was measuring. Elijah looked numb as Hades wrapped his talon hands around his now bloodied wrist and my hand. The vessel lay capped on the bed. Hades started to chant and I could hear Elijah chant with him. What was he doing that for?

His hands fell away. He took the vessel then and went over to the window and hung it in front of the window. "The moon's light will seal this life."

Hades mood now was pleased and he even smiled at us. "See, that wasn't too hard, was it?"

He took a seat at the end of the bed. "Now let's see you two really fuck each other." His eyes were dangerous and erotic at the same time. Elijah pulled me close to him and started to kiss me. I tried to reach Elijah with my mind but there was nothing there but emptiness.

Elijah was rough and I had bite marks all over me. He fucked me hard and filled me with very hot demon cum. He was a raging inferno that couldn't be extinguished. Finally Elijah collapsed next to me.

His breathing was hard. I turned over to face him. I held his face with my hand. His black red eyes were glassed over like he overdosed on some drug. I kissed him anyway.

"That was good my sons. Let's keep that up. You two can spend the rest of the night pleasing one another. I want to hear lots of orgasms from down stairs." He chuckled and got up.

Before he went out the door he turned to us. "Don't ever try to deceive me again."

The door shut echoing in the room.

"Hold me Avian." Elijah's voice was small and scared. I pulled him close and told him it was all right.

After a while we kissed and Elijah said that he needed me. "Make love to me over and over Avian. I want to be covered with your sweetness."

Our love making was needy.

What Hades had done to him had affected him. He was so solemn that I just held him. I was angry at Hades for this. Where we were was not right. Our real life was traded for this underworld full of monsters. I kissed the top of Elijah's forehead and whispered "I love you."

A sharp voice barged into the room. "He's going to need your love more than ever."

It was Sebastian.

I leaned over Elijah this time.

"Back off vampire boy, this is demon business."

"He's my husband." My voice was barely above a whisper but I knew he heard me.

Sebastian lips curled up into a twisted smile. "I don't give a fuck that he is your husband."

Before I could blink Sebastian threw me to the side without even touching me. He leaned over Elijah who half slit eyes barely focused on him. He grabbed Elijah by the throat and hauled him up choking him. I couldn't go to Elijah, my body wouldn't move.

He sneered down at Elijah. "You and Zak thought you were going to mess with Hades and me. You know what happens to those that try. You should know more than anyone. You've killed a long line of traitors. Love has made you a bit weak love. I think you need reminding of who you are." He threw Elijah on the bed and before Elijah could fight back, Sebastian was on top of him and had sunk his teeth into his neck. I could smell the burning flesh. The screams from Elijah were enough to make me sick. When Sebastian rose he smiled a bloody smile. "Now that's better."

Elijah laid still for a moment, and then he let out a sick twisted laugh that made me want to run out of the room. Elijah's red black eyes looked at me with lust. "Come here love, we have a busy night ahead of us."

Sebastian was beside me now. "I hear you like threesomes." I could smell the iron from his lips. "It looks like you have a nice ass to fuck and I wouldn't mind having that cock of yours in my mouth. Hades said your cream is delightful." He reached down and took hold of my cock and started stroking me. "Get hard for me love, I can give you such orgasms that you never dreamed of. Shall we?" He gestured toward the bed where Elijah was waiting for me. I wanted to run.

But there was no place to run. I slowly walked over to Elijah who quickly held out his hand. I hesitated in taking it but then he frowned at me when I was not taking his hand. I took his hand and he pulled me into bed with him. His neck had healed to a point but was still quite red. The vibe in Elijah was different. "Oh love, I can't wait to taste you. Let me explore every part of you." His voice was velvety and seductive. Sebastian was now behind me with his hand between my legs massaging my sac. He stayed quiet while Elijah cooed away at me. I felt my cheeks part. I could hear a soft groan from Sebastian. His fingers found my hole and started to slowly play around with me. I couldn't help it but I was hard and wanting what they were offering. I moved closer to Elijah pulling myself away from Sebastian. I could hear a little growl from him but I think he thought it was me playing. Elijah kissed me deeply and that's when the room crashed.

Sebastian flew out of the bed. Hade's boys came in and they were dragging Zak in. At first it looked like he had been beaten but when I looked again he looked like he was wasted on drugs. No doubt with the aid of the boys that were dragging him in. They dropped him on the floor at the foot of the bed.

"You bastards have poor timing," yelled Sebastian. They didn't seem to care as they sauntered up to the bed to see Elijah. One, a white blond came up to Elijah. "We've missed you brother." His black blue eyes glossed over me. He nodded at me. "But we know you've been busy." Again his eyes moved over me. "We brought your little play thing back to you. Hades drugged him a bit but..." he shrugged like it was nothing. "He'll be back to his bad ass self soon enough. It seems fucking the vamp boy here made the two of you stray off." He looked me right in the eye.

"No offense love but I can't imagine fucking something dead like you." He smirked and laughed and by the look on his face probably thought I should be laughing at his joke too.

There was another figure at the door now-Hades. He didn't look too impressed by the little gathering. His eyes were storm clouds.

The blond one stepped back. "I think this is our cue to go. Catch up later with you Elijah." He threw me a casual glance. "You too Avian."

He gestured to the rest of the boys and they left without a word.

All that was left now was Sebastian. "I just fixed things, okay? You don't have to be pissed off."

"Give me one good reason I don't turn you to ash."

Sebastian sauntered up to Hades and circled him. "Because we both know you can't, that's why."

"Leave my two sons alone. I took care of the matter."

"Yeah, I see that. Do think that thing in there is going to be pure?" Sebastian flicked at it sending it twirling around.

"Why wouldn't it be?"

Sebastian rolled his eyes at Hades, "Because they didn't do it themselves. It wasn't made from their lust for each other like the other one that hangs in their old room. They need to be locked in here and left to nothing but their lust and need for relief from their hard cocks."

Hades smirked. "You have it all figured out."

Sebastian tilted his head to one side. "Since when do I never have things figured out?" He came back over to the bed and he reached out to me. He let the back of his hand fall against my cheek. "I almost had a taste of this little vampire boy. But I will give them one more chance to perform."

He glanced over at Elijah. "You won't disappoint me, will you?"

Elijah pulled me close. "I won't."

Sebastian smiled. "That's what I want to hear." Then he swirled around to Hades. "Let's decorate this room for the lovers. I see they like sex toys. We can get some more of them for them to play with. This room needs color for our lovers who are going to breed us many little demons with the blood lust in them."

Hades just sighed. "Come Sebastian and let's leave our lovers to have an evening of love making. I'm sure we will be able to hear their cries of lust and orgasms from downstairs." Hades looked at Elijah and the look made Elijah speak up. "I won't disappoint you." Hades smiled. He was satisfied. Sebastian left with Hades.

I let out a shaky breath.

In my ear I felt Elijah's hot breath. "We have work to do." His hand went down between my legs. He pushed me back onto my back and spread my legs. He had lust in his eyes. Whatever Sebastian had done to him with that bite he was transformed back into the Elijah I met that night in the forest. "What about Zak?"

Chapter twenty One

"HE CAN JOIN US LATER when he is out of his drug induced state."

His hand squeezed my sac. I got hard for him as I knew there was no escape from this. He was gentle which surprised me. Hades and Sebastian would not be disappointed. They got to hear quite a few orgasms.

I woke in the darkness to a moan that came from the floor. Zak was coming to. I heard him crawl around to Elijah's side and crawled in beside him. Elijah shifted over to me letting Zak cuddle up against Elijah.

The white ceiling reflected in the darkness giving it the effect of white mist. Instead of staring at it I got up and went over to the window avoiding the vessel. It seemed to hang there, dead. Maybe it was and Sebastian was right. The thing in there wasn't a live. I took a good look over the garden and the grey mist floated over the dead garden. I could see clearly the cemetery. I wondered if she was out there. The night seemed to be calling to me. I was a creature of the night after all. I decided to go and grabbed my jeans and shirt with my boots. I decided not to put on the boots until I got outside.

I just opened the door when a voice spoke to me. "Come walk with me."

I froze and looked back into the house but… nothing.

"Come walk with me." The voice was in front of me and now I could see her. She was about 50 feet from the entrance way. Her flowing white gown what was left of it floated round her like spirits. Her hair fell down to her waist.

I stepped out towards her. "Are you the death witch?"

Her face was pale like the moons light and her eyes were hollow black. "Is that what you want to call me?"

"I…I…just hear them…"

She waved her hand at me cutting me off. "Never mind," she said. She gestured for me to join her, "Come, and walk with me."

I walked silently beside her. It seemed like she floated as I seen no feet under her gown. We ended up in a dark corner of the garden that for some reason seemed familiar. It was a huge oak tree and there was a tire swing under it. My mind was trying to place it. She sat in the tire and that's when I see her feet-skeletal feet. "Push me dear."

I went behind her and took hold of the tire and let it go. Her long hair dragged on the ground catching on some twigs and broken branches. Her hair pulled out quite easily but she didn't seem to feel it.

"This was always my favorite part of the yard, you know."

"Was it? Was this your home?"

She stopped swinging abruptly. Her hollow eyes tried to study my face. "Don't you recognize it?" Her voice sounded a bit annoyed.

"I'm trying to remember it but it's hard."

She appeared to understand now. "Yes, I guess with what happened to you, you wouldn't know much."

"Maybe you could tell me." She looked surprised by that. "Why?"

"I'm trying to find out who Elijah and I were. We don't belong here." Now I had her full attention.

"I want Elijah and me out of here and away from Hades and Sebastian. They want us to do nothing but breed demons for them." She never took her eyes off of me. "Can you help?"

She stepped off the tire swing. Her bone feet crunched on the ground. She came to me without a sound. "It all depends on what you are prepared to do for me."

"What do you want?" I wasn't sure what she would be asking for but I was prepared for anything.

She circled around me getting closer to me each time, testing me to see how comfortable I was in her presence. "I want some things out of the house that belong to me."

"That's it? You want some things out of the house?"

"Don't sound too confident yet my dear. These things are cursed."

She was right. I should have known the task she would ask would not be easy. "What are these things?"

"They're locked in the attic in a room that used to be mine. Hades has cursed the room so anyone entering it would be killed."

I shook my head. "How am I supposed to get in then? I would die."

"You silly thing, you are the perfect one to go in there and get my things."

"Why?"

"Because you are already dead, my dear. You can't kill something that is already dead."

"I wouldn't be harmed if I went into this room?"

She sighed like she was getting rather bored with me or ticked off. "Yes," was all she said.

"So, if I get these things, you will help us out of this underworld trap?"

She smiled when I said that so I guess I amused her now. "My dear it is not quite that simple but I can give you what you want and I know what that is but you better make sure that is what you want for you and your husband. With my *help*, there is no going back."

I didn't know quite what she meant by that as it seemed she knew far more than I did. I wish she would just tell me everything but that wasn't going to happen. Anything that she would tell me had a price.

"Okay, what do I do?"

"First, come walk with me. Then when I am done I will give you the list of things I want from the room." Then that was it, she spoke no more. We walked in silence as she led me through every dark corner of the yard. Old paths led to a garden I think. It looked like a vegetable garden. There were carrots in the corner growing that had gone to flower. Herbs seeded in abandonment and lettuces dotted here and there. There was even a pumpkin patch growing widely in one corner. It looked totally chaotic just like the rest of the yard. She stopped and went around the garden picking this and that like she was tending to this 'garden.' I waited for a while and then suddenly she was leaving without a word to me. I followed her down another path that was probably used by fox and coyotes and such. It went to the cemetery. This is where our little walk ended. She pulled out of her dress a piece of paper and handed it to me.

I took it out of her hand. The paper felt gritty and brittle at the same time. It felt like it had been in her dress for a long time. "The items are there." With that she turned around and walked away from me. "Just one more thing dear." Her voice drifted back to me as she continued to walk farther into the cemetery where I couldn't see her anymore. "Don't take Elijah into the room with you."

"Why," I shouted at her.

"The curse will kill him."

Then all I heard was the wind. I turned around and headed back to the house. I put the paper inside my pocket. I thought maybe that now would be a good time to go to the room as everyone was sleeping.

When I got back to the house the door to the house was open and Sebastian was standing there.

"What are you doing out here?"

"I like the night, so I went for a …"

"Ahh yes, vampires like the night. Did you enjoy your night excursion?"

"Yes." I didn't want to engage in a conversation with him but he wasn't letting me through the door.

"You need to be back upstairs where you need to wake your husband up and start round two of your mating. I was talking to Hades and we both agree you two need more motivation on this little task."

"What kind of motivation?" I knew I shouldn't have asked.

He smiled at me. "Well, I'm glad that you asked. I always say that an orgy is a good way to get you in the mood."

I knew what kind of 'orgy' he was talking about. The memories flooded me with Demon orgy parties that entertained with watching group sex with all kinds of sex toys. Of course, tying up one of them and then they all get to have sex with that one is fun to them. The drugs flow like a stream and the whisky is poison. It's not exactly what I would call motivation.

"Ahh, you don't like that idea? I didn't think you would. So, I think videotaping the two of you and then the rest of us can watch would be fun. Hade's boys want to know what it's like fucking you. They think Elijah is crazy. I think he just has eccentric tastes." He came out of the doorway and down the front steps. He sauntered up to me. "You smell like sex love." He undid my zipper and smiled. "No underwear love? I like you. It makes it much easier for me to cup these wonder full balls of yours. Oh Avian, let me have one taste of your cream." He yanked my pants down. I stood still. He knelt down and took my penis into his mouth all the while squeezing my balls. I had no choice but to fill his mouth. When I came he took every bit I could give.

"Oh Avian, that was wonderful. You do taste so delicious. Elijah is one lucky husband."

He stood back up and took my hand. "Let me take you back to that husband of yours."

Chapter Twenty Two

SEBASTIAN STRIPPED ME NAKED and put me back in bed with Elijah and Zak. Elijah stirred and he looked at us both. "Don't worry Elijah, I'm just bringing back what is yours." Elijah pulled me down next to him. He rolled on top of me and started to kiss me.

"Now that is more like it. Have a good long fuck Elijah."

"I intend to." A soft chuckle erupted from Sebastian as he left the room.

"Now, why didn't you tell me you were going for a walk? I don't want you to be alone out there. You need to be protected."

"I was okay, really." I didn't mention the death witch.

"It don't matter, you will tell me from now on, understand?"

"Yes," I said. The possessive Elijah was back.

We kissed for a while and the weight of Elijah was pushing on me. His knee worked between my legs. Elijah slid down and pushed my legs farther apart. "We need to secure you love." He moved as fast as I could. That was a first. It must have been Sebastian's bite. He went and pulled out the drawer with the sex toys in it and I could see from the bed that there were more. Elijah came back with his silk rope and tied me up like he did before. He placed out his assortment of oils out as well. But first he came back into bed with me and started to play around with my hole with his tongue. The heat of his tongue tingled. I shifted but he held me still. "I intend to drive you crazy. That's what you get for not telling me that you were going out for your little walk." He held up a red ribbon. I could only imagine what he had in mind. He tied the red ribbon neatly around the base of my balls where he snugged the bow. I looked like an erotic present.

I didn't see him bring it over. "This is going to heighten things, love." It was a mask of black lace silk.

"You're going to put that over my eyes?"

"Your other senses will be more alive and being a vampire your senses will be over the moon." He flashed a wicked grin. I shifted again trying to free myself.

"Oh love, that turns me on, your little struggles to get away. This is going to be the best ride ever." Then everything was in darkness and I had no clue what Elijah was up to.

"Oh Elijah please, I don't know about this."

"Relax love, I promise you'll love this."

I felt warm oil on my chest and Elijah's fingers working their magic. He squeezed my nipples and moved his fingers down my abdomen. I could feel the edge of his talons. He wrapped his warm oil hand around my now hard cock. He stoked me making me moan. My balls were aching. Elijah teased the tip of my throbbing cock with his tongue, flicking and licking making me leak out. He took me all in his mouth when I did that. I was ready to fill his mouth when he pulled away. I protested and begged for him to come back.

"We've only just begun Avian love; your senses haven't even begun to be challenged yet."

His finger slid up my hole. I was so sensitive and then I felt something smooth being shoved in me. It filled me a bit. "Don't push it out." He twisted it slightly making me almost catch breath. My whole body felt like a live wire spitting out sparks. I was going to explode.

Elijah kissed a trail of hot kisses in my inner thigh. I screamed out when he hit that special spot. I begged again but he was unrelenting. He gave the sex toy in my hole another twist before removing it and replacing it with his hard cock sending me arching into the air. He filled me making me almost convulse. "Hang on

Avian, it won't be long and you will be another dimension that you've never been in before." He started to thrust hard into me. "Oh Avian I'm so ready to fill you."

Suddenly I felt this heat run through me. He pulled out and smothered me with his cream. My hole and balls were covered. Then I felt the bow being tugged at my balls. "It's your turn love." He took my throbbing member in his mouth and I moaned. Finally, I was going to get my relief. He started out slow moving his tongue to tease me. I was ready to explode. I felt this rush of utter euphorbia crashing through my body. "That's it love, give me more and more."

I did until I felt completely empty and exhausted. "Push some cream out love." I did and felt something cold against me. "What is that?"

He came up and took my mask off and my eyes couldn't believe it. He had a gold vessel in his hand. "Our life my love is here and I think we are going to have more than one. You did wonderful." I tried to pull myself free. Elijah held me with his black red eyes making me go still. Now he needed the blood. His talon finger went across my chest leaving a thing stream of blood. He pushed down on my chest and the blood slid down and he caught it inside the vessel. Then he slashed his own wrist with his talon and let the blood drip into the vessel. An eerie presence filled the room. Black magic was here and it was making the air electric. I tried to free my hands. Elijah closed his eyes and chanted something old. The room went cold so very cold. "Please Elijah, let me free."

He looked down at me, "In just one moment, my love." He went over to the window and hung the gold vessel in the window. The moons light grabbed hold of it and the thing seemed to change color from gold to pale silver. Elijah smiled and was back in bed with me with his face in between my thighs kissing me and licking the cream from my hole. "I'll let you go after I've cleaned you all up. Maybe with any luck you will be hard again."

With his magic touch I did get hard but at least he didn't hold back on me and I released in his mouth giving him the taste of my soul.

The room was warm and Elijah and I were wrapped in each other's arms. The world was calm now. The room was bathed in pale white light. It was odd or it was just my eyes trying to adjust. When I moved Elijah and Zak stirred. Elijah rolled over on his back with lazy smile on his face. He looked smug and sexy at the same time. He glanced over at Zak and laughed. Zak told him to fuck off. It seemed like I was missing something between them.

I scooted down to the end of the bed and climbed over the footboard.

"Where do you think you're going love?"

"To soak in the tub…alone," I said.

"Should we let him bath alone Zak?" Elijah's grin was wicked.

"Fuck no, we're joining you." Zak's black eye shone in the pale white light.

There was no rest from the wicked or these two anyway. They followed me into the bathroom. Zak went ahead and turned on the water and poured bath salts into the water.

The air filled with jasmine with a hint of musk. He poured a small amount of liquid in creating a froth of bubbles. The bathtub was big but I wasn't sure if it would fit the three of us. Elijah crawled in first and gestured for me to sit in front of him. Zak went to the opposite side with no problem. We sat there soaking in silence. Elijah had wrapped his arms around me.

Zak sighed. "So, I see you did the real deed last night Elijah."

"Of course I did. I'm good at what I do." He sent a trail of kisses down my neck. "Isn't that right love," he whispered in my ear.

"Poor Avian, you must have almost done him in." His eyes filled with black water stared at me. "Being a vampire an all, your senses are so well…sensitive."

I let my head fall back onto Elijah's shoulder. Zak chuckled.

"He survived quite nicely, as you can see." His hand slid down and found me. He started to gently stroke me and it felt good. I closed my eyes and enjoyed Elijah's touch.

I had almost shut them out when Zak started to speak about their father.

"I took care of that little matter and father is none the wiser."

"Sebastian?"

"That pampas bastard knows nothing." Elijah chuckled. "Just be careful around him, okay? Knowing nothing can be his game." Elijah's tone was a warning. Zak didn't reply.

"I think our boy needs to be dried off."

"Well, we better take him to the bed then."

Zak got out of the tub first and held his hand out for me. I took it.

"That's a nice hard on". Elijah was out and pushing me towards the bed. Zak got some towel and brought them to the bed. They both started to dry me. My breathing had picked up speed. I liked what they were doing. Zak got some oil out and started to massage me. Elijah rolled me over onto my stomach and I got a nice massage on the neck and shoulders. Zak was good at this. I was relaxed.

Elijah was now behind me. His oiled fingers slipped between my cheeks and fondled my hole. "That's good love you stay relaxed."

His fingers worked their magic and went deep into that special spot. Then without warning he slipped his hard cock inside me and went deep. He picked up an even rhythm. He moaned with pleasure. Zak continued to massage my neck and shoulders.

I felt myself being rolled back with Elijah hanging onto me and still inside me. My hard cock was in the air. Zak went down and took me in his mouth. The two sensations were making me crazy. "I'm going to come."

"Let go then love, smother his face with your sweet cream."

One stream after another came from me making totally me spent. Elijah started his thrusts again and soon I felt his release.

I got to watch Elijah please Zak in a rather rough way. Zak likes it rough and Elijah knows how to deliver. Zak screamed as Elijah devoured him. "Tastes just as wicked as ever," Elijah quipped.

"What? I'm not sweet like your husband?" Zak's grin was laced with wickedness. Elijah laughed and pulled me into his arms. "No, you bastard you will never taste like my beloved."

The door flew open and Sebastian and Hades walked in. "Well, isn't this cozy? Our boys have been busy." Sebastian stopped short in his tracks. Elijah and Zak shared a look. Sebastian flew to the window and touched the vessel. "Hades, come here. You have to see this." Hades was there in a split second. He swirled around to face us. "You *have* been busy."

Sebastian looked at Hades. "There's more than one, I think there is three."

Hades smiled, "Really, now." Hades came over to us and sat down at the edge of the bed-inches from me. "Avian, it seems you are quite fertile." He ran his cold fingers through my hair, "My precious boy. I'm so happy that Elijah found you and you two got married. This has been the best union that could of ever have taken place. You two deserve to be rewarded." Sebastian was smiling. He nodded in agreement with Hades.

"Anything you boys want is yours. All you have to do is ask." He smiled like a proud father. I was relieved when he got up and backed away from me. His coldness that hovered over him made me shiver.

"I would like to take my husband to the other side for a few days where the hunt is allowed to wonder." Hades and Sebastian shared a look. Sebastian shook his head at Hades.

"I'm sorry my son but that I can't let you do that." His eyes cast down on the floor and his face was solemn.

"Why not," Elijah asked.

Sabastian answered for Hades. "Because you two need to be protected, especially now. The underworld will know about the upcoming births and I'm sure they will not be pleased. If you were to wonder out there, they would kill you. So you will stay here where you are under our watchful eye."

Zak sighed. "Great, what are we supposed to do here?"

Sabastian chuckled. "More of what you were doing this morning."

Zak just laid there naked and expressionless.

Hades stood at the end of the bed and took hold of the bed posts. His talon fingers wrapped around the wooden posts. He leaned in toward us. "I will decide a gift for you and it will be special I promise." He winked at us and then gestured for Sebastian to follow. They both left us, imprisoned in our room.

Zak rolled over to face us. "Well that went well."

Elijah snorted. "Yeah, just great."

"You two want to tell me what this is about?"

The two of them were silent for a moment. "Did you do something," I asked.

Elijah took my hand. "I was hoping to get a pass to the other side after our little demon baby making session but it seems with your fertile loins we did too good and now we are precious to them because of what we can do and give them."

"What did you want on the other side?"

"It wasn't what but *who* I wanted. Now I have to figure out another way."

"Who did you want to see?"

Elijah squeezed my hand. "It's nothing love, Hades is perhaps right. Your safe here and you mean everything to me." Elijah squeezed my hand again and leaned over and kissed me. I let it go to whatever this little mission was that the two of them had planned-for now.

"Can we leave this room?" I was starting to worry about if I was going to be able to do the death witch's wish.

Elijah shrugged. "I don't see why not. We are safe in this house and should be able to move around where ever we want. Why are you asking love?"

"I have something to do."

"May I ask what?"

I hesitated and that made them both stare at me. "Spill yourself lover boy," Zak said.

Elijah rubbed my leg getting closer to my inner thigh. "I met someone on my walk last night."

Both their eyes widened.

Zak sat up and moved in closer. "Do tell us who you *met*. I don't think he quite believed me that I actually met someone here.

"The death witch." I watched both their faces.

Zak rolled his eyes. "I'm surprised she didn't eat you."

Elijah pulled me close. "Don't go near her. She hates us and would feed you poison in a heartbeat."

"She appears to feel different about me." Zak coughed out a laugh. "You are his husband and anything associated with him would be hated, trust me."

"Zak's right, she can't be trusted so stay away from her. I'm surprised that she has wondered out. She usually stays hidden when Hades is around."

I didn't tell them about the list of things that she wanted me to retrieve for her in exchange for getting us out of here. I would have to do this on my own. I had to figure out something so that neither my husband nor Zak got suspicious of me.

"So, let's go see what there is for us in the kitchen. Your husband here looks a bit paler shall I say."

"Your right Zak, it's time he fed."

Zak leaned over to me and took hold of my chin. "Then after we are going to play with the new sex toys." He kissed me shoving his tongue deep in my mouth. He moaned. "Maybe we won't make it down stairs."

Elijah pushed him away. "Not going to happen. My husband needs to be fed, let's go."

The three of us went down to the kitchen to find a table filled with food and two pitchers of blood. "Well, someone knew what we wanted," amused Zak.

Elijah sighed. "Father knows everything." We sat at the table and filled our plates with meats, cheese and breads. Elijah poured me a big glass of blood. He dipped a piece of bread into the glass and popped it into my mouth. The blood woke up the blood lust in me. I jugged down the large glass of blood and Elijah filled it again. "Take all you need my love."

We sat around the kitchen table full. I felt elated with the feeding of blood. Elijah was happy and content right now and Zak seemed to be pretty content himself. I was wondering if I was going to get a chance to find the attic to the cursed room. I had to go in alone.

"What are you thinking about love?"

His black red eyes were trying to read me. "I'm not really thinking about anything."

"Liar," he grinned.

It was no use. "The death witch asked me to do something for her. Before you say no, just hear me out." He nodded.

"She gave me a list of things that she wants from her room in the attic." I didn't say this was a deal that I made with her in exchange for getting us out of here. I knew they wouldn't understand.

"I want to get them for, that's it. I know she won't hurt me."

"Oh God, she must be smitten with him. I would be careful Elijah, she wants your husband." He snorted.

Elijah just smiled. "You really want to give her these things?" I nodded.

He looked over at Zak. "Well you were looking for something to do here."

He rolled his eyes at Elijah. "Oh, I just can't wait." His sarcasm was choking.

"Please Zak. I need you to show me her room."

He sighed. "You're lucky you're married to him is all I got to say."

Zak led the way. Upstairs at the end of the hall way next to the study was a door. It was locked shut but that didn't stop Zak. He said a few words and the lock let go.

He opened the door and these small narrow stairs twined up and around. A pale light from a window cast a pale ghostly light on the dusty stairs.

"Shall we gentlemen?"

Elijah took my hand and we followed Zak up the winding stairs. They creaked with every step. We came upon the window that cast the pale light. Cobwebs draped across it but as I passed by it and the imagery I saw was not a dead garden but one that was full of life. I stopped short. Elijah was still holding my hand. "What is it love?"

"Do you see it?"

Elijah looked out the window. "See what Love?"

"The garden. It's so beautiful Elijah. The roses are in full bloom."

Elijah pulled me close to him. "You have a vivid imagination or hell of a good memory."

I was going to ask him what he meant but Zak's voice yelled down at us to hurry up.

We stood in front of a French door. Apart of the glass at the bottom was missing. You couldn't see in for the lace curtain on the other side that covered the glass door. Zak grinned. "Well this is it Avian, this was her room before she…well…you know."

I wanted to ask what had happened but it seemed he thought I already knew. "Okay Zak." said Elijah. "Open the door for us."

"Wait, you two can't go in, the room is cursed."

"If we can't go in then you can't go in either," said Elijah.

"She said I would be okay."

"And you believed her," Elijah asked.

"I think she was telling the truth." I tried to sound sure of myself but he just shook his head.

"You think she was telling you the truth love, I don't think so. Open the door Zak."

Like downstairs he spoke a few words and the door lock clicked. He pushed the door open and we could all see inside. The bed was made up with a bed doll sitting on top. A dresser with a tarnished mirror was sitting in the corner and a large armoire was against the wall with the door slightly open. An ivory rug laid on the floor at the foot of the bed. It looked hand made.

"Well, this looks real evil," Zak scoffed.

"You still can't go in, she warned me. I am the only one."

"The bitch is warped, what does she know?" Zak walked in a twirled around. "See? Nothing, the bitch lied to you."

He no sooner got the words out when he fell to his knees and started to choke and his skin went pale. He held up his hand and the skin now was disappearing and half his hand was bone.

"What the hell," Elijah yelled. "Get out of there." But Zak couldn't, he was choking again and deteriorating. I rushed in and grabbed him and pulled him out. He gasped for air and when he looked down at his hand he wasn't bone anymore. His black lacquered nails shone.

"I told you both that it was true."

Elijah's eyes were wild. "You sure as hell are not going in there."

"Elijah, I will be fine." And before he could stop me I entered the room.

The room I entered took on a new life when I stepped in. The still room had transported to another time. The room smelled like...lilacs. I looked around and the window was open. I walked over to it and looked out. Like what I saw in the stairway, the garden was alive. It took my breath away. I wanted to climb out onto the roof and jump down. The temptation was overwhelming. But I looked back through the door. I couldn't see Elijah or Zak. They probably thought the room swallowed me up.

I touched my clothes and when I looked down at them they were different. I was in a suit.

This was a suit fashioned from the past and I knew it was where I came from. She had transported me back to my time and it felt different. My hand flew to my chest. It was something I hadn't felt in a long time-my heart beat.

Something told me to reach inside my jacket pocket and the list was there and the paper wasn't gritty and brittle. It was fresh and crisp. I opened it and it read like a letter.

Dear Avian:

You reached my room. I'm so happy that you did this.

I hope you enjoyed my little 'gift' to you. You wanted to know about the past, well here is a little bit of it. This is who you were my dear. A young man about to be married to his beloved and yes that was Elijah who had just asked you to marry him.

Your favorite flower was the lilac. Do you remember?

In any case if you do this for me I will help you out of this underworld. You have to think about what I am about to do for you though, it will be forever this little wish of yours. There will be no going back. I just want you to understand that.

The following is the list and where you will find it.

I will see you in the garden where the old tire swing is.

Good luck.

Aria

Her name was Aria. It was a pretty name. I studied the list and set about looking for them. The first item on the list was a gold trinket box which was supposed to be on the dresser. I got it right away. The next item was easy as well-a hair brush which was puzzling.

The next item on the list was in the armoire in a drawer. I was to take out a wooden box with a carving on the lid. It was under some silky pieces that brought images to my mind. I quickly shook my head and pulled out the box. There was a carving there and I instantly knew it was the gazebo with the roses all around it. It was very beautiful. This box was locked so I didn't know how she would get into it but then again she was a witch. The other items were just personal items like her makeup and perfume. I guess she missed these things and I really don't blame her. It was a part of who she was. The last item on the list stopped me. It was the black velvet journal. That was in our old room. But my eyes wondered around the room anyways. What if there was another one? I looked everywhere but all I found was poetry books and a few Jane Austin books. It had to be the book that was in our old room. I went to the window and inhaled the lilac smell and held my hand to my chest just one more time. It was time to go back as I knew Elijah would be frantic. I gathered up the items in my arms and with one last glance at the room walked through the door to the other world. Zak screamed at Elijah who came rushing to me. His face was tear stained and blood red. He was in shock. "I thought I lost you forever."

"I'm sorry but I had to go in there. I told you I would be safe and I was."

Elijah gasped. "You're sorry? Love, you could have died and I would have lost you. I thought I did. How could you do that to me? Don't *you* love me?" His blood red eyes were wild and he was shaking.

"I do love you, more for than anything. I did this for us, believe me, please." I could see now he was shaking with fury. I could feel a tidal wave of anger coming my way. I had diffuse him.

"Elijah, listen to me. I would do anything for you and I promise not to go out of your site for the rest of eternity, I give you my word on that." He stood there for a moment in silence digesting my words.

"You give me your word?" His voice was steady and calming, at least I hoped.

I nodded. "See that you do love, because the consequences would not be pleasant, I give you my word on that." His words were cold and biting and I knew he meant every word of it.

Zak looked pretty shaken up. His black eyes had actually a hint of red in them. He calmly came up to me and took some of the items out of my arms. "Let me help you. I hope the bitch was worth it Avian because you crossed the line with your husband. I'll beat you myself if you ever try to pull a stunt like this again." He took a deep breath and walked toward the stairs. Let's get out of here."

I glanced over at Elijah who had calmed down. He took the wooden box out of my hand. He turned it around in his hands. He frowned at it shaking his head. I didn't want to know what he was thinking. He placed his hand on the lower half of my back. "Let's go love." His tone of voice left a chill on my skin.

We were back in our bedroom. Zak had laid the stuff on the dresser and Elijah placed the wooden box next to the items. I placed my items on a side table in the room. I felt hesitant to go near the two of them.

I barely turned around and Elijah was right there standing in front of me. He calmly took my hand. "Look me in the eyes Avian." I did. "Starting tonight we will be spending every waking hour in that bed." His talon finger pointed to the bed. "We are going to make another child. You will pleasure me and stay in my arms Avian. That is where you belong, in my arms and in my presence always. Do you understand?"

I nodded. "Good, now go and have a long hot bath my love and then come back to the bed when you're done. I want to gaze at your naked body for a while before you and I start making another child." He pulled me close and kissed me hard driving his tongue in my mouth. The heat of his tongue scorched the inside of my mouth but I didn't complain as I knew it would bring on more. He undid my pants and reached in and took hold of me. "Avian my love, you don't realize what you mean to me. You have to be taught to stay by my side and obey me for your own safety. Are we clear?" I nodded. "I want to hear you say it, give me your vow."

"I promise to stay by you and …obey." He smiled and then kissed me again and this time quite gentle. "I love you Elijah."

"I love you too. Now go and relax."

I went into the bath and started the water. I poured in the same salts and same liquid that Zak had used, letting the water run over my hands while I heard their voices.

Zak was loud and clear. "We should get rid of those things, you don't know what she has planned. She could harm or even kill him."

Chapter Twenty Three

ELIJAH'S VOICE WAS LOW and even though my vampire hearing is quite sharp, his words were not meant for my ears.

I heard footsteps coming into the room. I knew it was Elijah. He shut the door quietly behind him. I didn't turn my head I just stared at the water frothing in front of me. Elijah shut the water off. He chuckled softly. "You're going to overflow love." I stood up beside him. His expression was soft and relaxed. He gave me a warm smile and I smiled back at him. "You're not mad at me anymore?"

"Oh, you don't know how mad I am at you but I will deal with it and *you* will deal with it as well."

"What do you mean?" I was starting to get nervous at what he had in mind.

"I want you to feed off me for a while."

I swallowed hard. His blood was different than human blood. It could send me on quite a frenzy.

"Why do you want me to do that?" He started to undress me and when he undid my pants he pulled them down so I was naked in front of him. He cupped my balls and squeezed. "Then I can control you. You will be obedient to me and stay safe."

I never knew his blood could do that to me. "Now let's get you into the tub. I don't think I can leave you alone now. I want to wash you and get you real good and hard."

That he did. He washed every part, even my toes. When he was done he escorted me back to the bed where he quickly got naked himself. He straddled himself over me and told me to suck.

I took him in my mouth and sucked hard. He moaned with a demon growl coming from him. He soon emptied in my mouth. I licked him clean. He laid on top of me, kissing me and sending his tongue deep into my mouth. "I will never let you go."

Elijah sat up slightly and placed his wrist against my mouth. "Drink my love." I had no choice as I sunk my teeth into his wrist. He hissed as my sharp teeth sunk deep into his flesh. The flow of his blood hit the back of my throat erupting the blood lust in me. I drank with a vengeance like a man dying of thirst.

When I let go Elijah smiled. "Oh love, you will make a wonderful father to our demon vampire children. They will have our mixed blood running wild in their veins." Gently with his hand he pushed my head to the side exposing my neck. I closed my eyes.

His hot breath hit my neck and then his teeth caught me and sunk into my neck. I flinched as he fed off me. I soon started to relax as his suck became gentle. I felt weak when he let go.

"How do you feel?"

I told him I felt weak and that I needed some blood. "I will give you some after I've made love to you. In your weak stage I will be able to do what I want with you." He flashed a wicked grin at me as my insides sunk.

He tied my legs up just enough to give them support so I didn't have to hold them in place. He warmed my balls and hard cock with warm oil. Then he massaged me. The combination of his hands and warm oil felt so good and I was ready to come. I told him. "Really love, hang on love." He left me and came back with one of those vessels. Where the hell did he get that? His black red eyes looked deep into me. "You ready to give lots of that sweet cream love?" He started massaging me again. He licked the pre-cum off me and very quickly I started to come.

One stream after another came and he directed all of it into the vessel. The last stream he put in his mouth and sucked everything he could out of me.

"You never disappoint me Avian. You filled it good. Maybe we'll have more than one." He came up on his knees in front of my face. It's your turn love to make me come and fill this vessel to complete our baby making." He was grinning. I took him in my mouth and I could taste him.

He pulled just in time to fill the vessel. Elijah capped it, setting it aside. I knew the procedure wasn't finished yet. "Here clean me off love." I sucked him as he wanted. He was hard again.

"That's what you do to me." He shoved his head in my hole and pulled out. He moistened his fingers in his mouth and shoved two fingers up my hole deep to find that sensitive spot. "Relax those muscles love and enjoy it."

His fingers fondled and soon he had my hole spread open slightly. He shoved himself part way in and then went deep inside of me. I caught my breath as he leaned against me pinning me from moving. It was a long slow fuck that brought us both to an orgasm that sent us shaking in each other's arms. He untied my legs and we rolled to the side wrapping our legs around each other. We kissed as our cream blended together between our bodies.

Out tongues played with each other tasting and exploring. Elijah started to lick my belly and took my cock in his mouth where I grew hard for him once again. I didn't realize it but when I came again I emptied yet into another vessel. We were going to have a whole army of kids.

He fucked me from behind this time pulling out in time to fill this vessel.

"Now we have to complete this little session of ours." He pulled out the small silver dagger and took my hand and turned it palm facing up. With one smooth motion he slashed my palm. I flinched but he held my hand firm and he dropped my blood into each vessel. Then he handed me the knife. I stared at it. "You do the same to me." Elijah held out his palm to me.

"I don't know if I can do this."

Elijah put the dagger in my hand. "Do it." I knew I had no choice so without thinking I slashed his palm. Black blood oozed out. "See, you did good. That's nice thick blood thanks to you after I fed off of you. Now take my hand and drop some blood in each vessel." I did as he said.

Once the vessels were capped he took my hand. Both our bloodied hands held each other as we went to the window and Elijah hung them up for the moon to cover with its eerie light. He never said any chants this time so I asked. "You didn't say any words."

"I did but you didn't hear it. I said them while I was fucking you. It worked quite well since you gave me yourself so willingly." My face blushed.

"Come back to bed and let me make love to you for the rest of the night."

"We're finished making babies?"

He smiled. "Yes, we are and you did wonderful love. Now you get rewarded with my love making and I promise you will enjoy it."

Between the massages and fucking me in every position he could think of I think the pleasure was mostly his. I did enjoy it but I think this was more about control and keeping me in place.

I was laying on my stomach spread eagle sleeping. Something soft across my buttocks made me twitch. It happened again making me groan in protest. I eventually rolled over and Sebastian was looking down at me.

"Good morning precious." His voice was low and soft like he was trying to keep everything quiet for me.

"You rest love, you did quite well last night, filling two more vessels. You are so good for Elijah. You're the perfect husband for him. You two will have a large family, I can see that now." He smiled warmly. "I look forward to that. Hades and I have a surprise for you both but you rest for now."

"Where's Elijah?"

"Don't worry love, he's safe. He'll be here to see you shortly."

He reached down and took hold of my balls. I froze. "You're so full of rich seed my vampire boy. You are a precious gift to us. Then he bent down and took hold of my cock and kissed the head as if he was blessing me or something. I let out a breath when he let go of me.

"Maybe one day Elijah will let me taste your seed again."

He started towards the door and then turned to me before he left. "Rest love and Elijah will come for you later."

The click of the door echoed in the room. I sat up searching for Elijah or even Zak but they were nowhere around and leaving this bedroom might not be the wisest thing to do giving Elijah's possessiveness.

My eye caught the items on the dresser. I immediately looked over at the little side table and with relief I saw the items I had placed there. They hadn't taken them. I sat in the quiet for a moment and closed my eyes but then the sound of a click echoed in my ears. The door very slowly opened and I watched. Elijah very quietly stepped in but when he looked over my way his mouth fell open. "What are you doing up? You should be sleeping."

"I was woken."

"Who woke you," he demanded.

"Sebastian."

Elijah frowned. "Bastard."

He came and sat next to me. He pushed me gently back on the bed. My legs were slightly apart. He enjoyed that. His hand drew patterns on my chest.

"Watch the nail, okay," I said to half jokingly.

He smiled. "I will love." He put his finger in my mouth. "Suck my fingers for a little bit."

When he pulled out his fingers he told me to spread my legs apart to show him my hole. His fingers slid in deep. "It works every time, you get hard for me." He kept his fingers in place while taking me in his mouth. I was turned on and came with such a shudder. I gave him a full load in the mouth and he took every bit of it. "That was the best treat ever love." He pulled his fingers out and I started to relax. "Now you've got me hard."

I whispered in his ear. "Fuck me then."

He did just that. His thrusts felt good and I got hard again, damn him. Of course Zak waltzed in and seen what was happening and jumped on the bed. "Suck him Zak, he has a full load ready to go." Zak didn't need any more encouragement. He took me in his mouth while Elijah continued to thrust inside me. We were both ready to explode. I came first and then Elijah filled me. Zak licked me clean and then went down to my whole and started licking up Elijah's cream. Elijah laid beside me while Zak did his thing.

"Isn't this sweet Hades. This trio of yours can't get enough." Zak stopped and watched them.

"Don't stop Zak, I want to watch. Lick every morsel of that sweet cream up. Push some more out for him love." I did and Zak licked it all up as if he didn't there would be consequences to pay. Elijah just held me and when Zak was done he laid on the other side of me. He and Elijah shared a kiss. Then Zak kissed me. I don't know what that was for but my guess was for a show for Hades and Sabastian who were very pleased by what they saw.

"You see my boys are very lustful and will give us many children."

"Yes, I know, Elijah and Avian were busy last night. I think Zak should be rewarded as well."

Hades smiled. "I've already taken care of that. He will get his surprise tonight. It will be wonderful."

Their conversation between them carried on like we weren't even in the room. But finally they looked over at us and smiled. "You boys," said Hades. "Will get to have a party tonight with a special few invited. The party will start in a couple of hours. You can spend the two hours however you want." Of course we all knew what he thought. More of what we were caught doing would be in order.

Chapter Twenty Four

THE NOISE DOWNSTAIRS WAS getting loud. We, the guests of honor weren't even there yet and the partying was in full swing. The three of us had got cleaned up and were ready to face whatever was down there.

Zak was looking at the vessels. "You two have been busy." Zak touched the gold one. "This one has more than one life in it-maybe three." His black eyes shone at us.

Elijah smiled proudly. "Yes, we made that one in pure passion. Avian gave a part of his soul to me for that one."

My head jolted towards Elijah. "My soul?"

Elijah wrapped his arms around me. "Yes, love you did. That gold vessel holds three very powerful demon vampire children."

A cold shiver went through me. I had to get us out of here before they were born.

The smell of cigar mixed with some drug that was being brewed burnt the back of my throat as we walked down the stairs. Some of Hades boys pulled Zak into their own party. I took a hold of Elijah's hand for support. My look at him told him exactly how I felt about all this. His small smile tried to reassure me but this was going to be one tough party to get through.

"There's our boys." Sebastian's voice made everyone turn their heads toward us. He waltzed out in front of us like some peacock. "These two are precious gifts my fellow demons. Upstairs as we speak there are demon offspring from these two growing stronger every day and soon will be born to us." A shoveling of bodies and muffled voices slithered through the room.

A sudden shadow caught my eye. It moved about the guests like black mist. My eyes never let go of it. Then I lost it. Elijah squeezed my hand. "Are you okay?"

I nodded but my eyes were searching for what I saw. When Sebastian was done spewing his poison everyone raised a glass in a toast to us. That's when I saw it. Right in front a young woman all dressed in black leather with eyes as red as blood-a vampire. She held her glass up to me in the toast. I remained frozen staring at her wondering why she was standing in a room full of demons.

"Kiss your husband." It was one of Hades boys yelling out half drunk or drugged. Sebastian smiled at us. Elijah sighed and turned me towards him. He cupped my face very gingerly in his talloned hands and kissed me. An eruption of cheers and claps filled the room. Another one of Hade's boys yelled out. "You can do better than that Elijah, come on let's see something."

I stared into Elijah's black red eyes wondering what the hell they wanted to see. Elijah pulled me in close to him and kissed me deeply driving his tongue deep into my mouth. I was tense but Elijah didn't let me go until he had given them a show. I gasped for air when he finally let me go. There was no cheers this time, only more whispers that chilled the room.

"Let's let our boys enjoy the party. The rest of you go and enjoy the rest of the evening." Everyone grew silent at the sound of Hade's voice. I remained close to Elijah. He smiled down at me. "You did great love." He kissed me on the forehead taking the chill off my skin.

Elijah led me around the room with eyes staring at us from all direction. It was like we were on display or something. As it turned out nobody came near us. I guess they weren't allowed to.

If that was the case I was relieved. Elijah poured me a glass of wine and himself one. "Well, so far?"

I smiled. He grinned and I think he felt the same way. I started to relax a bit but my eyes searched for her. I think she returned to mist to hide. What was a vampire doing here? I walked around the perimeter taking Elijah with me of course. "What are you doing? It's like you're looking for someone."

"I am," I replied quietly.

Elijah didn't say anything, just followed attentively close to me. I ended up going out onto a porch from the back of the kitchen. The night air was cold and crisp. Elijah wrapped his arm around my waist as if I felt the cold. Then I felt her. Elijah knew as well. "Whose are visitor?"

I leaned my head against Elijah's shoulder. "Another one like me," I whispered. Elijah stiffened.

"Are you sure love?"

"Yes, she is here."

"A female vampire? What in the hell would she be doing here?"

"What? Are you discriminating against my kind?" Her voice floated over to us from the back lilac bushes.

"Show yourself," Elijah yelled out to her.

A shadow came forward. She blended into the darkness so much that we could barely see her.

When she came into form her leather shone in the dark and her red eyes shimmered. "How did you get here my dear?"

"That was easy, those drunk drugged up boys that you hang out with let me in. They're so stupid." She flashed a wad of cash in front of us.

"I see you fleeced their pockets while they were letting you through," Elijah said.

She shrugged and got a little closer to us. Her coal black hair was tipped in blue matching her painted blue lips. A small blue stud was in her nose as well as a silver bar in her eyebrow. Long blue claws adorned her small hands. There was an air of predator in her. She was what I heard some call her type as hunters. They were vicious killers.

She tilted her head slightly and settled her red eyes on me. "So you married a demon boy. What the hell were you thinking?" Her tone was acid and as she got decidedly braver and closer. Even though she was still a good six feet away from us, I could smell her breath. It smelled like mint but if you breathed her breath in you would be poisoned. She was the pure example of what a hunter was and why was she here, to hunt one of us?

"Why are you here," I asked her.

Her blue lips smiled at me. "To have fun at a party." That was a bare face lie.

"I don't believe you," I said never taking my eyes off of her.

"You like parties…your name?" Elijah inquired.

She ignored him. Then without warning she flew within a foot of me startling me. Elijah growled. She breathed on me choking me. Elijah lashed out with his sharp claws but his talon hand went through mist. She formed a few feet away. "You'll have to do better than that demon boy." She chuckled shaking her head. "You demon boys are so stupid and that's why I can't figure out why you married this this thing." She showed sharp teeth when she looked at Elijah.

"We knew each other from our past lives," I blurted out. Her eyebrows raised then. "Really? Wow, you must have it bad for one another then." I think this sounded more disgusting to her though. Her nose twitched as if she smelled something she didn't like.

Zak should have known better as she hit him with a gust of air throwing him hard to the ground. Zak laid there for a moment lifeless before stirring. "Get up you sac of crap," she hissed at him.

He coughed and sputtered for a moment before sitting up. "Who let the fun bitch in?"

"It seemed she followed one of the boys in," Elijah said.

Zak snorted.

"What do you really want here love because if Hades finds you here he will fry your pretty little ass."

"Ooh, scary." She rolled her eyes at him. "Where is the big boy anyway?" She licked her lips as if she could taste him.

"Would you like for me to get him then?" Elijah offered in a rather sarcastic tone.

She giggled. "Don't bother yourself love, I'll find him on my own." With that she vanished.

Zak straightened himself out and came up to the porch where we were. "Man, I hope Hades gets her."

Elijah scoffed at him. "You were just pissed that she didn't give you a taste of her hot vampire lust."

Zak's black eyes shone like a cat. "I don't think so, I don't wish to wake up in a pool of my own blood."

"Let's go back in love, Hades will be looking for us."

I took Elijah's hand and Elijah took Zak's hand and we went inside shutting out our little encounter. The party was getting quite lively inside. Some of Hade's boys were half naked dancing to the music that played rather loudly. Some in the corner where playing cards. I would hate to hear what the stakes are. Zak grabbed a bottle of whisky off the table.

"Well boys let's go have our own party."

Elijah smiled. "That sounds okay to me. In fact, let's leave here and go somewhere else."

Zak grinned. "And my love, where do you have in mind?"

"Follow me?"

We stood in front of the metal gate. I frowned. "Are we going to the pub on the other side?"

Elijah smiled at me. "No, this is a place that my love liked to hang out on the other side."

The graveyard looked the same. The night air here was fresh and kissed my cheeks welcoming me back. The tombstone I rested on was still there and that is where we sat with a bottle of whiskey in front of us.

The mist danced around us. We took turns drinking from the bottle. The warmth from the whiskey settled into my cold body. I leaned back on the stone and let the dampness from the mist settle on my face.

I felt Elijah right next to me. He traced my jaw line with his finger then kissed my damp cheek. "I love you," he whispered in my ear. I smiled.

Zak started to dance on the stone. He was feeling the whisky. Elijah leaned against me as we watched him. It seemed like we had shut the other world out but I knew that this was only for a short time and we would have to go back. I knew that and I was okay with it as long as I had Elijah by my side. Elijah sat himself right in front of me and started to kiss me. His kisses tasted different here. My tongue licked his lips and even the tip of his nose. We both laughed.

Zak looked down at us. "Well lovers, we have to go back and be the center of attention and remember?"

"Remember what," Elijah asked.

"Hades has a special surprise for me," he slurred.

"Oh that, yeah, well I guess we better get back. There's a surprise waiting for us too."

When we walked in Hades and Sebastian stood there looking at us. I thought we were caught and in trouble but both of them smiled. "Come with us boys. It's time for your gifts."

We shared a look and then followed them into the small study. Sitting in the corner was a young slim fellow. He looked up when we all came in but we couldn't see his face too much for his hair fell across his eyes. He stood up to greet us. I could tell he was nervous.

Sebastian went over to him and smiled at the all of us. "This is our first surprise and this is for you Zak." Zak's black eyes went wide. "Hades and I were talking and we think it's time that you had a mate of your own. We hope that Jamie here will be perfect for you. Jamie, this is Zak." Zak didn't move but Jamie did. He came up to Zak and offered his hand. He was very delicate, almost feminine. Zak didn't offer his hand, he just looked at the two of them. "Did I hear you right? This is supposed to be my mate?"

"Yes," said Hades. "Come Zak, take Jamie's hand."

Zak reluctantly held out his hand and Jamie was about to bend down and kiss his hand but Zak snatched his hand away. "No, I don't want any of this."

Jamie backed up not sure what to do. Hades came up to Zak and placed his hand on his shoulder like he was being fatherly. "Now Zak, just try and get to know Jamie."

He pushed Zak closer to Jamie and Jamie smiled at Zak trying to soften him up but Zak wasn't budging. "I can't even see your eyes."

"Then touch Jamie and pull his hair to the side and look into his eyes." Jamie waited for what Zak was going to do but Zak wasn't doing anything.

"You're going to have to try a little harder Zak." Hade's tone was getting a little more urgent now meaning he was not about to put up with much more of Zak's behavior.

Chapter Twenty Five

I GUESS ZAK KNEW IT too as he reached up and brushed Jamie's hair to the side revealing his eyes. They were as black as Zak's. Jamie offered a smile again and this time Zak gave a small smile back. Jamie seemed pleased by that. Jamie also took the bold move and leaned over and kissed Zak on the cheek. Zak froze. Jamie went in for the kill this time and kissed Zak on the lips. Their kiss lasted for a moment. I think Jamie just swept Zak off of his feet. Zak was flushed and for once couldn't say anything.

"Now that's better," smiled Hades. "We have a room for the two of you down the hall from Elijah and Avian. The bed is made up."

"I will show them to their room Hades."

"Thank you Sebastian." Jamie took hold of Zak's hand and led him out the door following Sebastian.

Elijah and I were stunned. Hades whirled around to us and smiled. "Wasn't that wonderful? Zak now has a mate and who knows maybe they will have children too."

I just about fainted and I think Elijah felt numb. He and Zak had been lovers for a long time.

"I now have given you two the gift of a real marriage. Now that you have a family on the way I think it is important that it just be the two of you from now on. But this is not my real surprise. I'm going to give you a home of your own."

"Where," Elijah asked.

"Oh, deep in the underworld where you will both be safe and oh don't worry Zak and James will be there with you. We'll have their wedding there, a big huge celebration. Doesn't that sound wonderful boys?"

I felt weak. If he was to send us there we would never be free. I had to get those items to Aria and fast. I just had to get that black velvet book out of our old room.

Hades excused himself to see how the new couple were getting along. He just wanted to see if they had made it into bed yet.

Elijah let out a deep breath when he left. "Well, this turned out to be an evening of surprises."

"I don't know if I want to go deeper into the underworld Elijah. That scares me."

"It's not exactly appealing to me either."

"Have you been there?" Elijah shifted his weight in uneasiness.

"Yeah, I've been there and it's very dangerous to say the least."

"Why would he send us to a dangerous place?"

"Well, it won't be dangerous for us because we will be protected by Hades and we will have a lavish home that is for sure. Our children will have everything they ever wanted."

"That sounds like a paradise you're describing."

"In a way it is but when we go there we will never see this place or the other side again."

I looked right into his eyes. "You sound like you don't want to go. We don't have to go love." I brushed his cheek with the back of my fingers. He took my hand and kissed my fingers. "I wish it were that easy love but the choices in our lives have been made."

I wanted to tell him about the deal I made with the death witch or what I prefer to call her now-Aria. But I didn't, as I didn't think he would understand but I was running out of time now. I would have to either make him understand or force him into it.

"Let's go upstairs to our room where we can be alone." Elijah nodded and we both slipped our arms around each other's waist and walked upstairs.

Elijah threw off his coat and sat in a chair with his feet outstretched in front of him. I poured him a glass of spiced wine. He took it and sipped slowly. I pulled up a chair beside him.

"Elijah, do you remember who you use to be?"

"What do you mean love? I am who I am."

"No, I mean who you were before Hades turned you."

Elijah's black red eyes settled on me searching in my own eyes for answers to what brought this on. "I don't know what you are getting at but if you are trying to search for who you use to be before the blood lust then I suggest you forget it because there is no going back. This is it for us. We are bound by our blood and love and we have children that will be born soon. We have obligations to fill now in this world. You have to understand that love."

I understood all too well and I fell silent. I didn't say anything more on the matter.

Elijah took me to bed and made the most passionate love to me like he really wanted to get across to me that I was his and belonged to no other but him. I laid in his arms contented as he caressed my temple and ran his fingers through my hair. He kissed my temple. "You are so mine love and I will love you for all eternity." I fell into a darkness that led to restless dreams. It was like someone was trying to wake me up to tell me something.

My eyes flew open and I felt this presence in the room. Elijah was a sleep next to me.

"Don't worry he won't waken."

It was Aria.

She had her stuff in her arms and she was putting them into a bag. She didn't look too happy. I watched her. After she had finished her hollow eyes looked around the room.

"It's in our old bedroom." She stared at me. "It's the journal you're looking for right?"

Her boney fingers wrapped around each bed post and leaned in to me. "Get it," she hissed.

"Why are you mad? I got everything you asked for."

Aria ignored me. I got out of bed and pulled on some jeans and t-shirt. She waited for me to lead the way. She followed behind me in a safe distance.

The door to the room was shut and when I tried to open it, it was locked. Aria was a short distance from me. "What is it," she asked impatiently.

"The door is locked," I told her.

Aria let out a huff and marched up to me and then looked at the door. "Open it." Her breath was ice.

"I can't, I've tried. Hades must have spelled it or something." It was like the entire door was sealed with iron because it stood before as solid as could be.

"Can't you break the spell Aria?"

Her eyes widened when I said her name as if she never thought to hear that again. Her empty eyes blinked a few times. "I can't, they will know I am here in the house. I'm not in the mood to see Hades or that other one."

"Sebastian?"

She snorted. "He's nothing to Hades but an obedient puppy." There seemed to be an edge of jealousy in her voice.

"Try again love, I need that journal and if you don't get it, I won't help you."

"What?" I shook my head at this useless attempt. I knew the door would not open no matter what I did. But the strangest thing happened. When I turned the knob, it clicked.

"See? You obviously didn't try hard enough."

I pushed the door open not quite sure what to expect. The first thing I saw was a pair of my jeans hanging over the chair and the bed was a mess. Pale blue light bathed the room. The next thing I know she's shoving me through. I turned around and looked at her. "Why did you do that?"

My answer was a raised eyebrow. I glared at her. "You thought the room was spelled like your room. So better for me to die than you?" She just sniffed and shrugged. I was starting not to trust her.

I walked over to the bookshelf to get the journal. It wasn't there. I went across each row of books and I could not see it. "It's not there."

Aria practically threw me to the side. "What do you mean it's not there, look harder you fool!"

I looked again but nothing, it was not there. I even went over to the bed and looked through the sheets and into the nightstand and it was still not to be found.

"Is this what you're looking for?" Both of us startled and looked at the figure who filled the doorway.

Hades came into the room with the journal in his hands. I think I heard a hiss and it wasn't from me. Hades chuckled. "Shouldn't you be in bed with your husband Avian?"

Before I could answer he continued on. "I see you have met my dear Aria. She must like you Avian and trust you to retrieve her things for her. I knew you were in her room."

Aria stomped her feet. "Now, now Aria, you should have come to me for these things. I would of given them to you darling. You knew that."

I froze. Now I wondered what else he knew. Did he know of our deal? Then a thought came to me. Was this the reason we were being sent away so I would not escape?

He walked up to Aria with the journal and handed it to her. She snatched it and shoved it into her bag. She then very carefully walked around Hades to make her get away but Hades stopped her. "Not so fast love, you and I have not spent much time together. I think it is time, don't you?"

She almost cowered before him but at then threw up her chin at him. "Make me tea."

Hades laughed. "Anything for you darling."

Hades held his hand out to me. "You need to go back to your husband."

I took his hand and his talons sealed around my hand. He escorted us both out the room with the door shutting firmly behind us and I didn't need to know but it locked again.

He delivered me back to Elijah. As I was undressing in front of Hades, Elijah stirred.

"What is it father, what has happened?"

"It's okay Elijah, I'm just returning your husband to you. He was running a...errand for someone."

Elijah didn't ask any questions although I knew I would be asked plenty when Hades left. Hades stayed until he saw me in the arms of Elijah who was now on top of me kissing me. Elijah moaned and that satisfied Hades and he left I presume to have tea with Aria. I wondered what she would tell him.

Elijah was hungry and I could feel his hard cock pushing between my legs. I willingly spread my legs so he could find his special spot. I felt the tip of his hardness push against my hole. "You're tense love, we'll have to do something about that." He reached over for his oil and started massaging me all over. Soon I was hard and I was ready for him.

"I plan on giving you a long fuck love." That he did. I was left exhausted in his arms with him whispering in my ear. "You'll have to tell me about this errand love."

I woke up with Elijah's hand massaging my sac. "That feels good."

"It's supposed to love. You're already hard for me." He took me in his mouth and sucked hard almost bringing me to a climax but stopped. "You're going to have to work for your orgasm this morning love." I moaned in protest.

"You have to tell me about this little errand first and then I will reward you with an orgasm love. So tell me all about it." He continued to massage and stroke me. It was too late, I came anyway.

Elijah took me in his mouth and sucked everything out of me that was left. "Well, that didn't go as planned but you tasted like heaven." He kissed me tenderly then without warning pinned me down. We were nose to nose. I pulled him in for a deep kiss and when I let go of him he gasped. "My love is hungry this morning but you still aren't off the hook love. What happened last night?"

I whispered in his ear. His eyes went wide. "Really Avian, I thought you would want a bit of a break from that considering what we have already started."

Then he narrowed his eyes at me. "You don't want to tell me." I shook my head but he wasn't buying it. He sat up and pulled me up with him. "Are you keeping secrets from me?"

"No, of course not." I was caught in hard place here. I couldn't tell him about the deal with Aria.

"Then, tell me and I will give you that wish for another child." He was testing me. "I met up with the death witch last night." His eyes flew to where the objects I collected where and noticed they were gone. "You gave them to her without me being there?"

I didn't tell him she was in the room last night. "I was alright, really."

His black red eyes went a little redder.

"It was okay." He grabbed hold of me by the arms and I could feel the tips of his talons piercing into my skin.

"You have to listen to me, okay? I'm only going to say this once." I nodded.

"You will tell me where you are going at all times from now on. We have had this conversation before and you didn't exactly listen did you?"

"I'm sorry Elijah but…"

"But no love, you will be a part of me from now on and by that I mean I will be in your head at all times."

"What?" I was wondering what he was going to do to me.

"Let up Elijah." Zak walked into the room followed by Jamie.

"Who the hell invited you here? Don't you have your own room now…with Jamie?"

Elijah was pissed and wanted to deal with me on this little matter of going behind his back.

Another voice joined in and that was Hades. "I agree with Zak, Avian is fine and I was with Avian last night when he was with the death witch so everything was in control, I assure you."

Elijah let go of me. "I see father. Well, I guess then everything is fine." He still looked pissed.

Hades looked at Zak and Jamie. "Why don't the two of you go downstairs to the kitchen, I think you will find some things on the table that you will enjoy?"

Jamie took Zak's hand and led him out the door.

Chapter Twenty Six

HADES SAT DOWN AT THE EDGE of the bed. "I want to talk to you two about the death witch. She and I had a lovely evening last night and we discussed that it was maybe best you two went to your new home in the next few days." My insides sank. Did she tell Hades about our deal? I was done for if that was the case. Elijah remained quiet and just listened.

When Hades left, Elijah looked at me and smiled. "Well, I guess I don't have to worry about you anymore as we will be going to our new home and there I will know where you at all times."

"You will?"

"Yes darling, when we are deep in the underworld we will be more aware of each other more than ever. We will be able to talk to each other through our minds and be able to feel each other's presence which I welcome. To have you inside me all the time will be a great pleasure love."

"We have two days left here then?"

"Yes, it seems so love."

I had two days to find Aria and find what the hell was going on and if she just went back on our deal. Tonight I would go talk to her even if I had to tell Elijah.

Elijah was now in a better mood and seemed quite anxious to go to our new home. We bathed together and he dressed me touching me making me hard. Before we went down to join the rest of them he took me in his mouth. His suck was seductive and the way he worked his tongue made me crazy. I shuddered as I let go. Elijah licked up everything I had given him. "Now that was the best breakfast I could ever have." He grinned as he zipped up my pants.

When we joined Zak and Jamie in the kitchen we were greeted by a pleasant smile from Jamie but Zak was a bit sour. Elijah sat down beside him. He leaned over to him and winked. "How was your first night together?" Elijah appeared to be more accepting of Jamie.

I think I heard a low growl from Zak. "Oh, come on Jamie seems so right for you."

Zak stuffed his mouth with some bread and cheese telling Elijah he had no intentions of talking about the situation. I looked over at Jamie whose eyes were on Zak. He seemed very much interested in Zak. So we sat around in silence for a while when Elijah decided to break the cold ice in the room that had settled in between us all. "Avian and I will be going to our new home soon-in a couple of days."

That got a reaction out of Zak. "In a couple of days?"

Elijah nodded.

"Then what about us?"

Elijah just shrugged. "What, you don't know? Hades must have told you something."

Elijah placed his hand on Zak's shoulder. "It's okay love. Hades will look after you and Jamie. You will be coming to the same place as us. That is where you will be married."

Jamie smiled when Elijah said married. Zak didn't.

"You two need to spend more time together. Why don't you take Jamie for a walk in the garden and maybe share a kiss or two?" Jamie's dark eyes shimmered.

"I guess so," Zak drawled out. Zak looked over at Jamie. "Can we just hold hands for a while before anything else?"

We heard Jamie's voice for the first time. "If you like my darling but I hope I can convince you otherwise." His voice was soft as a girls but very seductive all the same. Jamie got up and went around to Zak and I think Zak just froze. This is the first time I ever seen Zak be so quiet and reserved. He got up and Jamie took him by the hand and a firm hold it was.

They left with Zak glancing over at us for a rescue.

When the door shut Elijah laughed. "Zak is so scared of him. Jamie will have to do a lot of convincing I'm afraid."

"Maybe they aren't meant for each other."

Elijah grinned. "Oh they are meant for each other, Zak just doesn't see it yet but he will."

"Can we go for a walk in the garden?" Elijah looked over at me with mischief. "Do you want to spy on them?"

"No, I don't, there are other parts to this garden that I didn't see before."

"Oh, what part did you see that we haven't seen?"

I gestured to the back of the house. "The death witch showed me some gardens behind the house."

"I can't imagine what she showed you," he scoffed.

"Well, I admit it was dark at the time but it appeared to be an old vegetable garden and some others but I wouldn't mind going there in the daylight before we go."

Elijah sighed. "If that is what you want then we will go for this little walk."

Elijah slipped his arm around my waist and was giving me tender kisses on the temple and on the cheek. He was clearly not interested in this little adventure.

We came to the garden where I broke away from him. I opened the gate to the garden where all kinds of vegetables had seeded themselves. It was something that the weeds never took over but it was like someone maybe tended the garden to some degree. I walked around a large patch of herbs that stood very tall. My view of Elijah was blocked. Elijah didn't like that. He whipped around to where I was slipping his arms around to the back of my waist pulling me close kissing me. He whispered in my ear. "Do you want to make love in the garden?"

"Right here?" I cleared a strand of hair away from Elijah's eyes giving me a clear view of his red black eyes. I kissed him. "That might be interesting but I don't think this spot would be suitable."

Elijah didn't say anything. He kissed me and held me for a long time before letting me go.

"What was that about?"

He shrugged. Elijah took a step back from me with a mischievous grin. "Maybe I could convince you if I showed you another part of the garden that you haven't seen and you might like to make love there with me."

"Well, show me the way," I grinned. Elijah took my hand and led the way.

We went out of the gate and down another path that looked to be well used. Tall grasses towered over us on either side of the path. I couldn't help but wonder who used this path.

When we came to the end of this lined grass path it was all open and up a head was another garden that was enclosed with a white fence and gate which was somewhat standing still. In the middle was a large aspen tree standing quite proudly. Old buildings were fallen not too far away. My guess was this was a pasture by the broken fence that laid half down not far from the fallen buildings. The whole view seemed to take me back to another time-my time.

"What's wrong love, you don't like this spot? Let me show you first." He went ahead of me and held out his hand to me inviting me into this part of the yard. I took his hand. "Elijah, does this garden bring back memories to you?"

He was silent for a while. "It doesn't matter now love. It's gone but we have each other. Come."

He led me to the enclosed garden. The garden was divided up into rectangle beds made from brick that was crumbled now or grown over with moss. In fact the paths in-between these tangled beds were a lush carpet of moss. At the back of the garden was a carpet of this lush moss that covered the entire width of the garden. In the middle was an old wrought iron daybed. Moss had crept up onto it and made itself a nice bed where the cushion should have been. The white paint had chipped off but was still clinging to it in places.

"See love, a nice soft spot for you to lay," Elijah whispered into my ear. I took in an uneasy breath. Something felt wrong here and also something told me that we just shouldn't be here. I shivered. Elijah immediately wrapped his arms around me.

The wind picked up and the old aspen tree that was still had come to life. The old buildings sang a mournful tune as if they had been woken. The moss under our feet moved with the wind's dance.

I half expected it to swallow us up. I frantically grabbed Elijah in an effort to run but this black mist whipped past us. Elijah held me protectively in his arms as the wind got stronger and the wind now had an awful howl to it. The black mist came back and hovered in front of us. It formed a decayed corpse with its mouth open revealing sharp teeth. Its long claws were ready to strike.

It let out a horrible screech and then shot up into the air. The wind died down at once. Left standing was the female vampire that we had encountered us at the party.

Her red eyes were fire. "You can thank me later."

"What are you doing here? Didn't you leave with the rest of them that night?"

"Don't get your shirt in a knot Elijah. I can come and go as I please."

"What was that thing," I asked her.

"The death witch's pet. It guards this place against the likes of you." Her blood red lips smiled.

My gut feelings of us not being here was right. "This is her garden then," I said.

"Yes Avian, this is her garden and you're not welcome." Her red eyes settled on me. "*You* shouldn't be here at all." I think she meant more than just being in the garden but overall.

"Are you her pet too?" Elijah scoffed at her.

She chuckled at Elijah. "I'm nobody's pet love but I do have a soft spot for your husband here."

Elijah growled. "He's not yours to take and I would suggest that if this is why you are hanging around, you better leave."

She laughed out loud this time. "Oh Elijah if I wanted to steal your husband, he wouldn't be standing by your side right now. I would have had him a long time ago."

"Then why are you here," Elijah asked. His tone was acid and I could feel the tension in his body traveling down to his hands that would form tight fists.

She didn't offer any explanation to Elijah. I guess she didn't feel like she owed him anything.

Her red eyes settled on me again. I could tell she wanted to talk to me-alone. I was curious as to what she wanted. Elijah placed his hand on my shoulder with a firm grip. "We're going love." I felt my shoulder being pulled back all the while I never took my eyes off of her. I turned to walk beside Elijah out of the garden. I threw a quick glance back but she was gone.

I slid my arm around his waist and started kissing his temple and cheek like he was doing to me earlier but his mood was shaken. There would be no love making from him right now.

When we got to the front of the house Jamie and Zak were there. They both looked at us and knew something had happened.

Elijah was a little less tense when he saw the pair of them. He even smiled. "So, did you share any kisses?"

Zak's empty black eyes answered that question. Elijah frowned and his bad mood was back.

"You really need to try harder Zak. You will be married soon. You need to be a husband to Jamie in every way."

Zak narrowed his gaze at Elijah. "I don't need your help love."

Chapter Twenty Seven

JAMIE WRAPPED HIS ARMS around Zak from behind. "Don't worry about Zak Elijah, we did share a kiss and his tongue was deep inside my mouth tasting me. Didn't you darling?"

Elijah backed up and grinned. "Well, you have made progress. Jamie loves you Zak, that is obvious and you are very interested in him. You don't have to deny that in front of me."

I could tell Zak's teeth were gritted even though he didn't show it. Jamie pulled Zak back. Zak looked up at Jamie who took the opportunity to kiss Zak in front of us. It was a deep kiss. Zak started to relax in his arms. Jamie whirled around to the front of Zak and led him into the house. We knew where Jamie was taking him. Zak shot us a glance but disappeared behind the door.

That put Elijah in a considerable good mood. "This is wonderful isn't it, they're about to finally make love. I'm happy for both of them."

I didn't say anything but I think Zak was not going to be exactly a participant.

We went into the house and Elijah took me upstairs to our bedroom. The bed looked freshly made with the comforter pulled back slightly waiting for us.

Elijah threw his coat over the chair. His white shirt was half undone revealing his bare chest to me. His nipples looked inviting. He poured himself a drink and sat down in his favorite chair stretching those sexy legs of his in front of him.

I sauntered up to him with no pants on and flung my one leg over his and straddled myself over him. Then I sat on his lap. I still had my shirt on. He didn't move. Elijah watched me intensely through half opened eyes. I spread his shirt open and licked those nipples of his and then took his nipple in my mouth and sucked. His fingers threaded through my hair and I heard him moan.

Then I went to his other nipple and did the same thing. I could feel him getting hard underneath. I slid down slightly and rubbed his increasing bulge. "Take my cock out Avian."

I didn't do as he said, I just continued to rub him and take another suck at each of his nipples. He was getting impatient so I slid down and undid his zipper very slowly spreading his pants open revealing his bulge under his underwear. My hand cupped him, rubbing his increasing bulge against the fabric. Finally, I slid his pants and underwear off. I got back up on his lap and rubbed our cocks together smearing each other with our wetness. I rubbed Elijah's cock with our pre-cum lubing him up good. I raised myself above him and lowered myself on to him. I guided him carefully inside me. He filled me pretty good. My muscles were tight around him at the moment and he liked it. I swayed my hips slightly adding to the pressure. "More Avian more," he demanded.

I moved another way making Elijah moan with pleasure and I hit my own special spot sending a quiver through my legs. Elijah took hold of my cock and started stroking me encouraging more of my wetness to leak out.

"Let's get you on your back love." He brought up his legs and without too much effort lifted me and laid me on the floor all the while he was still inside of me.

"Now let's give you a proper fuck." He pushed my legs back giving him a full view. He moved in and out slowly at first then pulled out and went down and tongued my hole. I was ready to come if he kept this up and I told him so.

"Then we can't have that, can we?" He pushed deep inside me again and his thrusts were not so slow now. He was fucking me in a good hard rhythm. His breathing was faster and I was prepared to feel his warmth filling me. I was going to explode with him.

We locked eyes and I watched him come first. His warm cream filled me. Then Elijah pulled out he spilled his cream over my balls and cock which was now in his mouth. He sucked hard making me scream and convulse. "You were heaven love and I enjoyed that immensely." We wrapped each other's arms around each other on the floor and kissed savoring each other's touch and taste.

I woke to a black pair of boots in front of my face. I blinked. I was resting on Elijah's chest. I looked up to who was wearing them and I looked into a smiling face that was Sebastian. "I see our boys had some fun on the floor. I have come to invite you two for a special get together." He nudged Elijah with his foot. "Get up my fuck boy. You have to get ready for a special dinner. I expect you two in two hours downstairs in the formal dining room."

He whirled around and threw his head back at us before leaving. "The death witch will be there."

I bolted up. Elijah was right beside me. "What was that about and did I hear him mention the death witch?"

"Yes," I said. "We have been invited to a special dinner in the formal dining room and the death witch is going to be there."

He rolled his eyes. "I will be glad when we are in our own home. There won't be any of this."

"Why did he invite the death witch?"

Elijah held me in his arms. "Well love, she and Hades were lovers at one time but things went sour. He keeps her here though but it seems that maybe the romance is back on."

Then one thought dropped on my toes. The deal I made with her was off.

We were dressed in our finest as we walked hand in hand down the hallway. Elijah stopped at the door where Zak and Jamie were. The door was partially open and Zak was sitting at the end of the bed. Elijah pushed the door open making Zak look up. It looked like he had just come out of the shower. He had a towel wrapped around his waist.

"Is Jamie here," Elijah asked.

Zak nodded. "He's just coming out of the shower."

Elijah's eyebrow raised. "You didn't shower together?"

Zak's black eyes went blacker. Just before Elijah opened his mouth to say something Jamie came out with a towel wrapped very low around his waist. Jamie stopped short and stared at us. I felt intrusive.

His dark eyes didn't look pleased to see us in their room. "Elijah we should go, we are expected..." Elijah held up his hand stopping me from saying anymore. He walked up to Jamie. He didn't move. "Have you made love to him?" I thought Jamie might tell him it was none of his business but instead he said a very quiet "no." Elijah looked at them both. He came back to me and took my hand. "I will tell Hades and Sebastian that you will be a little late then."

We left the room with Elijah shutting the door firmly behind us. He slid his arm around my waist and led me downstairs. He kissed me before we reached the dining room and whispered in my ear. "You can make love to me like you did this afternoon again. That's what I want for dessert."

We entered a decorated room full of flowers of almost every kind but mostly roses, the ones that reminded me that use to grow here. Tables dressed in Chantilly lace served as displays.

There were displays of many kinds of sweets and champagne glasses that teetered on each other in a crystal glass trickery that made you think they would fall all over. The grand dining table was set up with the finest china and crystal. Candles flickered on the table in between the many bouquets of roses. In the corner a strange quartet was starting to play music that soon filled the air.

Elijah sighed as if already bored. "You aren't fascinated as to what this is all about," I asked him.

"I only care about you and I can only think of one thing." Elijah's hand slid over my crotch and grabbed a firm hold of me.

"We have to get through this dinner." He dropped his hand and just in time as Sebastian was coming over although I'm sure he seen everything by the smile on his face.

"You made it, wonderful. Dinner will be served shortly but first we have to gather in the large study." He looked around a bit then addressed Elijah. "Where is our other couple Zak and Jamie?"

"Oh we just left them a while ago but they will be a tad late. Hopefully they're fucking."

Sebastian snorted then he looked confused. "You said hopefully, what did you mean by that?"

"They've been a bit slow in that department but I'm sure they are working on it," Elijah said.

Sebastian smiled. "I certainly hope so. Hades and I hope that they will be as fruitful as you two." He waved his hand at us to follow. As he was walking he glanced over at Elijah.

"My Elijah you have one thing on your mind tonight. You can go right after the meal as I don't think you will make it."

When we got to the study my eyes just about fell out of their sockets. Aria was standing by the window with Hades in this elaborate gown that was all ivory and lace. Her dark hair was all piled up in layers with flowers in place. She looked totally different. Aria didn't look like a decayed corpse at all. Did Hades revive her or something?

She looked over at me and smiled. I smiled back because I had no choice but I wanted to go up to her and have a little conversation about our agreement we had. Instead, we all had to gather around for some event. Sebastian came into the room with Zak and Jamie. Both of their hairs were upheaved so maybe they did or maybe not as Sebastian had a scowl on his face.

"I'm glad everyone could make it for this special night. Aria and I are having a special ceremony tonight to celebrate our commitment to each other. After tonight things will be different. My boys will be moving on to their own homes with families and Aria and I will be here all alone so we are going to start spending more time together and who knows what that will bring but we both welcome it." She smiled at us all with a certain gleam in her eye like she was up to something. Maybe she was deceiving Hades. I had to talk to her.

They had written little vows to each other and they made their little commitment to each other in front of us all. I think this little ceremony could be taken with a grain of salt. There was a flavor of deceit in the air. After they were done Hades and Aria led us back into the dining room to begin the festivities. Elijah was super irritated. He kept looking at Zak trying to get him to look his way. Zak wasn't giving out one glance.

Until we sat at the table, then we were together and that is when Elijah nabbed Zak. When Zak sat down he bent over and kissed Zak who responded with a moan. When Elijah pulled away. He shook his head. "You don't taste any different."

Jamie wasn't long coming to Zak's rescue. "We almost did it but then *he* came barging in."

"Jamie, what is almost? Where you inside him fucking him? Sebastian would not have dragged you down here if you were busy fucking him."

Jamie's face flushed. "No, I was not *fucking* him but we might have been if we weren't disturbed."

Elijah couldn't believe what he was hearing. "You two need help."

Zak shot Elijah a look. Then he smirked. "Are you going to join us and show us some pointers?"

"You don't need pointers love, you know all too well how to please," Elijah cooed.

That was the end of their little conversation as now the meal was being served. Ghost like creatures floated in with trays of steaming foods. Trays of stuffed pork and chicken were laid out before us. Tiny potatoes smothered in butter and seasonings were brimming in crystal bowls along with orange glazed carrots and baby peas smothered in cream sauce. Rolls of bread fresh from the oven by the smell were placed in front of us. Jamie grabbed a few for him and Zak.

Then this thin skeletal creature poured blood into our crystal goblets. The smell made my throat ache.

Hades stood up and the room went quiet. "Let's toast to this evening and to my Aria." Aria flushed. I'm sure as fake as can be and then proceeded to bat her eyes at him.

We clinked our glasses together and drank our blood which awoke the blood lust in me. I wanted more. Elijah handed me his. I took it without question. Elijah leaned over to me. "You can feed off of me love as part of our love making when we get away from here."

"I can't wait," I breathed. I could smell the blood in every glass in the room and I wanted to empty them. "Eat something and maybe that will help," Elijah urged me. I wasn't going to make it. "I can't eat food, I want blood." I practically shouted at him making a few heads turn including Hades.

"Calm down love, I will get you more blood." The skeletal creature was there instantly probably by Hades doing and left a pitcher. Elijah poured my glass and I drank greedily. I noticed when I sat down the glass that pitcher had filled again to where it was before Elijah filled my glass. It seemed I had a never ending supply so I continued to drink until the blood beast in me was satisfied. Elijah set a plate of food in front of me then. "Try to eat something."

The food tasted really good actually and I did enjoy it as long as I had the endless supply of blood. Hades came over to us.

"Everything is alright with the two of you?"

"Everything is just fine father. Avian needed to feed."

"I could see that, you must keep your husband well fed Elijah." His cold fingers cupped my chin and lifted my face so he could see me. He smiled. "Your eyes are a lovely red now, that is the way they should always be, not that pale color I'm used to seeing."

"I will make sure he stays fed from now on," Elijah assured Hades.

"Good, let's keep those beautiful deep red eyes of his." Elijah nodded.

Chapter Twenty Eight

I LAID ON MY BACK WHILE Elijah thrust inside me ready to fill me. I cried out his name when I felt his heat run through me like a wild fire. Elijah laid on top of me while he was still deep inside of me. "Feed love."

I sunk my teeth into his neck and let the blood flow into the back of my throat. I almost couldn't get enough of Elijah tonight. When I let my head fall back I was dizzy and high at the same time.

Elijah got off of me but remained inside of me. Blood trickled down his chest. I ran my finger over his chest and placed my finger in my mouth and sucked the blood.

Elijah pulled out and turned me over and he fucked me from behind this time filling me again and pulling out in time to smother my balls with his warm cream.

I rolled back on my back and Elijah took my swollen cock in his mouth. His tongue was hot. I arched in the air as he sucked hard then would flick his tongue at the leaking cum. I filled his mouth with my full load that never ended. I just about passed out.

Elijah came up and held me tight. He gave my balls a massage and slid his finger in my hole far to that special place making me almost gasp. He went down and licked me and tongued me lapping up all his own cream cleaning me. By this time I was hard again.

Elijah laid down on his back and spread his own legs letting me deep inside of him. It wasn't long till both of us came. I went down and lapped up all his cream over his stomach and chest and then went down to his hole and cleaned him up.

"Oh Avian, you have such hunger tonight. I love it," he moaned.

I couldn't resist and I bit into his inner thigh. Elijah flinched but laid there and let me feed. If that wasn't enough I bit into his other thigh and fed some more. I was so sedated that I could barely keep my eyes open but I took his cock in my mouth and sucked him till he fill my mouth. Then I think I passed out.

When I woke it was the middle of the night. I felt more alive than ever. It had to have been all the feeding I did. I felt stronger and I could hear the garden sounds from inside the house. I just laid there and listened. It was exhilarating. I sat up and Elijah was sleeping beside me. I wanted to go out into the darkness where I belonged. I remember him telling me that I should tell him.

I leaned over and kissed him making him stir and respond back to my kiss. I could taste both of us. "I'm going out for a walk." Elijah's black red eyes reflected in the moons pale light.

"I don't want you to be away from me but I will go with you but you have to do something first. "I'm hard. Suck on me for a while and then sit on me like you did before."

I took him in my mouth and sucked and took all of him in my mouth moving up and down his shaft. His breathing picked up and I knew he was near. He arched and filled my mouth with his sweetness. I laid beside me and held him. "Now, can I go out?"

Elijah grinned. "Yeah, but not without me."

"You could sleep." His eyes went soft in the light. Something was different here. "I could go out and you can stay here and sleep. I think you should sleep love. You won't remember any of this." He nodded as his eyes fell closed. I kissed him and soon he was sound asleep.

I guess I had forgotten the compulsion I could so but you had to be a heavy feeder to pull it off. Feeding with Elijah gave me the power.

As I breathed in the chilly air I walked alone on the path that went out to the gardens behind the house-the ones I was supposed to stay away from.

The moon tonight was bright and lit up the entire garden. The festivities had all died away. There was no sign that there was anything that had taken place. But that was how this place was. It was alive one minute and dead the next. I wondered if Aria was with Hades now or where she was.

I was hoping to find her. I went past the vegetable garden and down the grassy path to the open pasture and to the enclosed garden. I stopped at the end of the path and stared.

The large aspen tree was lit up in silver light. Around the tree small globes of silver light floated around the tree and garden. A few wondered over the fence. One of the globes of light went into the air as if it got caught by a draft of air. I went closer to the garden. It was a magical sight and I wanted to get closer to the globes of light. The one that had gone into the air settled back down in front of me and hovered in front of my face like it had eyes that saw me.

Then it flew away in a blurred light back to the garden. I had to be closer so I walked up to the gate entrance. The glow of light shone on my face. Behind the tree came out a figure. She was all a glow as if part of the light herself. As she got closer she reminded me of someone but the name wouldn't come. The globes of light swirled around her as she came closer to me.

She offered me a small smile. "You came back Avian."

My mouth opened but no words came out. "You found Aria's special garden." She knew who Aria was. Was she a witch?

"You don't remember my name. It's Rebecca. "I'm Aria's younger sister."

The name Rebecca settled on my tongue trying to dissolve into the empty crevices of my past. I felt a panic on my skin that made me shiver. The past wanted to tumble out but couldn't. I looked at her. She was but a foot from me. Her eyes were ice blue and so where her lips. "I can bring you home Avian where you belong, not here where you certainly don't. You and Elijah were set to be married in your and Elijah's time. I can give you that back."

"Why," I whispered.

"You helped Aria get her things back. This is her thank you. You did ask for her help, did you not? Perhaps you have changed your mind?"

I shook my head without saying any words.

She smiled like she understood. "Then I will help you but you have to understand what Aria and I can do will not give you eternity together. You will go back to the day before you were to be married and then after that I do not know how long your time will last. It could only be a matter of days or even one year. One day the sun will not rise and both of you will turn to ash and enter into the spirit world for eternity"

I could feel a tear roll down my cheek

"How do I do this," I asked her.

"You simply follow me into this world into the tree of light here." She gestured towards the old tree. There is a portal I can open that will take you through back to your own world. You and Elijah…or just yourself."

"I won't leave without Elijah," I blurted out.

Her ice blue ices shimmered in the moons light as if her eyes were nothing but water. "Then you must follow me."

"Can I take the others?"

The globes of light were pulling up strands of hair pulling her back. I suppose my red eyes frightened them and they wanted her away from me.

"You are giving them the same fate as you. If Zak and Jamie are willing then I will show them."

She knew their names. Of course she would, I should have known that.

"Then I will bring them," I said.

"You haven't much time as Hades will be sending you deep into the underworld. There, you will be lost to this world forever. Remember that."

"I will, I won't forget. When do I come?"

"You will know when it's time to come Avian." She disappeared behind the tree.

I turned and started on the path back to the house. Elijah might be awakening soon I thought. I just got past the old vegetable garden and was getting near the back of the house when I saw it.

A black blur flew past me and then back at me again and this time took direct aim at me knocking me to the ground. I laid on my back facing her, the female vampire.

"You should just try say *hi* instead." She offered me her hand. I stared at her black claws and imagined what she could do with them if I placed my hand in hers.

"I won't tear you to shreds darling, I promise."

Somehow I think her promises weren't that good. I got myself up. "You must like it here."

She shrugged. She was up to something. "I see you were talking to Rebecca from the other world."

I narrowed my eyes at her. "How do you know about Rebecca?"

"I know everything about her dear. You can trust me on that."

"So, what about it?" She came right to me. "You're eyes are deep red, you've been feeding well darling. Why do you want to follow Rebecca when you can have eternity with Elijah deep in the underworld?"

"We don't belong here." My voice was weak and unconvincing as she smiled at me. "You don't want to leave here."

"How do you know what I want," I retorted back at her.

"I don't think you know what you want." She was now in my face. I could smell her breath, it smelled like demon blood. I backed up. "You were feeding on a demon."

"They can be tasty as you know." She threw a wicked grin at me.

"Who are you and why haven't I seen you around on the other side?"

"You can call me Jax and this side is more fun although I do go over to the other side to feed on the humans."

"So, why are you hanging around here?"

She came up close to me again. "Aria and I are girlfriends."

I choked out a laugh. "Yeah, I bet you are."

She scowled at me but I didn't care and I had enough, I was going back to Elijah. I went to go when she blocked me.

"What's the hurry love?" Her blood red lip pouted. "Don't you want to play with me?"

She showed me her fangs and ran her tongue along those sharp incisors.

"Leave the boy alone dear, he's taken." My eyes flew to the voice that came up behind the shadows. It was Aria. She lazily sauntered up to us in a bored fashion.

Jax huffed. "But he's cute peaches."

Peaches? These two had a history together obviously and that explained why Jax was hanging around here.

Without a word I left the two of them behind but before I got too far Aria's voice trailed after me. "So, you talked to my sister."

I stopped and looked back at her. "You have your chance to go back to your time. It comes with a price as I'm sure Rebecca explained but it's yours to take or go deeper into the underworld love-for all eternity."

I swallowed hard hearing the words. I turned and left them.

When I got to the front of the house there was someone sitting on the front steps of the porch. I panicked for a second thinking if it was Elijah but I knew as I got closer it wasn't. It was Jamie.

He looked to be deep in thought and I didn't want to intrude but I had to go past him anyway so…

He looked up as I came close. He was surprised to see me I knew. "I went out for a walk."

"Oh…yeah, you're a vampire." He spoke the words under his breath.

"You need some company?"

He didn't offer me to sit so I thought but then he spoke up before I got past him. "I would like that."

I sat beside him and we just stayed silent. "You love Elijah a lot, don't you" he said suddenly.

"Yes, I do love him a lot. I see you care for Zak a lot too."

"I was so happy to have Zak in my life but…"

"Zak can be difficult," I finished for him.

He chuckled softly. "Yeah I guess but I think he's scared".

"I didn't think Zak was scared of anything," I said amused.

Jamie's black eyes told me otherwise. "I want to make love to him like you and Elijah do but he only goes so far and pulls away."

"Well, Zak isn't used to commitment so maybe that has something to do with it but …"

"I'm not scared."

We both turned around to see Zak standing there with his hands stuffed in his pockets. Jamie gave him a loving look. He came and sat down next to Jamie and gave him a kiss. Jamie kissed him back. Zak appeared more loving towards Jamie. Hades would be pleased.

Zak faced Jamie and I knew he was going to tell him something. "I should go," I told them but Zak held up his hand. "You can hear what I have to say to Jamie."

"When I first seen you, I didn't know what to think. There was something about you that was familiar. I was confused."

This sounded weird to me. Did these two have a past like Elijah and I? Hades liked reunions it seemed.

"But now I love you so much Jamie, I don't want to be without you, ever." Jamie's eyes lit up and mouth fell open. I think Zak's confession shocked us both.

Zak took Jamie's hand and kissed it softly. "Come to bed with me." They both got up and went inside. They were kissing all the way up the stairs. I just shook my head in awe.

Chapter Twenty Nine

I SNUCK INTO THE ROOM where everything was still. Morning was only a few hours away. I slipped in next to Elijah who stirred and rolled over to face me. "Good morning love."

"Good morning to you." It appeared that he remembered nothing of last night so it worked.

We kissed for a while.

"I wonder how Zak and Jamie are making out and I mean that in the literal sense."

"I think they are together now, I have a strong feeling about it," I said.

Elijah smiled. "That makes me happy to hear. I can't wait for all of us to be in our new home. It will be wonderful Avian."

"Yeah, a new place for us." But we were of course thinking about two different places.

Elijah and I laid in the tub soaking. Elijah was very happy and content. His half opened eyes stared at me. I knew he was thinking something.

"What?"

"Today I have a little surprise for you love. I can't wait."

"Tell me." I wanted it out of him in case there was something I needed to be alerted to. He just smiled. That told me he wasn't going to tell me a damn thing. So I moved closer to him and leaned into him till we were face to face. "You will tell me."

"Good luck love. Try and get it out of me." That was a challenge I would accept without thought. I leaned in and kissed him. Our tongues explored each other.

I let the back of my fingers fall against the outline of his jaw line down to his neck and to his shoulder where I started to massage him and with my other hand started to work the muscles on each side. He let his head fall back closing his eyes.

"This feels so good but I'm still not telling you." He grinned at me but I was not discouraged. My hands continued their massage over his chest and nipples. I bit and sucked on each one making him groan. I could feel his erection against me. It was working. I kissed him again but more deeply this time. I let my tongue trail along his jaw down his neck where something else stirred in me. I instinctively sunk my teeth into him. He moaned encouraging me to feed. There was something sensual between us when we fed off of each other.

I was dizzy when I pulled away. His blood was worse than any poison. "I love your now beautiful deep red eyes. You are so mine love." He was about to pull me in for a kiss when something in our bedroom exploded. In a blur we were both in the room. "Look Elijah." I pointed to the window where the vessels were. All the vessels but the gold one were leaking blood. They had all cracked and turned black.

"What happened," I asked Elijah.

He was almost shaking. "The three children in the gold vessel killed them."

"Then get rid of that gold vessel. They are more evil than evil itself."

"I don't know if I can, it is so powerful. Black magic protects it."

I wrapped my arms around him. He sighed, "I'm so glad that we are leaving tomorrow."

That was the secret. We were leaving this place sooner than what I thought. "We're leaving here sooner?"

His black red eyes went through me. They were full of hurt. "That was my surprise love. We are going to our new home then."

"I see," I said. My mind was whirling. My plan to get everybody to the garden had to happen today. I kissed Elijah on the temple. "It will be okay, I promise."

We went downstairs to the kitchen but no one was there. My eyes gazed at my surroundings and a strange feeling in my chest settled in. Something was different. The house was like it was when I first came here. Dust and cobwebs had settled in and some of the kitchen cabinet fronts were missing. Broken china laid on the shelves. I rushed into the hallway and looking into the study, it was the same thing. Everything was decayed once more.

I went back to the kitchen to Elijah. He was looking down at a broken cup. "What has happened to this place?"

Elijah set the cup down on the table. "It's time to move on. This place is dying."

"Elijah, it was dead when we got here. It only came to life when Hades showed up." He didn't respond. I think he was stricken by what happen upstairs. If this world was dying then that gold vessel could die with it as far as I was concerned. Then another thought entered my mind, if this place was dying, then what about the garden where I had to take everybody to? Was it dying too?

"We have to go and get Zak and Jamie." Elijah looked confused as if the names didn't ring a bell.

I ran upstairs to their room. I opened the door and found them in bed. Zak was sucking Jamie's cock. They paid no attention to me. Jamie soon came. Zak was enjoying his treat. Then they both noticed me. Zak grinned. "Would you like to taste him?"

"We have to go now," I said.

"Where are we going," asked Zak.

All I could say was someplace special. Zak fell over Jamie. "I don't want to go anywhere. I want to stay in bed with Jamie. We fucked for the first time last night. I want more of that."

"You can do more of that in the special place," I said. Zak chuckled.

"What is this special place you talk about? Is it kinky?"

I had to get around Zak. "Maybe, you have to come with me to find out."

Jamie sat up moving Zak over to the side. Jamie had a look in his eyes that looked right through me. It was as if he knew what I was up to. He then smiled down at Zak. "Let's go find out what this special place is, maybe we can do all kinds of things there."

Zak grinned. "Anything for you my love."

"We'll meet you down stairs Avian," said Jamie. Somehow I couldn't shake that weird feeling that Jamie gave me. I went back down to Elijah. "Did you find them?"

At least he knew who they were. I nodded. "They'll be down in a minute."

Elijah sighed. "I guess Hades has left for some reason."

I wonder if he was coming back or not. Maybe the promise to take us deep into the underworld was a lie. Jamie and Zak came into the kitchen. They were both dressed in black suits and shirts. It was a style that was of our time. Jamie only passed one glance over my way. Zak didn't seem to be any the wiser. He ran his black lacquered finger along the counter and looked at the dust with disgust. His black watery eyes narrowed. "Hades is gone isn't he?"

Elijah nodded. Jamie went up to Zak's side and gently brushed aside his dirty blond hair from his eyes. "We have another special place to go to now darling." Zak's eyes lit up like he was reminded.

"Well, we can go any time to that special place you promised Avian. This place is dead," said Zak in a bored fashion.

A rumble from outside shook the old china in the cupboard sending one to the floor crashing. Everybody looked at one another. Elijah and Zak sighed. "Hades and the death witch are fighting again. I guess all bets are off. One of them tricked the other. Let me guess who" said Elijah in a sarcastic tone that was acidic. I was putting my bets on Aria. I knew she was up to something when she had that little ceremony with Hades. I just hoped her sister was still going to hold up her promise.

Zak sneered. "That stupid bitch, why didn't he get rid of her a long time ago?" Jamie rubbed Zak's lower back whispering in his ear. Zak peered up into Jamie's eyes like a love sick pup. Jamie had Zak in the palm of his hand.

"Well," Elijah said to us all. "We will not let that miserable bitch ruin our last day here. We will party and celebrate the upcoming marriage of Zak and Jamie." Zak and Jamie smiled.

Well it did buy me time. I could find out what was going on out there and if the special garden was still there with Rebecca. Another rumble from outside shook the cupboard again. "We should go into the garden before she starts to rain hale on us," Elijah said.

Jamie didn't look so sure about this now. The rumbling was getting louder and the wind had picked up. Jamie came up behind me when we were heading out. "Where is this special place," he asked in my ear.

I turned my head to speak to him. "It's the old garden behind the house with the old aspen tree in it." He didn't ask about it, it was as if he understood what I was talking about." He just nodded. Jamie was a mystery that I wish I could remember from the past. I didn't know if I should trust him or not. I guess I would find out.

We went into the garden near where the gazebo was. It had half fallen in now. But it didn't stop the boys from going in. Jamie and Zak went through to the other side and leaned on the railing together. Zak let his arm rest around Jamie's neck. He couldn't stop kissing him. Elijah walked around to where they were. "Stop it, we're supposed to be celebrating you're upcoming nuptials. It's not your honeymoon yet although I hope you are practicing," he grinned. Zak shot him a look. "I'll have you know we've certainly worked on it." They all laughed except for me who shared a look with Jamie. He quickly looked away and kissed Zak.

The wind now was getting stronger. "Elijah," Zak yelled over the wind. "Let's go over to the other side and catch up with the boys."

My chest sank. I couldn't let this happen.

"Hades won't allow us to go over," I said.

Zak scoffed "Daddy isn't here, he had a fight with his bitch so he is otherwise occupied."

"What about Sebastian then?" I was grasping but I needed to stall them.

Zak laughed again, "That asshole is gone too, back in the underworld screwing something-kinky bugger." He grabbed Jamie's hand and together they leaped over and landed silently beside us. "Let's go boys and have some fun," Zak said while grabbing Jamie's ass.

Zak and Jamie went ahead of us and I caught one quick glance from Jamie who had this rather smug look on him.

I took Elijah's hand. "If we go is this place going to be here when we get back?"

"Of course it will love, Hades is the only one that can make it disappear and he's not going to do that when he knows his boys are here."

"You're sure of that?" Elijah took me in his arms and held me. "My beautiful love, you and I will have a far better place to live than here. Look at it Avian, it's in ruin because it's dying. We have to move on to where nothing will ever die again and that's our paradise waiting for us deep in the underworld love." He kissed me deeply taking my breath away.

"Stop making out over there," yelled Zak. "We're ready to cross over now."

When we crossed over it was dark out in the human world. The night sky was filled with howls. Hades boys didn't sound too happy. Even Jamie was sticking close to Zak. Elijah and Zak shared a look that made myself and Jamie nervous. "What's going on," I asked Elijah.

Chapter Thirty

WHAT WAS HAPPENING ON THIS side of the world appeared to be worse than what we came from? We had met up with a small group of Hades boys who informed us that word had got out that Hades was making an army of demons. That would be via us of course. Jarvis, one the boys said that if they caught us they would fry us. That news was all I needed to hear to go back. I pushed on Elijah's chest. "We have no choice, if you want to see our paradise you have to come back with me." Jamie had Zak by the hand as well and was urging Zak to do the same thing. Zak swore in some ancient demon tongue and kicked at the gravel. "Maybe some of the boys can come to our side where we will be safe," said Jamie. Jarvis and others seemed to like that idea. Zak smiled at Jamie. "Perfect, that's why I love you." He kissed him and that's when hell descended.

I never felt such heat. Two large hounds with fangs that dripped blood was in front of us. They towered over us. Two demons flew in front of them. Their eyes were fire. I remembered these ones when I lived here. They were ruthless and ate anything including other demons. Hades boys disappeared into black mist.

The one with straight blood red hair came forward smiling at us revealing a row of sharp teeth. His red lacquered claws grazed along his chin. "Look at what we have here my puppies. I believe it's the baby makers for Hades. How many have you spawned off so far my sweets?" His dark tongue slipped along his bottom lip. "I would certainly love to spend some time with you in my bed." We all backed up as he got closer.

"None of them could fuck as good as me darling." The demon just smirked like he knew who it was.

"My darling Jax, you've come out to play with us."

Jax came sauntering out all dressed in black leather with sharp high heeled boots that could go through a throat if she wanted. Jax went up to him. He looked down at her like she was a tasty morsel. She ran her red painted lacquered claws up his chest and around his neck. He was almost salivating. The pups of hell backed up from her. The other demon stayed in the darkness, His dark straight navy hair blew in the breeze revealing his red blue eyes. They were narrowed in on her. He didn't trust her I could tell.

"Ty, why are you bothering Hade's boys for? They're not worth it love." She threaded one of her claws through his hair. He let out a low growl. "Have you got something else better in mind my love?"

"Oh love, I always have something better, you should know that," she purred.

Ty grinned at her. "Why don't we watch the pups feed on them first then you can entertain me like only you can?" He grabbed her ass and pulled her tight against his lean body.

The other demon was clearly not amused by this. He walked within seconds to where they were. He was standing behind Jax very close. "Get rid of her," he hissed at Ty. Jax rested her head on Ty's chest. "I could do a threesome Luke if that makes you feel not left out." Ty chuckled but Luke just showed his teeth. She hissed right back at him showing sharp teeth. "Now you two lets calm down. Luke, take it easy, you know she's fun to play with. I'll even give her to you tonight so you can have her all to yourself. My gift to you love. Ty leaned over Jax and kissed Luke. Luke backed up. "I don't sleep with vampires who feed on demons."

Ty looked down at her. "You don't do that still do you?"

Her red lips pouted. "Not ever, I promise." He grinned and in a blur he grabbed her wrist and sunk his teeth in. She couldn't fight back as Luke held her tight while Ty tasted her. When he let her go he grinned and shook his head. His mouth and teeth were blood stained. "You lie my pretty, what punishment should I give you?"

"Take her head off, love," Luke said grinning. It was obvious Luke would love nothing better than to do away with one of Ty's play toys.

Jax managed to free herself from both of them. She twitched her nose at Luke and the next thing Luke is flying through the air crashing into a large tree. Ty just smirked and then laughed out loud. "You were always a feisty bitch Jax." Luke came crashing back but as a wolf with blood red eyes. "Luke," cooed Ty. "Come here love." Luke came padding over to Ty who ran his red claws through Luke's bristle. "It's okay love, she means no harm, just some fun. I'm all yours love tonight. I'll even let you tie me up and play that little kinky game you love so much." A little whimper came from Luke. Ty chuckled. "I thought you would like that."

But now his attention was back on us. "We have other matters to take care of first and I believe that is to take care of a few of Hade's boys. That's always fun to see them burn. They scream so loudly, don't they love?" Luke growled. The large monsters behind then licked their lips. "Oh don't worry my pets, there will be plenty of blood for you to lap up."

I pushed Elijah further back and Jamie did the same thing to Zak. Both Zak and Elijah were ready to fight but I felt a bit outnumbered and given that demons don't fight fair, I was looking for a way out. I was hoping Jax had one more trick up her sleeve.

Ty and his killing team started to come for us. Jax was standing behind Ty coming with him. So much for any more tricks from her.

Elijah and Zak were ready to fight but Jamie and I just looked on in horror. Jamie was terrified. Suddenly the wind got up and hale started to pound on us. "What the hell" growled Ty. Where did this come from?" Even the large hounds backed up shaking their huge heads. The large balls of ice got bigger and bigger. Soon there was a huge a mass of ice between us.

"Let's go," a voice from behind me hissed. It was Jax who was gesturing for us to follow her back through to the other side. I grabbed Elijah and Jamie grabbed Zak and we pulled them through following Jax. It was bitter cold and the howls of the demons chased us. Jax pulled at us even making us go faster. I thought I was going to be shredded into pieces. Then the next thing my face is in the gravel. We are on the other side.

"Damn bitch, you didn't have to go that fast. We are capable of going as fast as you, you know," Zak growled at her.

She walked up to him and kicked him in the ribs. "You aren't capable of keeping up to anything."

When we got up the sky above us was churning. Black mist whipped around us like ghosts that had risen from the grave. The garden was alive but with the dead. I had to get to the garden. I grabbed Jax. "You have to help compel them to go to the garden where Rebecca is." Her red eyes showed concern. "I think love it might be too late. Rebecca will not come out with this going on and if this world is disappearing then she will disappear with it."

Jax had just confirmed my fears about this place. Maybe Aria did have the power to destroy it after all. "We have to try anyway," I yelled back. She very lightly shrugged her shoulders and walked towards Jamie and Zak. Jamie instantly caught her on his radar. I wondered if she could. Jamie grabbed Zak and started pulling him away but she was faster. She was in there faces and they were both mesmerized by her. I sighed and went to Elijah before he noticed what was happening. I faced him and cupped his face with my hands making him look directly at me. "My love Elijah, it's time for us to leave here for good. You have to follow me to the garden that will take us away and give the peace that we need. Come love, come with me." I took his hand and he very willingly came. Jax led Jamie and Zak behind me and I took them to the garden. There was no light coming from the big tree, no globes of light floating around or no magic to be found. The guys stood around in a daze.

"Call Rebecca out Jax," I pleaded.

Jax walked up to the gate. "Rebecca, it's me Jax. I need you to come out. Avian is here." She got no reaction. Jax looked back at me. "Maybe she is already gone love."

"No, she can't be, you have to try again." Jax turned again to the garden. "Rebecca love, if you're here you have to show yourself right now, this world here is going fast." Lightening lit up the dark clouds now and the wind was swaying to its own music taking everything with it.

There was still no response. The guys now were starting to look around now and I could tell by the looks on their faces our compulsion was wearing off. Jamie was the first to seem to notice that something was wrong. He looked straight at me. "What have you done to us?"

"I'm trying to save us," I said. His black eyes shimmered in the lightening. His eyes were storms themselves. "Saving us? What the hell are you talking about? Elijah loves you and gave his soul up to have eternity with you and this is what you do in return to him?" Jamie did understand all this and he knew the story of us all.

"I don't want to spend eternity in Hell," I said. Elijah was beside me now. "What are you and Jamie talking about?"

Jamie wrapped his arms around Zak who was still not completely with us. "He's trying to kill us all," Jamie spit. Elijah frowned at Jamie. Then he spotted Jax. "What is she doing there?"

"It's okay love, we're going to another place," I said. I placed my hand on his chest clinging to him. "Get away from there vampire, don't you know what kind of garden that is." She didn't pay any attention to him. None of this was working.

"You're right Avian we are going to another place and *now* is when we are going." Jamie shot him a look. Elijah looked at us all. "We're going to go deep into the underworld where our new home is, Hades showed me the way in case something happened and since it has we're going now. Follow me." Jamie smiled and kissed Zak who was finally coming back to us.

"But we can't," I said. Elijah stopped and looked at me confused. "What do you mean love, that we can't? We certainly can and we will. When we are on the other side I will show you our bedroom, it's beautiful and I will make love to you tonight in it. Come love, now."

Jamie was looking smug. Him and Zak were hand in hand and were ready to follow Elijah. Elijah took my hand and kissed it and started to lead me away.

When we turned away that's when the tree started to glimmer and the aspen tree started to come to life making everyone stop and turn. Jax was still there standing at the gate. She stood there and smiled. "She's still here."

"Elijah," shouted Jamie. "Take us away from here and take us to our new home, now." The light from the tree seemed to come alive but not like before but maybe it would work. I would have to try and compel them again. "Elijah, you have to follow me into the garden to a new and better place love. Just for you and I." Elijah, for a minute appeared confused and when I took his hand he came with me. And I had him at the gate where Jax was. We were all but ten feet from entering the gate. There was still no Rebecca. "Bring her out Jax, Rebecca needs to come out now."

"How do you know Rebecca's name Avian?" Elijah's tone was dangerous. "Avian, please tell me what you have done."

"I'm just trying to take us to a better place," I said.

Jamie yelled over at us. "He's trying to kill us and send us to our graves Elijah, you have to stop him."

Elijah's eyes were blood red. "Is this true?"

The bark of a dog saved me. Zak ran to the garden past us and on the other side of the gate was a dog who ran up to him wagging his tale. Elijah gasped. "No Zak, get out of there!"

He ran towards him and I followed along with a horrified Jamie. It was too late as Zak went past Jax to the dog and kneeled down on his knees and started petting it. Behind the dog was Rebecca. Elijah stopped short and stared at her. Rebecca never wavered. Jamie whimpered and begged Zak to come back. Zak looked back at us.

His eyes weren't pools of black anymore, they were a pale blue and he looked like he transformed into the person he used to be.

His dirty blond hair looked wavy and thicker than here. His smile was brilliant. It appeared Zak couldn't hear Jamie's pleas and then Jamie turned to me and yelled with tears in his eyes. "You did this, you killed him and took him away from me!"

Elijah was in shock now. "Go get him Jamie and bring him back, don't just stand there. He's not gone yet, we can still see him," I yelled back at Jamie hoping to encourage him to cross.

Jamie looked at me with suspicion in his dark eyes. "You're running out of time," I told him. He looked at Zak and then me trying to decide. At the end, he went for it and when he crossed the bright light took him, Zak, and the dog. They were gone. Elijah fell to his knees inside the gate, screaming. The light in the garden was fading. Jax threw me a desperate look. "Something's wrong Avian, it's not working."

"What do you mean, Jamie and Zak are gone home now to where they belong."

Jax shook her head, "no they didn't go there, and they went to another realm."

I looked at Rebecca. "You said we would all go home."

She scowled at me. "You don't deserve to go home and die peacefully, you deserve an eternal existence of what you've became." Her eyes were navy blue now and shimmered like the lightening above us. "You brought this hell to this garden and you will suffer." The wind howled around us and I threw myself over Elijah. The blinding light was almost searing. Where was she sending us?

I had failed and now I was going to die in some god forsaken hell place. Maybe it would have been better if Ty and his pups had killed us. I realized I could not go back anymore and where ever Jamie and Zak went I at least hoped they were together.

I clung to Elijah's body that seemed lifeless in my arms. I took his hand and noticed that his claws were gone. He had normal hands. I noticed I could see the veins in my own hand again. What was happening to us? Then the world went white and I was alone-all alone. Elijah wasn't with me anymore. Was this my punishment? I would never see my love again. I felt a thump inside my chest. I remember placing my hand over my chest and I could feel something there that hadn't been alive for a long time-my heart. But what good was it when I was in this eternal white ghost world. Maybe all of this was happening before I truly did die. I closed my eyes and waited.

There was a noise. Then I felt someone shaking me and my eyes tried to open but there was this blinding thing in my eyes. "Get up already." The voice seemed familiar and then someone or something was licking my face. I shook my head and when I could open my eyes there was two guys standing over me and a dog who licked me again. My hand went up to the dog. It was a golden retriever. He barked. "Good boy, you found him." The two guys standing over me were Jamie and Zak. I bolted up. "You guys are okay." I frantically looked around for Elijah but I didn't see him. "Where's Elijah?"

Chapter Thirty One

"WE HAVEN'T FOUND HIM YET," Zak said. My heart sank and I really did have a heart again. Jamie held out his hand to help me up. His dark eyes were sea blue. He smiled and I took his hand. He didn't hit me anyway like I expected.

"What is this place," I asked them both.

"It some kind of tropical island," Zak said. "How we got here I don't know." Jamie just shrugged.

It seemed like neither one them remembered what happened. Maybe that was for the best. They had both shed their jackets and rolled up their sleeves and pant legs. We walked along the shore that was endless and blue. The tropical breeze blew our hair and warmed our faces. Would I come across Elijah? As we walked I felt like we would not find him. This was hopeless and then we saw a house on top of a hill. Zak pointed it out. We almost ran to it. It was a clean white house that had palm trees around it with a bunch of tropical flowers greeting us with their sweet scent.

Zak's mouth dropped. "Look at this place. There is even a swimming pool." The pool was a clear blue and reflected the clear blue sky above. There was a row of glass doors that Jamie opened and went into this open living room and kitchen. There was windows on the other side as well giving a spectacular view. This was certainly paradise but I couldn't wrap my head around that this was the place that Rebecca had sent us unless it was a way to torment me since Elijah wasn't here. Maybe he was in some place horrible and I had to live with it. That thought made me sick and want to die.

Jamie came up to me. "Don't worry we will find him. He has to be here." I just nodded.

Zak had opened the fridge and took out this tray of tropical fruit. "Look at this," Zak said.

Jamie's eyes widened. Zak brought the tray to the table where we all sat around and enjoyed this fruit. I looked out the window every once in a while to see if I could see him-even a tiny black speck to give me hope. But all I saw was endless beach.

"We're going to go exploring, do you want to come?" I felt a tail wagging against my leg. I looked down at two big brown eyes. I let my hand fall on the dog's head and let my finger run through his soft fur letting him nudge his nose into my hand and that is when I clued into that someone had spoken to me.

"Are you alright Avian?" Zak's hand was now on my shoulder. I looked up into his pale blue eyes. It was like looking into the face of a different person.

"Sorry, I'm fine." I tried to sound convincing.

"We're going to go exploring, did you want to come with us," Zak asked.

"No, you guys go ahead. I'll walk around the house and explore it," I said. Jamie came up beside Zak. "You know we will keep an eye out for him and we'll bring him back to you first thing, you know that," said Jamie.

I smiled at them both and the dog. "I know you will." I looked down at the dog. "So Zak, what is your dog's name anyway?"

"Max is his name," said Zak. He barked when Zak said his name. Rebecca was sly in bringing back Zak's dog to entice him to cross the gate. It was still confusing to as why we ended up here and not some place in Hell. I guess I would never have the answers.

Zak, Jamie and Max left me alone at the table staring out at the view. I shook my head shaking out any thoughts that I would see Elijah. It was hopeless. He would have been here with them when I came. I had to live with the fact that I would be alone now without him.

I got up and decided to look around this large house. There were steps going up to another floor. This is probably where I would find the bedrooms so I thought I might as well pick one for myself. Soft carpet underneath cushioned my feet. I first came to a bath that was pretty standard. Next to it was a rather small room. There were some boxes in it like who ever had this place was storing some things in this room. I went on and I could see light that I knew it was from a window and a large one at that. When I entered the room my mouth dropped. The whole wall facing the beach was all window. In the middle were glass doors going out onto a balcony. A large oak four poster bed was up against the wall with two antique night stands, one each side. Two wall sconces were above them. The creamy white walls reflected the tropical feel and lush lighting. It was beautiful and this was going to be my room. There were two doors in the room. I opened one and it went into a large walk in closet-complete with clothes that I could wear. I shook my head as if I was in a dream. The closet was completely organized with shelves. I couldn't help but stare at the nicely stacked jeans and sweaters. I guess the nights were cool. Next to the shelves were different shirts from long sleeve to short sleeve. It was unbelievable. There was even a row of shoes that I could wear. I wanted to pinch myself. I backed out and went to look where the other door opened into. This was jaw dropping as well. A huge spa bathroom. The tile floor reflected the ocean from the huge glass windows.

In the corner was a huge whirlpool bathtub and in the other corner was a huge glass and tile shower. On the other wall a double sink vanity with a large mirror. Against the wall near the tub was a fireplace built into the wall. I stood there in a dream state day dreaming about Elijah and I in here soaking in the tub watching the fire crackle while we kiss and share a glass of wine. I gasped and turned abruptly and ran out and tore back the doors. I grabbed onto the metal rail and breathed in the sea air that I needed. But it didn't stop the tears. My grief over took me. I thought that I would break. I gasped for air cursing the world for keeping me here without him.

I continued to hang on to the rail and I glared out at the ocean with blurry eyes. I wiped my face with my shirt. I decided to take the damn thing off when I noticed something. I wiped my eyes again. I thought it was one of the guys. I went to go in when something stopped me. Did I notice long hair? Neither Zak nor Jamie have long dark hair. Who did I see? I grabbed onto the railing again and leaned in narrowing my gaze on the individual. It was a woman. Was she owner of this place? There was stairs from this balcony going down to the beach. I took them and I was almost running when I slowed down. I didn't want to scare her. She must have seen me by now and she kept coming towards me. I waved at her and she waved back at me with a smile. Where have I seen that smile before?

"I'm so happy you made it here," she said as she got closer. Her long raven black hair billowed behind her. Her white sundress blew against her lean tanned body and tall lean legs. She was barefoot. Above her ankle was a thick ankle bracelet.

I stopped and let her come closer. I wasn't sure that I heard what she had said to me. She smiled and held out her arms out, for a hug? I smiled even though I was confused. I suddenly forgot that I was clinging to my shirt. I was standing in front of her shirtless but it didn't appear to bother her because she knew me.

Her arms fell to the side as I guess she saw by my face that I didn't know her. She stood all but a foot from me. Her eyes were deep brown with freckles around her nose. They looked cute. Then she smiled again. "Hi, my name is ..."

My eyes suddenly went wide. "You're Jax, oh my god!" I dropped my shirt and took her in my arms this time and whirled her around. "You're alive!"

She grinned at me. "Of course I am, silly." She seemed relieved that I knew her now.

"Come, walk with me" she said. I quickly threw on my shirt and joined in step with her. "I'm happy that you made it."

"How did you know we were here," I asked. "It was Rebecca that sent us here?"

From out the corner of her eyes she looked at me with mischief. "It wasn't her who sent you here, I did love." My mouth dropped open.

"You did? How and why?" I was really confused now.

"When Rebecca went back on her word I intervened and sent you to this dream realm. This darling is one of my hangouts so you can thank me again." She chuckled.

I couldn't believe it.

"I see the others made it too," she said. Up a head was Jamie and Zak. Max was running ahead of them towards us. That's when my heart sunk again. "Well Jax, we all didn't make ..."

Max was at Jax's feet barking and wagging his tail in excitement.

"I'm sorry miss, about that. He's very friendly as you can see" said Zak. "Come here boy and don't bother the lady."

I looked at both Zak and Jamie. They smiled politely and shook hands with her and introduced themselves. "Nice to meet you," she said. "You can call me Jax and your friendly friend here, what's his name?"

"His name is Max," said Zak.

I was confused. The guys didn't know her. Jax just looked over at me and gave me a friendly wink to let me know it was okay.

"Do you live on this island?" Jamie asked her.

"Oh, I live in a lot of different places but this is one of my hangouts that I come to sometimes," she told them.

"Would you like to come up to the house," Zak asked her. Jamie chided in, "yeah, we're new here and are just starting to get to know the place."

"I would be pleased to come. I can tell you of some cool spots around."

"Great," said Jamie. "We'll meet you at the house. Avian can show you the way."

They both took off with Max in hot pursuit. I turned to her. "They didn't know you. What is going on?"

Jax sighed. "Let's walk some more. Sometimes love when we pass into these dream realms we lose who we were. As I'm sure you noticed, I'm not a vampire here."

"I noticed that, that's why I didn't know you at first," I said.

"There was a good chance like Jamie and Zak, that you wouldn't have known me. It was a chance I took."

"You call this place a dream realm, does that mean it doesn't really exist?"

"Oh, it existed at one time but no one lives here anymore. There are no more houses here anymore, it was all abandoned over two hundred years ago. This was what it looked like about hundred years ago when I found it."

"Will we die here like we were going to die in our world?"

She shrugged. "I can't tell you, really. But dream realms last for a long time so you might spend near eternity here."

"I see, well you picked a pretty good place for us anyway."

She gave me a smug smile. "Yeah, I did." We both laughed but then I remembered something.

Chapter Thirty Two

"THERE IS SOMETHING THAT you don't know. I should tell you about…"

Jax had stopped.

"What is it or do you already know about…" She was looking straight ahead. I looked to where she was looking. There was someone walking toward us. It was a guy and it was not Jamie or Zak. His dark mass of curly hair was blowing in the wind. He had cut off jeans on and a white t- shirt. She looked up at me. "I think this now completes your little family."

My mouth hung open in shock. "I thought that he was …was…"

"Dead," she asked. "Not quite love. I managed to fight Rebecca off."

She continued on. "I managed to grab Elijah at the last minute and send him here with me. We arrived here at the same time. I wasn't too sure about the rest of you. I thought maybe you were burned in the light and all that was left was Elijah."

"But we all made it," I said. She smiled that beautiful smile. "Yeah, you did." Elijah was getting very near us now. Jax touched my arm. "There is something love that you need to know."

"What?"

"When he came here with me, like Jamie and Zak, he didn't know me. He did mention your name to me but his past with you as demon and vampire is gone love, okay? His mind is still foggy. He probably will never know. His old life in your world where you came from is also fuzzy and I don't think it will come back to him. But he has you, he never completely forgot you."

It was a lot to take in. I so badly wanted to run up to him and throw my arms around him but I couldn't.

He smiled at me when he got closer. "Hey," he said.

"Hey, yourself," I said.

We stood there and stared at each other for a moment then I couldn't resist I put my arms around him and hugged him. He hugged me back. He smelled like the ocean and his hair was sun warm. I kissed him on the cheek. He smiled rather shyly at me when I did that but I think he liked it. This certainly was not the aggressive possessive Elijah that I had married in the demon world. I took a deep breath.

"You want to come to the house where I live?"

He nodded. "Yeah, I would like that."

We walked side by side with Jax beside Elijah. The backs of our hands would every so often brush up against each other. It was electric and I think Elijah felt it. There was a twinge in my crotch. I had to control myself until Elijah was ready.

When we got to the house Max barked and jumped all around us.

"Who's this," asked Elijah laughing.

"This is Max our welcome committee of one." Zak came to the glass door to call him back when he saw who was with us. He must of yelled back at Jamie because he was there right away and both guys were smiling.

"You found this guy," Zak said.

"Yeah, apparently I belong here with you guys. My memories are a little off," he told Zak.

"That's okay, we're all new here to this place. I'm sure Avian will help you out with sorting stuff out."

We all gathered in the living room and Jax helped the guys cook up a feast of seafood and steak. There was even cold beer to drink. It was a great evening. My world suddenly had come back to me. I had my true love back even though he had not much memory of us. That was okay. We would have a long time to get to know each other again.

The sun was setting so the guys made a fire out on the beach. We all sat around it while Max jumped at the flying sparks. Jamie and Zak were sitting on a blanket wrapped up in each other's arms. I noticed Elijah taking glances at them every once in a while as if maybe he was trying to remember them and then we locked eyes. He smiled and his smile sunk my heart. He moved closer to me and my heart started to race. "Can I?"

"Of course you can," I said. I smoothed out the blanket for him and he sat down all but a few inches from me. He smelled so good. I wanted to kiss him on the cheek again but I didn't want to scare him off or push him too much.

"This is a great place isn't it," he said.

"Yeah that's for sure. It's paradise especially now that you're here." I cringed when I said that, I was pushing it. "Oh, I didn't mean to push." He placed his hand on top of my. I froze.

"It's okay, I want to reconnect with you and it makes me happy that me being here makes you happy."

"Oh, it does believe me, in more ways than you know." My words were starting to stumble along with the loud beat in my chest.

"I want to try very hard. I feel a connection with you and it's strong. I can't ignore that," he said.

My heart was singing and I sure he could hear it. He looked over at me out the corner of his eye. "Can I do something Avian?"

He was getting closer to me. His lips were all but touching me. I went closer to him and then our lips touched and I thought the world was going to explode. Our kiss didn't last long enough.

"Thanks for letting me," he said softly in my face. "You can do it again if you want."

He grinned. "I will, I promise."

We sat there quietly enjoying the fire and each other's closeness.

When we went in the house. Elijah wanted to know where he was to sleep. I so wanted to take him to what would be our room but I knew I couldn't. "There are different rooms upstairs, you can choose one." I took him up and showed him a few rooms." Which one is yours?"

My heart skipped a beat. "It's over here."

I don't know who turned on the sconces over the bed but they were on casting a golden glow over the room and I never noticed it before but there was a fireplace in the bedroom and it was burning. The whole atmosphere was almost more than I could bare.

"This is a beautiful room you have," he said as he walked around and when his eyes settled on the bed I walked over to his side. "I hope this will become our room soon."

He smiled and his beautiful chestnut brown eyes took me all in. "I'll be looking forward to that."

He bent down and kissed me again. I hungrily took his kiss and returned it with passion. He pulled away slightly.

"I'm sorry, I didn't mean to …"

"It's okay, it's just that I'm not quite ready yet and I'm sorry for that, I shouldn't have done that to you, I'm sorry."

"It's okay love." I called him love. That was his name for me.

He smiled. "I want to be your love, love," he said. I should find a room of my own and let you sleep." I nodded and then I watched him leave and with every fiber of my being I wanted to drag him back and let him sleep with me in the same bed. We could just lie there as long as he was there and this wasn't a dream. I was afraid when I woke none of this happened and he would still be gone.

I think I laid awake for most of the night in fear that he wasn't here. Sleep finally did take me and I think I dreamed of storms clouds and Rebecca's eyes and Max's wagging tail that made Zak come rushing up to him. Then there was the blinding light and that's what finally woke me. I bolted up in a cold sweat. The bright light was the sun shining into the room. I was still here in this paradise place, was Elijah?

I got up and when I went to the door I could hear laughter. My chest thumped. I rushed to the stairs and stopped halfway. They all turned to look at me. "Good morning sleepy head, you almost missed breakfast." Jamie got up to get me a plate.

I raced down to the table. "Where is…"

Zak pointed to the balcony where Elijah was standing with his coffee looking out at the view. I let out a big sigh.

"What's wrong with you, did you have bad dreams," Zak asked.

"I thought this was all a dream but it's…"

"It's very real buddy and even though I don't know how we got here but…"

Chapter Thirty Three

ZAK COULDN'T FINISH his sentence but I just smiled back at him. "We'll all figure it out together."

Zak smiled back at me satisfied with that. Jamie came up to me with a plate full of eggs and hash browns with toast. This was unreal. "Thanks, I'll take this out there." I nodded towards where Elijah was. I couldn't wait to see him. Jamie opened the door for me and Elijah turned and his face lit up sending my heart racing.

"Good morning, I thought I might have to go up there and get you."

I sat my plate and coffee down at the table. "Sorry, I had a restless night."

He frowned. "I'm sorry about that, I thought being here would give you sweet dreams."

He sat down opposite me and he took my breath away. The ocean breezes played with his dark curls and those beautiful chestnut eyes melted me. His face was even a little bit tanned. I could see the pores along his nose and I so badly wanted to touch his face.

"I'm alright now that I know you are really here."

He smiled and his face was all a glow. "Well, I'm glad that me being here with you has chased away the bad dreams." Elijah took a sip of his coffee and gazed out over the view. "We should go for a walk down the beach after your done eating."

My heart skipped a beat. "That sounds great, I would like that."

The glass doors opened and Max along with Zak and Jamie came out. Max seemed to like our new addition to the family. He wagged his tail quite lively until Elijah patted him and ruffled him up.

"We're going for a walk down the beach and see if we see Jax or not. We were going to get her to show us some places around here. Do you guys want to come?"

Before I could say anything Elijah turned to Zak and said, "Avian and I want to go for a walk alone up the beach but maybe we'll meet up with you guys and Jax later."

Both Jamie and Zak smiled and nodded. They both went down the steps to the beach with Max running ahead of them.

I could barely finish my breakfast but I did. Elijah picked up my plate and I followed him into the kitchen with mug in hand taking my last sip. When he set the plate down he turned around to me taking the cup out of my hand and without notice took me in his arms and kissed me deeply. When we pulled away I was shocked and I think it showed on my face.

"I'm sorry but I couldn't resist and wanted to do that since I saw you this morning."

"You don't have to apologize Elijah, I didn't mind and you can do that any time you want."

He grinned. "That's good because I intend to do just that." He winked at me sending my heart into overdrive. "Let's go for that walk…love."

This couldn't get any better. I was walking along a beach with the love of my life in a paradise place. We walked in silence for a while until he threaded his fingers through mine. I think an electrical jolt went up my arm. He gave my hand a gentle squeeze. "I know I don't' seem to have much memory of the past but I was wondering, was I good to you? I mean I can feel your love for me but I keep wondering about myself and what I was like."

That was a loaded question. How much was I going to tell him and keep back? Would he understand the whole demon thing? I decided that it was too much information and given that Jamie and Zak know nothing either, I think this part of the past would be best left untold.

"Don't worry Elijah." I gave his hand an assuring squeeze. "You were good to me, always, and that's why I love you." All the possessive behavior that Elijah showed as a demon and what I can remember in our world what he was like which was a guy who liked to be in charge but had a kind side to him. I remembered that much.

"Let's just deal with the now and moving forward in this beautiful place." He smiled at me making my heart race again. "That sounds good to me."

We didn't walk too far when he stopped me and pulled me close to him giving me one of those deep kisses again. I moaned this time. His breath picked up and our hold on each other got tighter. His hand traveled down my back and was almost going over my buttocks when we heard shouts. We pulled apart and saw the guys and Max coming toward us. They also had Jax with them. I stole another kiss from him before they got to us. "Hey, I'll get you for that."

"I hope so," I said grinning like a fool. He laughed.

Max was the first to get to us of course wagging his big tail at Elijah for attention. Jamie and Zak were both grinning at us. They of course saw us. Jax was hanging in the back a bit smiling at us too. "I see you guys have gotten a lot closer," said Jamie. Elijah smiled back at him. "Yeah, it's been great, I'm so happy."

"That's great" said Zak. "Because we have more great news, Jamie and I are getting married."

We all hugged and then I asked, "But who's going to marry you?"

"I'll do that," said Jax. "I performed such things before in my past." She smiled at me and I knew there was a pile of things that I knew nothing about concerning her life.

Elijah came forward then. "That's great to hear Jax because I think after these two tie the knot there will be another couple needing your services as well." He winked at me.

"Anytime you're ready," she said.

I was stunned and elated at the same time.

It was a beautiful evening and Jamie and Zak looked so handsome in their white suits. Candles glowed around us on the deck with tropical flowers lending their scent to the ceremony. Jax looked radiant in her off white sundress and she wore a white orchid crown on her head making her raven black hair shine. Jamie and Zak made their own vows and made us all tear up. I don't know where they came from but they exchanged gold wedding bands that had a design engraved on them. I suspect Jax had something to do with this. They kissed and Max barked.

We celebrated with great food and spent the evening around a fire on the beach. I went over and sat beside Jax for a moment. "That was a beautiful ceremony you gave the guys."

'Thank you," she said "I hope your turn will be soon."

"Oh, I think that will be sooner than you think, Elijah needs to be connected to you. It's the one thing that keeps him going and sustains him."

"That sounds like a bit of a life line," I said.

She sighed. "In a way it is, his spirit is attached to you because it is the only thing that he recognizes. He wants to complete his union to you by a marriage sealing his connection."

It sounded complicated but I didn't care. "Well, the sooner the better. Whatever awaits us I want us to face it together." She smiled. "There is something you should know as well. I can't stay here with you guys forever or however long this realm lasts. I have to go back to the other world."

"Why can't you stay here with us and be away from all that evil?"

"My vampire side is too strong and no matter how long I fight it I have to go back to it and be a vampire for a while but don't worry, you haven't seen the last of me, I'll be back sometime and show up on your door step."

"I look forward to it but I hope you stay with us for now."

"I will," she said.

Jamie and Zak disappeared into the house before midnight. We wouldn't be seeing them for a while. Jax also left. I suspect she was going off to meet someone but I wasn't sure. I wondered where she stayed and what her place looked like.

Chapter Thirty Four

THAT LEFT ELIJAH AND I in front of the fire. I was wrapped up in his arms. He kissed my neck and started a chain of kisses down my cheek. I was hoping this would lead to something more but then he stopped. "I do love you Avian and I want us to get married very soon."

I pulled him down on the blanket and kissed him letting my hand slide down his chest to his pants where I stopped and just slipped my fingers under his pants to his skin. He reacted with a groan and I took that as a yes to keep going. I slid a little further and the tips of my fingers touched the growing bulge in his pants. I popped open his pants and unzipped him. I massaged him on the outside of the fabric. His eyes were closed obviously enjoying it so I slipped my hand under the fabric to feel his hard cock. I released him took him in my mouth. That's when he bolted up. I startled. "I'm sorry, I thought…"

"No, it's okay, I liked it. You felt really good but a part of me is so nervous."

"You don't have to be nervous with me love, we'll take our time."

He nodded. "Why don't we go in, it's been a long day."

So we went upstairs and went to Elijah's room. Jamie and Zak were making some noise. I grinned at him. "You know you are not going to get much sleep with those two. Why don't you stay in my room, no pressure?"

I could have taken him to another bedroom but I wanted him in with me. "You okay with that?"

"Of course I am, let's go."

A cool breeze wafted in through the partially opened glass door making the white curtain billow out softly. I could hear Elijah's soft breathing. It sounded silly but listening to his breathing sounded like music to me.

I rolled over and kissed him on the temple. He stirred and rolled over and faced me. I so badly wanted to run my fingers through his thick curls.

"I'm sorry I didn't mean to wake you."

"That's okay. I wasn't sleeping much. I couldn't stop thinking about what you felt like on the beach."

"Felt like?"

He took my hand and placed it over his very hard cock. "I want you to make love to me so bad. I want to be naked next to you." I rubbed him and wetness came to my fingers. "Then let's get naked."

We let our bare skin touch sending electric shock waves through us. There was no stopping now. We both wanted this. This time when I took him in my mouth he didn't stop me but I knew he was going to come right away so I stopped to his protests. I kissed his inner thighs testing to see if that was still a sensuous place and it turned out it still was. I sucked at his sac making him crazy. I knew I was soon going to have to give him his release so I took him in my mouth and sucked hard. He quivered sending his sweetness into the back of my throat. I took every bit of him. He laid back trying to catch his breath.

"It's my turn now," he grinned. He took my cock in his mouth and enjoyed every bit of it. His other hand slid around to my back and grabbed my bottom squeezing and then his finger slid inside my cheeks finding my hole. Elijah rolled me onto my stomach and spread my legs apart and shoved his finger inside of me. I moaned as he played with my hole for a while until I felt his once again hard cock sliding a little in. I wanted him to take me now. He pushed a little farther and kept going till he filled me. "You feel so good Avian." He took hold of my hard cock and started rubbing me all the while sliding in and out of me in a slow motion. I didn't last long when I came.

Elijah started to pick up his pace. His sac hit me with each thrust. He screamed out my name as he filled me. He pulled out and shot a few streams over my butt and hole. He went and licked me for a while. His tongue felt good. He rolled me over and kissed me. "I want to taste more of you." He slid down and took my cock in his mouth. I soon grew hard in his mouth and gave him what he wanted. He licked everything off of me.

After we laid in each other's arms satisfied and beyond happy. "I think we just had a pre wedding night."

I chuckled. I hope every night is like this," I told him.

"I think I can make that promise," he whispered in my ear.

Zak looked at me funny. "What," I said.

"You're tie is all wrong. Let me fix it." Jamie came into the room with a small orchid for my lapel.

"You're almost as nervous as the other groom in the other room. I think I did his tie twice."

"We better get these two married right away then," chuckled Zak.

I just took a deep breath. Elijah had moved into my room the night of Jamie and Zak's wedding. We fell in love all over again but this time it felt real and alive. I know Elijah didn't remember any of his demon self and not much of his other self as well but that was okay. What was important was the now and we had each other. Today was our day to seal our relationship with marriage which seemed very important to Elijah.

Jax was waiting for me. Elijah stood there with Jamie looking very nervous but smiled when he saw me. Zak delivered me to Elijah where we faced each other. Elijah took my hand and looked deep into my eyes with those beautiful chestnut brown eyes that I appeared in so many times of my dreams.

Jax had given us the same gold rings as Jamie and Zak. They had the same design engraved on them as the guys. This meant something I was thinking. I would have to ask her what it meant before she left and I had a feeling that was going to be soon.

She first handed Elijah his gold ring for me first. "I give you this ring as a symbol of my never ending love for you and I will stand by you in this time we have till it fades and our spirits leave forever but not apart. I love you more than anything my love and I give you my heart for safe keeping." He slid the ring on my finger. I felt a slight tingle go through my hand. I glanced at Jax who didn't give any clues, she just handed me my ring for Elijah.

"I give you this ring as a symbol of my never ending love for you and I will stand by you forever till we fade into this light but never parting. My love for you is strong enough to get us through any storm that comes our way and I will always keep your heart safe inside me. I love you darling now and forever." I slipped the ring on his finger and then we sealed our vows with a kiss. I swore I seen a light like the one I came through but it disappeared. I think I was the only one that seen it besides maybe Jax who knew more than she let on.

We celebrated into the wee hours of the night. Elijah led me upstairs before our first night as a married couple was over. He undressed me slowly and then offered me a massage. I laid back and Elijah did his magic with the warm oil. I thought I was going to explode before he was done. Elijah fucked me from behind while rubbing my cock. We both came together. I was in heaven.

We woke up the next morning wrapped up in each other's arms. Elijah kissed me. "Good morning my beautiful husband."

"Good morning to you my sexy husband."

Elijah smiled. "Oh I like that." He slipped his hand around and squeezed my butt slipping his finger into my hole finding that special spot that made me groan. He switched his position and with his other hand he took my cock in his mouth. I grew hard in his mouth. The two sensations made me quickly come. "I don't think you're done yet love." He spread my legs back and exposing me. He took some of that oil from last night and rubbed it all over my hole and his hard cock. He slipped inside me and started this erotic motion, swaying his hips and going deeper and deeper till all of his hardness filled me. He was getting great pleasure from this. Then he picked up his thrusts and fucked me till he came filling me so much that his cum leaked out of me. He collapsed on top of me. I wrapped my legs around him hugging him. We kissed for a while before getting up. We decided to go into the tub. That was a favorite of ours, of course it always led to more love making.

Elijah went ahead to start running the water. I looked out the window to take in our view and that's when I noticed her. It shocked me at first to see Jax as I first met her-as a vampire. She was standing out on the beach in front of the house. I threw on a robe and went out.

"Hey, Jax, what's up?"

"You do know me. I wasn't sure if you would or not."

"Why wouldn't I know you?"

"I guess you are different than the others."

"What does that mean?" I was confused.

"Her blood red lips smiled. "Avian, the others will not know me. I am but a distant memory to them. They might talk about me like I was from many years ago. That's just the way the dream realms work. They play with the mind."

I didn't know what to say. "Well, it hasn't played with my mind yet, I still know you. I'm sure Elijah would still know you. Why don't I go and get..."

She held up her hand and stopped me. "No, love trust me he will not know me."

"It's this isn't it?" I held up my hand with the ring on it. "It has something to with these rings we wear."

She grinned at me. "Maybe love but more importantly it binds all of you together here in this dream realm. I fore warn you not to take it off-ever. It's what keeps you safe and my magic will keep you *alive* till this realm is done. Then it will be up to you, if you want to die with it, that is your choice but if you want to move on then I could probably find you another dream realm." She paused for a moment and I knew she had one more important thing to say. "There is only one thing and that is even though you are the only one that knows me now, in time you might not know me either and will choose to stay away from me thus sealing your fate with this realm."

It was a lot to take in. "I understand what you have told me but I can't fathom not ever knowing you because you're not going to just disappear on me forever-right?"

She didn't answer right away and I knew by her blood red eyes that she didn't want to answer it. "You said that you would show up on my door step again," I reminded her.

She nodded like she remembered. "I promise you that, I will come back here before this realm is done, that I can guarantee you. What I can't guarantee is that you will know me. I might look different and you won't recognize me."

I couldn't believe what she was saying. "But you would know me, your memory will stay, right?"

"I should Avian , let's just hope that's how it works out." Her voice had some sadness to it. With Jax there was no getting any story out of her. She took a deep breath. "I'll make a pack with you. When I come back, I will do my best to get you to remember me, if you don't."

"That sounds good to me."

"Good" she said and held out her hand to shake on it. I did and when her cold skin touched mine, a shiver went through me.

"Hey, what are doing out there by yourself love?" I turned and Elijah was standing at the glass door. I turned to back to Jax but she wasn't there.

All I saw was the endless ocean.

Epilogue

ARIA SIFTED THROUGH THE DEBRIS of the old house looking for treasures. The fight in her was gone-for now. Hades had pissed her off rightly and in return she let herself destroy the only world that was a link to her past. She had collected old chipped tea cups, a few silver spoons and paper. She didn't know why she kept the paper but she did.

With her skeletal toe she over turned an old book and underneath was a silver dagger. She smiled and bent down and picked it up. This was the dagger used by the boys to cut each other and seep their own blood into vessels to make demon children. She held it up in front of herself. The engravings in the knife handle were in good shape so it still held black magic. She would sell it or trade it in the underworld for pretty things she thought.

She sighed as she looked around. She would have to find a new home and let this world finally die, probably the way it should have always been.

"Finding things are you?"

Aria didn't bother to turn and acknowledge Hades.

"You know darling I could put this garden and house all back together the way it used to be-really use to be. You would have all your flowers again and your beautiful Victorian house would be restored to its former glory."

Aria still ignored him. How many times had she heard that song? Probably thousands of times. She lost count. This time was going to be different. There would be no more listening to his lies, she was going to be on her own now.

"Come my darling, please turn around and talk to me. I want to make you happy. Wouldn't you like to be your young beautiful self again?"

That she would like but if she allowed that then she would start this whole cycle of his courtship and lies and she would have no more of that. No, this would end now.

He was right behind her now. She could feel his cold breath and the touch of his cold fingers on her shoulder. "Let me do this for you, my love." His voice was velvety sweet but underneath she knew his words were laced with poison.

She whirled around and faced him. She laid her skeletal hands on his chest. "You make me pretty and beautiful again?"

"Of course," said Hades. "Anything for you, my love," he cooed softly. His dark eyes glimmered and he smiled. He was so handsome. "Well, my darling love, what are you waiting for?"

He chuckled. "That's my girl." He took her skeletal hands and chanted softly. Aria could feel the black magic slither over her skin. She remembered how it felt, like a snake's cold skin slithering across her body. She always held her breath. He always kissed her forehead when the job was done. She looked down at herself and she was dressed in the most beautiful gown-a lovely emerald color to show off her dark eyes. To finish it off he placed a large emerald necklace around her neck. "Oh, it looks so beautiful on you, but I admit I can't wait to take it off of you and delight in what is underneath." His cold lips kissed her deeply making him groan.

She knew he wanted her now and would soon whisk her away deep into the underworld if she didn't act now. She smiled sweetly at him and battered her eye lashes at him.

That always got to him. "Oh darling, you are so sweet to me, giving me things."

"You can have anything you want, you know that. You just have to do one thing and that is give me a child."

It was always the same thing. He wanted a child from her that would be truly an heir for him. He would have his own flesh and blood to carry on his work and have babies with some other poor girl that would be lured in the same way that she was.

She cupped him with her now delicate hands and kissed him letting her hands fall to his chest after. She gave him the sweetest smile ever as the black magic in her hands pushed on his chest. He gasped and before he could fight back he was sailing through the air turning into nothing but black mist.

She laughed. "Bye, bye love, I'll catch up with you…in maybe 500 years or so."

Her toe hit something. She tilted her head at the object. Aria looked around and then bent down and picked it up. She stared at the gold vessel. The words that were engraved around the engravings were still readable. She figured it must have fallen out of his coat pocket.

"Well, it appears my pets that *daddy* dropped you and left you behind. Now you're nothing but poor orphaned demons." She giggled and then she grabbed hold of the vessel and it steamed under her touch. "I always wanted children. I could be your mommy my little darlings. But I will have to take you far away from here. Let's see, where could we go? How about a nice warm place, like a tropical island?"

Thank you for reading!
Come on over to Elizabeth Baillie's website.
http://www.elizabethbaillie.blogspot.com

Other works by Elizabeth Baillie are:

The Dark Heat Series (Novellas)